BLOOD BOU

Presents

BLOOD RITES

An Invitation to Horror

Edited by Marc Ciccarone

"The Unbeliever" reprinted with permission – first appearance *Fantasy Book*, Vol. 2, No. 31983.

"Saturnalia" reprinted with permission – first appearance *Left Hanging: 9 Tales of Suspense and Thrills*, 2011.

Artwork by Andrej Bartulovic.

ISBN: 978-0-9849782-7-4

First Edition

Visit us on the web at:
www.bloodboundbooks.net

Available now from Blood Bound Books:

Night Terrors II: An Anthology of Horror
D.O.A.: Extreme Horror Collection
Steamy Screams: Erotic Horror Anthology
Rock 'N' Roll is Dead: Dark Tales Inspired by Music

Novels available now from Blood Bound Books:

Sons of the Pope by Daniel O'Connor
Monster Porn by KJ Moore
At The End of All Things by Stony Graves
The Sinner by K. Trap Jones

The Blood Bound Staff:

Marc Ciccarone
Joe Spagnola
Theresa Dillon
Karen Fierro
G. Winston Hyatt

CONTENTS

Cold Comfort of Silver Lake
Nathan Crowder
1

Shine On, Harvest Moon
Monique Bos
14

A Grave Matter
Joe McKinney
22

The Candle and The Darkness
Aric Sundquist
33

The Lullaby Man
John McNee
42

The Final One Percent
Desmond Warzel
57

The Philosopher's Grove
Brad C. Hodson
63

The Unbeliever
Brian Lumley
73

The True Worth of Orthography
Lisa Morton
85

Falling Past Thessaly
Christopher Hawkins
97

Sleep Grins
Chad McKee
104

The Lady With Teeth Like Knives
Mark C. Scioneaux
115

The Binding
Daniel O'Connor
121

Cry
Jeff Strand
145

Corpse Lights
Ed Kurtz
151

Life and Limb
Adrian Ludens
162

Who Is Schopenhauer?
Bryan Oftedahl
171

Phantomime
Gregory L. Norris
185

Never Say No
Angela Bodine
192

Saturnalia
Maria Alexander
204

The Butterfly
K. Trap Jones
219

The Leaving
Matt Moore
225

The Trapdoor
Douglas J. Lane
241

COLD COMFORT OF SILVER LAKE

Nathan Crowder

They passed their child's projected birth date in total silence, Steven with the novel he was writing, and Anne curled up in a comforter on the couch, crying softly. He saw the look in her eyes, the silent questions. She wondered if it was her fault. And despite the reassurances and platitudes, he found himself wondering the same thing.

Gone was the sunny, laughing wife he had known. She didn't sing along to the radio any more or delight him with bad puns while discussing the news. In fact, she rarely bothered with the news at all, instead pulling deeper and deeper into her shell. More often than not, Steven found himself wondering if he was in love with her. Was he just in love with who she had been? He told himself that her black moods wouldn't last. Eventually, the storm would pass.

After almost a year of crumbling relations, Steven made one last gamble and put their house on the market, much to the surprise of everyone who knew them. A year earlier it had been their dream home, with a view of the coast, a brightly painted nursery, and good schools nearby. Now it was just an unpleasant reminder. Anne rarely left the house, leaving Steven to make excuses to friends and family as the move approached. Some days, Steven could almost believe the excuses he made.

Silverdale was supposed to be their new start, their last chance to save a marriage. Anne and Steven had driven through the sleepy mountain town on their honeymoon four years earlier and fallen in love with its picture-postcard beauty. That night over dinner, they agreed to move there someday when their lives slowed down. Neither of them expected the move to be motivated by the ghost of an unborn child slowly eating away at the foundation of their marriage. He reasoned that the constant reminder of happier times would somehow revive Anne. At this point he was willing to try anything that might give him a respite from the sullen moodiness broken only by unpredictable crying jags that could last for days. And the relative seclusion would work to his advantage as he finished writing his latest book.

He had been surprised to find that the only home in their price range anywhere close to Silverdale that wasn't a trailer or a ramshackle hut was the old, gray Victorian by the lake.

Steven disliked it almost immediately. It sat in the all-but-permanent shadow of the surrounding hills, with narrow windows that looked out from faded gray walls like eyes on a spinster's face. It had a vaguely cadaverous quality that no amount of sprightly gingerbread trim could disguise. If the last book had sold better, or if he or the publisher had confidence that the next one would take off, it might have been different. Steven might have risked one of the smaller and more run-down homes that were more expensive because of their proximity to town. He even considered a mobile home on the other end of Silverdale, but the hard look on Anne's face made it clear that that would never do.

For reasons he couldn't fathom, Anne liked the house by the lake. She gasped the first time she looked out the kitchen window and saw a sliver of sunlight on the icy surface of the water. *Early April and still frozen*, he thought. Even with the sunlight on the ice, the lake looked black and impossibly deep.

"Look, Steve! It's our own private lake!"

Steven looked at their agent. Valerie was studying her clipboard a little too intently for his comfort while her teenage son, Hank or something, ignored all of them, lost in his handheld video game next to her. "Is the lake private?" Steven asked.

"Private? Not really, but it might as well be. The lake is on public land, but this house has the only easy access to it. And the access is private." Valerie glanced nervously up from her notes. Not at Steven, he noticed, but toward the lake.

Anne was the most vibrant she had been in over a year, flush with the excitement of starting over. “Can I see the rest of the house?”

“That’s why we’re here,” Valerie said, laughing.

Steven gave his wife a quick kiss as she walked past. “Okay, hon. I’m going to stay down here for a bit and soak it all in.”

He waited until the women were well out of earshot, their footsteps sounding on the stairs and then in the halls and rooms above their heads. “So, someone was killed here?” he asked. “That’s why it’s so inexpensive?”

The kid looked up, surprised to be spoken to. “What? In the house? Not that anyone knows about. You’d think a place like this would be haunted just looking at it from the outside, wouldn’t you? Major letdown.”

“With full disclosure, your mom would have to tell me that kind of thing anyway.” Steven nodded, familiar with real-estate law by way of movies and television. “How about the lake? Has anyone died in the lake?”

The kid got a bit cagey. His eyes flickered nervously to the door as he suddenly wondered if he should be talking to one of his mom’s clients. “Well, that’s kind of tricky.”

“Tricky how?”

“Well, you know how the lake got its name?”

Steven smiled, trying to put Hank at ease. “I didn’t realize the lake had a name.”

“Silver Lake. There used to be a road that goes past the house to the Adderson Mine, but it grew over forever ago. One day the miners broke through into the lake and like, a dozen people drowned. The mine shut down and never reopened. The mine owner lived here with his wife until she vanished. Some people think she drowned. Or that Old Man Adderson dumped her body in the lake.”

Steve suddenly realized he had stopped looking at the kid and had stepped to the window. Silver Lake dominated his view. Steve felt cold looking at it and had to tear his gaze away. “They never figured out what happened to the wife?”

Hank shrugged. “After the mine closed down, they kind of kept to themselves. She was a lot younger than him, and neither of them were what you'd call social. They'd been up here all alone for a few years, just him coming down to pick up groceries and stuff. No one realized she was gone until he died and people went looking."

"How did he die?"

"Pneumonia," he scoffed, turning back to his game. He continued to talk, accompanied by intermittent beeps from the small device in his hand. "He died down at the store buying groceries. So he must have been pretty sick to keel over in public like that. The sheriff came up to give the widow the bad news, and he couldn't find any trace of her."

Steven looked back out the window again. He felt his gaze drawn deep into the cold blackness of the lake. It spanned just over a hundred feet at its widest point and was perhaps three or four times longer than it was wide, more like a loch than a lake. Nothing grew around the gray, rocky shore, but the mountains had a climate all their own. With ice still on the water, he didn't exactly expect to see flowers. But any plant life, a leafless tree perhaps, would have been reassuring. "You said she might have drowned? Why is that?"

"I take it you've heard the Adderson legend, then?" Valerie said from behind him. He had been so consumed by the view that he hadn't heard her come downstairs. Steven turned around and saw only the agent, a look of disappointment on her face as she tried not to wring her hands too visibly.

"A bit," he said. "Heard that the husband died of pneumonia and the wife was missing, so maybe she drowned. That's all."

Visibly relieved, Valerie moved to the window and pulled the curtain cord to close off the view. "Well, there was no sign of any violence. If she was killed here, her husband covered it up very well. She had a pair of suitcases under her bed—"

Steven stopped Valerie with a hand on her arm. "Wait. 'Her bed'? "

"Her husband was old and old-fashioned. He might have married her just to take care of the house. They had separate bedrooms. Her suitcases were empty and under her bed. Her shoes were in the closet. She hadn't run away, and if she had, no one had seen her come through town. That's the only way out of Silverdale from here."

"But they never found the body?"

"They dragged the lake, but it's just too deep. Drowning victims…" She shuddered, then smiled as if to cover the involuntary response. "I heard that they rise to the surface as they start to decompose. But they never found her."

Steven pictured a young woman, naked and pale, bloated like a fish belly as she bobbed to the surface. "How long ago was that?"

"It's going on eighty years now. This house has had a succession of owners since then, but none of them have kept it for very long. It was even rented out periodically during the tourist boom in the seventies. But it has been vacant for several years."

Steven paused to listen to excited "oohs" and "ahhs" from upstairs as Anne tramped back and forth in the room above him. "So, the house is in good shape, it doesn't have a history of violence, and it's certainly priced to sell. Your son tells me it isn't haunted. Why so many owners?"

Valerie bit her lip. She didn't give him an answer, but her eyes flicked back to the closed window. Steven could feel it too. There was something about Silver Lake, something cold, unwelcoming, something that had nothing to do with the high rocks bordering it on three sides or the ice on the surface. He doubted that the lake was ever warm—ever inviting.

"Is the lake safe?"

Valerie was startled out of whatever deep contemplation she had been in. "Safe? What do you mean safe?"

"It's not poisonous or anything? I hear there are sometimes problems in mining areas with runoff."

"There was a mine up the way that closed over eighty years ago, and another one nearby that continued off and on up until the fifties or so. There was some concern about heavy-metal poisoning in the seventies. The lake overflows into a creek along the northern edge, so they had to test it, but it came up pure. It's just glacial runoff from up the mountain. Nothing wrong with it. But it doesn't get a lot of direct sun, so it's pretty cold. Even in the middle of summer, Silver Lake never really heats up much."

A breathless Anne appeared in the doorway behind Steven, startling him. She grabbed his upper arm for support, and buried her face in the back of his shoulder. He could feel her smile through his shirt. "Tell me you've already bought it."

"Not yet," Valerie said cheerfully. She avoided looking at Steven's hard-eyed smile.

"Please?" said Anne. She put her chin on her husband's shoulder, her breath warm on his neck. "You haven't even seen the upstairs yet. It's gorgeous, and it has the most amazing view."

Steven climbed the stairs to see the second story. He didn't feel there was much choice in the matter. He found that the "amazing view" amounted to an unobstructed view of the black surface of the lake from the wide bedroom window. He thought of a dozen men trapped in the darkness of a mine as their lungs filled with watery death. Steven saw his wife's enthusiasm, such a rare flower he almost didn't recognize it, and he conjured up a forced smile. "It's lovely." He knew his options were pretty limited, so he bought the house. If he denied Anne the first thing that made her happy in a year, he might as well just throw in the towel.

Their worldly possessions arrived by truck within two weeks. By early May, they were completely settled, and things started to look up. Steven had set up his office in the spare bedroom on the second floor away from the lake, and Anne set about instilling the house with a homey, lived-in touch. He spent his mornings writing while Anne slept in, and in the afternoon they went down the mountain and explored their new hometown. But eventually Anne grew tired of being out in public, and they retreated back to the house, back to the silence of the lake.

Early attempts at gardening proved fruitless. There was too much shade for anything to grow aside from choking fingers of ivy that crept around the foundation. The few hours a day when the front lawn got any sun at all left it scrubby and thin. Anne planted bulbs and lavished attention on them, but a month passed, then two months, and when they were well into June, there were still no signs of flowers. The only things that she had planted with any degree of success were a pair of low pine shrubs. They crouched, twisted and gnarled along the southern end of the driveway as if mocking her. Her inability to coax life from the ground seemed to be a reminder of the miscarriage and she slid quickly back into depression.

As the days got longer and warmer, Anne spent more and more time in bed with the lake view stretching out past the windowsill. If she wasn't there, Steven could often find her sitting at the edge of the lake itself on a large flat rock she called "the beach." She was crying as often as not. She stopped going into town, unwilling to pass through the front door. It was a conscious avoidance of the patch of barren dirt near the front porch where her lily and crocus bulbs lay, stillborn in the long shadows of the mountain.

While she slept and wept, Steven walked on eggshells, fearful of saying something that would initiate another storm. He wanted to help but felt that there was nothing he could do but ride it out. He blamed himself for not stopping Anne when she wanted to start gardening. Nothing grew up here. Even the weeds were anemic.

To make matters worse, the ice had thawed on the lake by the end of their first month and the warming waters seemed to wake in him deep, barely remembered nightmares.

Steven had been an excellent swimmer as a child but would only ever swim in pools. There was something about swimming in a pond or lake that always bothered him. The mud under his feet, the water weeds grasping at his legs, the occasional brush of a fish beneath the water, it was all too primal. As the ice thawed, he began to wake in the middle of the night with a strange, lucid-dream logic that escaped him in morning, a sense that he was being watched as he slept.

And some nights, he awoke to see Anne framed in the window with moonlight shining through her nightshirt and long brown hair. Her gaze was invariably cast down on the still surface of the water, so it couldn't have been her who had been watching him. She didn't even turn as he jolted awake in the twisted sheets. He blamed sleepwalking for Anne's behavior; by morning, she was always next to him in bed, with no recollection of having gotten up at all during the night.

As an unusually hot July settled upon Silverdale, Steven's temper became shorter in the dry sauna heat of his office. Several times Anne knocked on his open door, interrupting his work for the purposes of small talk, to ask him how things were going, to offer to bring up a beer. Or worse yet, she lurked quietly in the hallway outside the room, shifting from foot to foot, saying nothing before turning to leave again. Steven knew there were things on Anne's mind, things that troubled her. But even direct questions, asked when he found the time between chapters, wouldn't draw Anne's concerns out into the open.

The crying dried up and was replaced by a cool distance. When Steven returned to the shared spaces of the quiet home, he was met with a wave of mild disconnect. It was as if he wasn't even there anymore. Anne took to sleeping on the downstairs sofa several nights a week. She rarely initiated even the slightest bit of contact.

Their new beginning felt more like an old ending every day. A month of this disintegration and no side claimed victory.

On a particularly hot day in August, Steven left the office and couldn't find Anne in the house. The sound of splashing yanked his gaze out the kitchen window and onto his wife's bare shoulders beneath a cascade of wet hair as she swam near the lakeshore. Unreasonable horror gripped his gut so tightly that Steven found himself at a loss for breath. Before he knew what he was doing, he was out the back door, shouting at her to get out of the water.

She looked up, a complicated ballet of emotions on her face—joy from the swim turning to terror at her discovery, turning to concern as Steven's ankle twisted in the gravel and pitched him forward. And there, at the edges of her eyes, was a look that held him so rapt that he forgot to get his hands out to catch his fall. It was a look of guilty satisfaction. Steven couldn't be sure if it was over his fall or the luxury of the swim.

When it turned out that his ankle was too sore for him to bear his weight, Steven had to rely on Anne to drive him in to the doctor. It was the first time she had gone past the end of the driveway in months. Unless Steven counted the lake—an incident he was still too shaken to address.

The injury wasn't as bad as either of them had feared. No more than a nasty sprain. Steven was advised to keep off his feet as much as possible for a few weeks. He was given crutches and painkillers. The crutches he could make his peace with, as they let him get to the bathroom without help. But the painkillers were another matter entirely. They upset his stomach and made him sleep too deeply.

Getting up and down the tight stairway was too much of an effort most nights. He solved that problem by spending most of his time on the sofa, curled up against the rose-colored cushions while Anne resumed sleeping in the bedroom upstairs. And at night, he dreamt of the lake.

In his sleep, the cold water surrounded him, ink-dark. He couldn't even see his feet beneath the surface. In the distance, he saw the house with the midday sun high over the eaves. The sky was crystal clear and perfectly blue. It did nothing to make the lake anything other than dark and unwelcoming. Ancient hereditary memory of deep-water predators like the shark crossed through Steven's mind, even if the idea of a freshwater shark was ludicrous. He could not shake the dream logic that sharks or maybe a giant octopus or blind cave fish swam below. If that were the case, he knew he would have no idea until it was too late. Steven knew he wasn't alone in the water, and that terrified him.

All life comes from the ocean, he thought over and over again, the words ricocheting crazily around the inside of his brain. Beneath the water his toes brushed against something. It was soft—jelly soft. Bloated-corpse soft. *They never found the wife*, he thought, and he imagined her long hair coiling around his calf, her cold, dead face pressed up against the sole of his foot. He felt her pale nose grazing the arch, her too-white teeth caressing his ankle. He remembered the dozen or so miners drowned by the lake waters in an adjacent mine shaft, and pictured their fish-belly-white eyes staring at him from the darkness below.

In his dream, he thrashed wildly about, almost drowning until his brain tried to impose logic over the situation. There was something down there. But it couldn't be her. Not after all these years. No, it had to be something else.

Before Steven could overpower the nightmare with his conscious mind, the shape beneath his feet writhed against him.

A cry woke Steven from his sleep. He sat bolt upright on the sofa, the sound of his own shout still echoing in his ears. He blinked back the night terror, trying to get his bearings. "Anne?" he croaked, knowing it wouldn't be loud enough for her to hear up the narrow staircase.

Steven fished around for his crutches and found them shoved halfway under the sofa. He pulled himself to his feet, wincing when his bad foot swung back and hit the edge of the sofa's wooden frame. He hobbled to the kitchen, where he could look out over the lake and reassure himself that he wasn't still out there in the water somehow. A quick look out the window showed no movement on the moonlit surface of the lake. As he flipped on the light, he heard Anne stir in the bathroom upstairs. He mapped her progress by sound—the flush of the toilet and quick hand wash at the sink, then her footsteps as she headed for the stairway.

He shifted awkwardly on the crutches to see the stairs, cautious of slipping on the hardwood floor in his socks. A cold wetness seeped into his right sock, oozing up between his toes.

On the hardwood floor, a single set of Anne-sized footprints led in from the back door, glistening wetly in the moonlight.

"Are you in here, hon?" Anne called down the hall toward the lit kitchen.

"I had a bad dream and got up for some water." Steven's voice felt hollow, but if Anne thought so, she didn't say anything.

She was in the kitchen only moments later, dressed in her green terrycloth robe, her hair falling limply around her shoulders. It was still wet. *Of course it was still wet*, Steven thought. *Who else could be tracking wet footprints through the house if not his wife?* "Do you think you can make it upstairs?" she asked. "I'll tuck you in all nice and cozy."

There was something about her smile that nagged at him. It contained an offer he hadn't seen her make in too long. He couldn't refuse. The trip upstairs was easier once he got going, and once in the bedroom, it was worth the effort. She made the removal of her robe into a striptease for his unasked-for benefit. When she slid into bed beside him, Anne's hands were cold despite the relative warmth of the night. They warmed up quickly as she slid them beneath his shirt to caress his chest and stomach.

In the back of his head, he wondered if this was just another dream from which he would wake up at any second. He worried briefly that he might wake before the anticipated climax. Reaching down to make sure that she was real—that this was real—he curled his hand in her damp hair. He was instantly frightened that if it was a dream, it might become a nightmare at any moment. Steven let go of the hair and wiped his shaking hands dry on the rumpled sheets at his side.

Anne's hands explored down across Steven's stomach. They slid inside the waistband of his shorts to find that he was more than ready for her. She traced cold, damp lines down his stomach with her hair. He was transfixed, powerless to stop her. He found himself engulfed in the warmth of her kiss and the cold of her dangling hair. It had been a long time since she had shown him any sign of affection, and now that he had it, he wasn't sure what to make of it.

He shuddered as the orgasm shot through him like lightning, hands knotted in the sheets to avoid touching her wet hair again. Anne crawled up next to him like a sleepy kitten, that same sexy, languid smile on her face as she put her head on his shoulder. Steven didn't move until the sun came up. If he slept, he didn't notice. If he dreamed, he didn't remember.

He was too busy remembering Anne's smile. It was an infrequent expression—infrequent enough that he could pinpoint when he had seen it before. The memory sat like a lead weight in his gut.

The next day, he fished Valerie's business card out of his desk. She answered the phone with a chipper "Bushnell Realty, Valerie speaking." She wasn't too surprised that it was Steven calling.

"You mentioned that there was some local history about this house," Steven began, surprising Valerie by not immediately wanting to sell the place and move on. He understood that that was how much of her involvement with the house had gone.

"It has some colorful legends and lore around it, yes. Why do you ask?"

"Who knows the most about local history in town? I remember seeing a flyer for a Silverdale Museum or something."

"That could be Ol' John. Let me look up his number for you."

While Valerie rustled through her day planner, Steven glanced down the hall to see Anne, dressed only in her robe, heading down the stairs, a towel over her arm. She was smiling contentedly, and looked up to see Steven watching her. She waved playfully.

He cupped his hand over the phone and smiled as calmly as he could manage. His smile felt fragile, but he suspected she wouldn't notice. "How long have you been swimming in the lake, Anne?"

"Since June, the second week sometime, I think. I'm pretty sure that was when it started to get really warm. Why?"

"No reason."

Anne looked at him strangely and then rolled her eyes. She disappeared from sight down the stairs about the same time Valerie came up with the phone number. "You have a pencil?"

Steven wrote down the phone number. It took him close to an hour to work up the nerve to dial and only a few minutes to get the answers he was looking for. He was still sitting quietly in his desk chair in the office when Anne got back from her swim. She fed him lunch, rubbed his shoulders, even read to him from a book they had been sharing.

That night in bed, Anne came to him beaded with water from yet another dip in the lake. She pleasured him with her mouth again before falling asleep. He didn't try to stop her although his heart wasn't in it. She lay back against the sheets and fell asleep with that same satisfied smile as her breathing grew deep and regular.

Steven had seen the smile before, though it had been well over a year since he'd seen it last.

His phone conversation with Ol' John had been rattling around in his head like batteries in a coffee can all afternoon.

"Oh, she probably did drown in the lake, or her husband did her in and hid the body real well somewhere else," Ol' John had said. "It's a shame about the baby, though."

"Baby?"

"She was well along in the pregnancy. Seven or eight months, I think. No one really knows for sure. But her husband, well, he didn't cotton to having a baby around the house. There are some who suspect that she was having an affair and that's why he killed her."

Steven reached out slowly and placed his hand flat against Anne's belly. He couldn't feel it yet, but it was there. That satisfied smile—that glow—it was her first pregnancy all over again.

Only this time he wasn't the father. He couldn't be. They hadn't had sex since long before moving to the lake.

"All life comes from the sea," he whispered. He couldn't feel it, the baby. But it was there, growing inside her, waiting. He thought about it, then thought again about that thing in the lake of his nightmares. His mind replayed the image of a bare foot touching something rotten-soft under the icy blackness as it scuttled away from him.

I may not be the father, he thought, *but she's still my wife. We can raise it...* He caught himself.

Not he or she.

It.

Rotten-soft and cold.

It would be so easy, he thought. A pillow over Anne's face, a few minutes of struggle, and it would be over. He left his hand on her stomach and cried. Eventually, Anne turned on her side away from him, holding Steven's hand to her stomach with her own. He hadn't seen her happy for so long.

With his free hand, Steven found a pillow.

SHINE ON, HARVEST MOON

Monique Bos

I attended high school with a girl whose mother had set her on fire.

We knew the story well before Tia Jefferson made her first tentative appearance at Woodrow Wilson Senior High. Her grandparents lived in our town, and reporters thronged their lawn for months—from the day Elaina Jefferson lit her three daughters and herself on fire, to the evening when a jury doomed her to pass the remainder of her life on death row. We knew that Tia's younger sisters had died in the tragedy—one in the hospital after several agonizing days—and that Tia herself had suffered third- and second-degree burns over more than half her body, including her face. We knew Elaina, Tia's mother, had escaped nearly unscathed; either her suicide attempt had been a stunning failure or she hadn't been serious about wanting to die.

We were never fair to Tia. I can concede that now. There are no excuses, just explanations: we were teenagers, cruel in our inexperience and lack of empathy and invincible youth. We had no concept of what Tia had endured, no realization of the difficulty she must have faced, starting a new school where everyone knew the worst thing that had ever happened to her. And on top of that, half her face was scarred, twisted, wrinkled. There was talk of skin grafts, plastic surgery, but Elaina Jefferson had carried no insurance for her children, and Tia's grandparents spent what little savings they had on the sisters' hospital care and the double funeral.

Some of us called her "Freddy," as in Krueger, because her skin resembled his. Some of us told her she should follow Jason Voorhees' example and invest in a hockey mask. Some of us said she should take a page from Michael Myers' book and cover her ugly face. From the beginning, we conflated Tia with the worst bogeymen we knew: the mass murderers of our favorite horror movies. We attributed her mother's unspeakable crime to her, rationalizing that because Tia survived when her sisters didn't, she must share some of the guilt. Living, especially in such a visibly damaged state, was an unforgivable sin to us.

Tia started school two weeks into sophomore year, which made her even more of a target of our ostracism. She had no choice about missing those first classes; she'd been testifying at her mother's trial, and then there had been a dispute about whether she'd live with her mother's parents or with her father, whom she hadn't seen since she was five. So when she finally showed up, we'd been expecting and talking and speculating about her. We all knew her recent history, and we poured the kind of intense scrutiny on her that drives teen Hollywood starlets to alcohol and drugs.

I might as well be honest here: I was among the worst. You know that saying "a face only a mother could love"? On her first day, I told Tia she had "a face only a mother could kill." This was before school shootings became so commonplace, before Columbine, and I'd like to say we weren't aware of how much damage our bullying could do. But that would be a lie. Of course we knew; the damage was our main motivation. Seeing Tia turn away—never in tears, she never cried; I guess the tears had been burned out of her—and hunch into herself, watching her brown eyes go blank and flat, enjoying the feel of her humiliation and our triumph: these were our incentive and our reward.

You hate me, I'm sure. Would it help if I tell you I loathe myself when I think back on the way we treated poor Tia? Or can you at least credit my honesty in owning up to my part of what happened?

If Tia herself never emerges as a player in my story, it's because I never conceived of her as anything except the girl with the maimed face. We called her "the Phantom of the Opera" and mocked her refusal to hide behind a mask. No one I knew ever had a conversation with her. Perhaps some of the teachers did, perhaps they tried to reach her, but even for them I suspect she was an object of pity and horror and revulsion. Or maybe one of the rejects tried to befriend her—the black-trench-coat boys who played Dungeons and Dragons, or the druggies, or the slutty girls. Maybe one of them approached her on the way home from school and asked her about herself, about who she really was beneath the face and beyond the news.

But maybe not. I never saw anything like that. What I remember is Tia Jefferson alone, always, in the back corner of the cafeteria at lunch, not eating the damp sandwiches her grandmother packed for her; at her own table during study hall, drawing pentagrams in her notebook with a chewed-up ink pen; changing clothes in a toilet stall before and after gym class rather than stripping down in front of us.

I've become a bit obsessed with Tia Jefferson recently. There's a surprising dearth of material online, probably because we attended high school just before the dawn of the information age. I did find one poorly written paperback, pages falling out, about her mother's crime. The author, attuned to the zeitgeist of the time, blamed the murders on Satanism; Elaina's drug habits and occasional prostitution received little more than footnotes, although I suspect they were far more likely contributors to her actions than some nebulous spiritual beliefs.

I briefly considered trying to interview Tia's grandparents or other surviving relatives, but I gave that idea up; the grandparents had moved away from our town, and if I told them who I was, they'd probably chase me off with a shotgun. And why not? It was less than I deserved.

So Tia, in my mind, remains an enigma, a blank slate, an absence behind a scarred exterior. Maybe she wasn't especially bright. Maybe she didn't have much spirit or personality. Maybe she'd been a surly, socially inept child before the tragedy in her life.

We gave her no chance to be anything else afterward.

Every fall, WWHS students held a hayride and bonfire the week after homecoming. The event always took place on a Saturday afternoon melting into evening. And because it wasn't an official school event, we managed to bring flasks and evade chaperones.

More than one baby was conceived in that hay wagon or beyond the sparks of the fire.

Everyone knew about it, including parents and police. We held it every year at the Lawtons' farm, and they'd been hosting it for twenty years, since the first of their twelve boys started high school. The second youngest was in my grade, and by the time the first generation had finished, the second generation would be about ready for high school. So we figured the tradition would continue forever.

Invitations never went out because everyone just knew. But someone lit on the idea to make sure Tia Jefferson heard about it, and for weeks we taunted her: "You oughta come; there's going to be a huge bonfire, and we hear you love those." The day before homecoming, in true *Carrie* fashion, one of the popular boys—Jason, the one I happened to be dating—decided to ask Tia to be his date to the hayride. I spurred him on. When he approached her with his offer, she said nothing, just turned away. She wasn't naïve; she knew he couldn't be serious. But he kept at her for the next week while the rest of us made cracks within her hearing: "Bring a blindfold because that's the only way you'll be able to stand kissing her." "The sex will definitely be doggy style." "Careful not to knock her up. The baby-killing might be genetic."

There was no defining moment in that particular torture campaign, no taunt that was worse than the others. Tia never gave in, never thought Jason's attentions were anything more than a cruel prank. He didn't try very hard to persuade her otherwise. But the Friday afternoon before the hayride, as I linked my arm in his and headed for the parking lot, I looked back at Tia and saw for the first time an expression on her face: a smoldering hatred, shocking in its intensity as well as its viciousness. I shuddered and nestled closer to Jason, pushing my breasts against his upper arm to distract him. I didn't tell him the reason for my sudden clinginess; I wasn't about to admit Tia Jefferson had gotten to me.

We were all shocked the next day when she showed up to the hayride. Everyone knew it was only for the popular kids, only for winners. The geeks and nerds never bothered to put in an appearance. Despite their plentiful offspring, the Lawtons were among the wealthiest families around, with sons who tended to be tall and golden-haired, who were inevitably awarded late-model convertibles on their sixteenth birthdays, who lavished their girlfriends with jewelry and flowers, and who would assuredly remain in our small town for the rest of their lives, working on the family farm or in one of the businesses that had sprung up around Main Street. They were not a family who associated with, or encouraged approaches by, high school losers.

But Tia clambered onto the hay wagon, which was hitched not to horses but to an old, red tractor, with the same bland imperviousness she had shown for the six weeks of her attendance at WWHS. She ignored the stares and whispers and outright taunts, turning her face outward to the view of pumpkin fields and dead cornstalks.

She did nothing, said nothing, as the hayride started. Did nothing, said nothing, as we laughed and sang, as couples began to get frisky and the booze came out. Jason, leaning over to stick his tongue down my throat, spilled Jack Daniel's onto his lap and cursed. Chuck Lawton, who had graduated from WWHS the year before and was the closest thing to an adult around, was driving the tractor with an open can of beer in his hand. He cranked the tractor radio up loud, and we were having a riotously good time. Then someone screamed.

Tia sat there, in the midst of hay and booze, holding a massive box of kitchen matches in one hand and a piece of straw, burning at one end, in the other.

"What the fuck—" someone said, and someone else lunged toward Tia, but Tia held the burning stalk down toward the bale on which she sat.

"Don't come any closer."

I realized it was the first time in six weeks I had heard her voice. It was soft, jarringly sweet.

"Chuck, stop the tractor," someone yelled, but he had the music turned up too loud to hear.

"I hate you," Tia Jefferson said in a clear, almost kind, tone. "I hate you all."

And then she stood, leaned over, and dropped the burning straw on Jason's lap. It landed just to the right of his crotch, on the exact spot where he'd spilled the whiskey, and his pants blazed up.

Chuck finally heard the screams, but by the time he'd stopped the tractor and turned around, Tia had lit more matches and scattered them through the straw and near the flasks. She aimed well; she must have spent the first part of the ride studying us, figuring out who was most drunk and where alcohol had spilled. She didn't waste matches on anyone sober enough to smack the fires out. People began piling off the wagon, jumping, rolling in the ditches beside the road. But more people were trapped, some even trampled, and in the middle of it all, Tia sat there beatifically lighting match after match until the entire box caught fire and her hand blazed into flames.

The fire caught terribly quickly and spread, consuming the desiccated straw bales on the wagon and, in the surrounding field, the dry yellow husks that once had been cornstalks. Later the inspectors said the whole thing was premeditated, that Tia must have come out the previous night and poured gasoline around the exact spot where she planned to start the fire. And we were in a drought, so even the irrigation ditches that normally held a trickle of water were cracked and barren.

Some of us got away. More didn't. Bones were broken when people leaped from the wagon. Kids landed on top of each other, cracking legs, arms, spines. And then the tractor exploded, so even those who thought they were safe, who were maybe still trying to help put out fires on other people or who were frozen in shock or horror, burst into flame.

I understand Tia now. I understand why she'd want to die, why, after what she endured, the continuing ridicule was simply too much to survive. Why, whenever she looked in the mirror, loathing for everyone and everything consumed her. She despised what she saw.

I live with the memory of her eyes on me, her calm voice saying, "I hate you all," and although I know it was true—she did hate us all—she hated me especially.

Although it's been nearly a quarter century, I'm still shocked when I look in a mirror. I still expect to see my old face, the one I wore until I was sixteen, until I got crosswise of Tia Jefferson. The red, puckered scalp where hair no longer grows except in patches, the eye permanently scarred into an uplift at the corner, the grotesque parody of a nose, the twisted lip: sometimes I have considered these my penance, my fair payback for the heartless, cruel bitch I was as a teenager. Sometimes I see them as a curse visited on me by a girl who was herself cursed. Sometimes I see them as destiny.

The Lawtons never held another hayride, of course. There were lawsuits and police investigations and talk of criminal charges. The parents sold the farm at a loss, and the sons scattered. Those of us with burns received generous settlements from our insurance companies, and some of us still live on disability checks. There's a memorial wall at WWHS, which closed in 2001, and a population of aging people with various scars, internal and external, floating like ghosts around town. I've heard that some of them have formed a sort of survivors' group, that they meet, talk, reminisce. I never speak to any of them; we avert eyes when we pass in the grocery store or at the gas station.

Sometimes at night, in mid-October when the air feels and smells like crisp leaves charring on a wood fire, I go to her grave. I stand beside the marker etched only with her name and the dates of her short, sad life. I never bring flowers, because I know if she were alive she'd throw them back at me anyway. I don't talk because there's nothing to say.

But I'd like to think that Tia's still out there somewhere, and that wherever she is, she knows. She knows a vigilante with a box of matches and a scarred heart roams the countryside, setting fire to carelessly cruel jocks and cheerleaders when they park in their gas-filled cars on country lanes, or ambushing them in dark parking lots. She knows about the house parties that end in flames, the moviegoers who choke on smoke as they blunder toward exit lights, the basketball games prematurely lost when the fire alarms shrill. She knows there hasn't been a hayride in this part of the state in fifteen years.

It's no kind of life, Tia Jefferson, this existence to which you've doomed me, doomed all of us, doomed our damned little town. But the little I can do, I do for you.

And the October moon watches always, a pregnant harvest moon, red as blood, red as fire.

A GRAVE MATTER

Joe McKinney

Even before he realized the junction signs were in German, Private William Bedford knew he was in trouble.

He was hopelessly lost. The zigzagging, mazelike warren of trenches was hard enough to navigate in the daytime, but at night, with only the red chemical glow of an occasional Very flare sizzling overhead to guide him, it was next to impossible. Add to that the rain and the incessant pounding of the artillery, and his position felt dire.

But being lost wasn't even the worst part. He couldn't remember anything from the last few days. Bedford had a dim memory of his lieutenant ordering him to take a message from their position to battalion HQ, but what that message was he didn't know. Scarier still, he couldn't even remember the name of the lieutenant who had given him the message.

He was confused, scared, alone. He didn't know what he was going to do. The rain had turned everything to mud. Every step sucked at his boots and made walking even a few steps a chore. His back ached. His head was a soupy mess. If he wasn't more afraid of drowning than of getting captured, or even shot, he'd just lie down here in the mud and wait for daylight.

But waiting would make him think of his hunger. For he was hungry, too.

That was the worst of it, the hunger. He was shocked that he could be so hungry amid all these rotting corpses, but the ache in his belly wouldn't go away. He had to have been wandering out here for days to feel this hungry, he told himself.

And maybe that was it.

Maybe he was so hungry it was affecting his ability to think. That wasn't so strange, was it? Without fuel, the body wouldn't work right. The brain couldn't think straight. A man could be driven mad by hunger, couldn't he?

Exhausted, he leaned against a trench wall.

Another Very flare lit the trench, and in its light, Bedford saw that he was not alone. A man was sitting just inches from where he'd stuck his hand, and the man was staring right at him.

Bedford jumped back, slipped, and landed on the edge of a sandbag seat and slid off into a shell hole six inches deep with rainwater. He looked up through the rain and realized only then that the man had not moved. His dead eyes regarded the same spot where Bedford had just been.

Relief washed over him.

"You gave me a good scare, mate," he said, and, groaning with the effort, pulled himself onto the pile of sandbags.

He regarded the dead man for a long while, unable to tell from his mud-soaked uniform if he was British or German. German, he suspected, from the boots. And dead a while too, for his torso had started to bloat and his skin to darken. Many of the corpses had been out here since the Monday before last, and between the heat and the rain a noxious odor of rotting flesh had seeped into everything, corrupting even the earth itself.

His fright gone, Bedford leaned toward the corpse, his thoughts once again turning to food.

"How about it, mate? You have any food in that pack of yours?"

His fingers trembling, Bedford reached for the shoulder straps of the man's pack but froze when the man started to move. His coat was pulsing, lifting and falling, lifting and falling, like some grossly exaggerated heartbeat.

Swallowing the lump in his throat, Bedford lifted the flap of the man's coat and pulled it back just a little.

Exit wound, he thought.

The man had been shot in the back and the bullet had come out here, leaving a hole in the side of his ribcage the size of a man's fist.

Bedford tried to figure out how the man had been shot in the back, clearly a fatal blow, and yet still found his way into a seated position, his back against the parados. Strange. But he didn't get a chance to reason it through, for at that moment an enormous black rat squeezed its way out of the wound, squirming to free its oily, engorged body from between the man's shattered ribs.

Bedford shrank back, hissing.

At first, the rat barely noticed him. It had eaten well and was sated. But then it raised its snout, as though catching the scent of something familiar, and it locked eyes on Bedford. The rat's demeanor changed instantly. Its hair stood on end, and angry popping noises came from deep in its throat. Working frantically to free itself from the wound, it set the dead man's body to shaking. The shoulders jerked and danced against the mud that held them fast, stopping only when the rat finally extracted itself and flopped into the man's lap.

It moved quickly after that. Still emitting those angry popping noises, it darted up to the man's shoulders and prepared to spring for the top of the wall.

The rat was fast, but Bedford was faster. There was a small jagged rock on the sandbag next to him. He scooped it up and sent it flying at the rat. The rock connected with a dull thud and sent the animal tumbling end over end into the mud, where it lay, dead as the soldier at whose feet it had landed.

Bedford roared in victory.

But then, feeling foolish, he lowered the fist he'd shaken at the dead rat. He fell back onto the sandbag ledge and blinked rain out of his eyes. He was troubled by his own behavior, but also by that of the rat. He had never seen one act the way this one had. For a moment, its yellow eyes had held more than fear, more than terror. Bedford could have sworn he'd seen an atavistic rage there, almost as though the rat had recognized him and hated him to the core.

But the rat wasn't the real question, was it? Why had he acted with such a spontaneous need to kill? He didn't like rats, nobody who lived in the trenches liked rats, but he could not recall feeling such hatred for them before. He had never thrilled at killing them before.

And since when had he been such a crack shot with a rock?

Questions, lots of questions.

He looked away from the dead rat and slowly realized that the artillery had stopped. He stood up, his head ringing from the sudden silence, swaying, staring up at a night sky full of tattered, gray smoke clouds.

The rain too had slacked off. It was little more than a light drizzle now.

Bedford looked up one side of the trench and down the other. The trenches were built into zigzag patterns. There were no straight lines, and no line of sight longer than ten or fifteen feet. The pattern minimized the damage caused by artillery shells and Mills bombs, and made it easier to shut off sections of a trench taken during a charge. Sound military strategy, perhaps, but it sure didn't help a fellow when he was lost.

Best to eat. That was the ticket.

He rifled through the dead soldier's pack and found a tin with no label. Hurriedly, he peeled back the lid and fished out a chunk of white potato that looked promising. He popped it into his mouth and chewed with such desperation that it took him a moment to realize how foul the food tasted. He couldn't swallow it. He hacked and coughed, and finally vomited thick chunks of potato all over the duckboards at his feet.

Only when his spitting and spluttering was over did he hear the sound.

Bedford looked around, uncertain of where it was coming from. Somewhere off to his right, it seemed, back the way he'd come. He wasn't exactly sure. But he was certain of what it was. Someone was eating over there. He recognized the sound of growls mixed with the tearing of meat from the bone.

No, he thought, not *someone*. A dog maybe, snarling and growling like that? But there were no dogs out here. Were there?

A sharp aching pang went through his gut, a need he couldn't resist. Bedford climbed up the parapet onto ground level, dimly aware that he was going against everything he'd ever been taught, everything the soldier in him knew to avoid. He was staggering into no man's land like a drunk tumbling out of a bar, but he didn't care. The sound of someone feeding drove him on like lust.

From somewhere nearby gunfire crackled. He ignored it. He saw the remnants of a burned-out church, only two of its walls still standing, and headed in that direction. He could see where the trenches had cut their way through the churchyard, the diggers giving no heed to the grave markers there. A few of the grave stones still stood, leaning like bad teeth in the orange glow of distant fires.

As he drew nearer to the church, another section of the trench yawned open in front of him. The sound was coming from down there.

He leaned over the edge and gasped.

Down in the mud was a ghoul of some sort. Naked and hideously grotesque, it only vaguely resembled a man. It stood on two legs, but it hunched forward like an ape. It tore flesh and rent the bones of the dead from their bodies with its two hands, but it crammed the pieces into a mouth that was closer to that of a dog than a man. And, like the rat Bedford had just killed, this one seemed to have eaten itself into a sated lethargy, for it moved slowly, heavily, like a glutton rising from the table.

"Oh my God," Bedford gasped.

The thing turned its head sharply toward him.

Move, Bedford thought. Come on man, move!

The ghoul—that was what it was; even over his fear Bedford was certain of that—made a series of hacking noises in Bedford's direction. It lifted one arm, streaked and oozing with mud and blood, as though in salutation.

Bedford, for his part, shook his head violently from side to side, backing up one step at a time.

The ghoul hopped toward him, its thick, rubbery legs carrying it forward not unlike a frog, and that was enough for Bedford. He let out a strangled yell and started running.

A shell burst to his left and knocked him off his feet. The horizon was lit with a sudden magnesium-white radiance, against which the black silhouettes of armed soldiers ran.

Germans, he thought. He was in trouble again.

Keeping as low as he could, Bedford jumped into the nearest section of trench and pulled some of the dead over top of him. And there he waited as the roar of the artillery started up again and the guns went rattling on.

He must have fallen asleep, for when he came to, a German soldier was standing over him with a rifle pointed at his face, yelling commands and questions.

"*Identifizieren Sie sich! Wer bist du?*"

The soldier pulled the corpse off Bedford and shouted again.

"*Was ist Ihr Gerät? Identifizieren Sie sich!*"

Bedford blinked at the man. "*Habt Ihr nichts zu essen*?" he said. "*Ich bin am Verhungern.*"

The soldier recoiled in disgust.

"*Oh mein Gott,*" he said. His expression was one of abject horror. "*Welche Art von Teufel sind Sie?*"

Backing away, the soldier raised his rifle to shoot.

Bedford lunged at the man, knocking his rifle away with the same blinding speed with which he'd hurled the rock at the rat. He knocked the soldier onto his back and hit him, thrashed him this way and that, brutalized him as easily as a wolf might overcome a piglet. The soldier made a few guttural noises, but then went silent. Bedford continued to pummel the man, stopping only because his hunger had made him too weak to go on.

Looking down at the ruin he'd made of the soldier, he saw blood everywhere. Bedford was up to his elbows in it. Some of it had even spattered on his face. He tried to wipe it away with the back of his hand but only managed to get some of it in his mouth. The moment the blood touched his lips he began to salivate. He breathed in the odor of death, the scent of blood, and he leaned in close to the dead soldier.

"No!" he shouted, pulling himself away. What in the name of God was he doing? Horrified with himself, he stood and looked around, as though someone might be able to help him.

Instead, he saw the ghoul, hopping toward him on those frog-like, rubbery legs.

The dead German soldier's rifle was leaning against the trench wall. Bedford grabbed it and leveled it at the approaching ghoul, which stopped and stared at him uncertainly.

"You go back to hell, you monster!" Bedford shouted.

He fired at the thing, but it was fast, and the unfamiliar rifle was hard to control. His first two shots only managed to hit the wall above the ghoul's head. The third plunked into the water at its feet as it rounded the next corner.

He lowered his weapon as the creature disappeared out of sight. Bedford was panting uncontrollably, his heart pounding against his ribs. He was disoriented, and he sat down next to the soldier he'd just killed with his bare hands. The soldier, God help him, that he'd almost eaten.

What in the hell was going on? What sort of madness had overtaken him?

Then another thought struck him. He'd spoken German to that soldier. How had he learned German? When had that happened? He tried to peel back the fog from his memory but couldn't. Nothing made sense.

The whole world seemed to have gone crazy.

And what about him? Was he crazy too?

Bedford roused himself when he heard German voices getting nearer. He had been lucky once, but he knew he wouldn't be lucky again.

He stood, and, still carrying the Mauser, went off in the opposite direction.

He'd nearly made it to the church when he saw the ghoul again.

It was crouched over a pile of bodies, its dog-like muzzle streaked with gore, bits of wet flesh still clinging there. A bib of blood colored its chest and ran over its distended stomach. Bedford lowered his rifle. He could tell the creature was in ecstasy. Its eyes had rolled up into its head, and it fed with an orgiastic joy that Bedford knew should horrify him, but it didn't. The smell of rotting flesh should have gagged him, but it didn't. He wasn't disgusted in the slightest. If anything he felt...envy.

And then the flabby skin of the creature started to twitch and vibrate. Bedford peered through the mist, uncertain of what he was seeing, for it seemed that the creature was changing, that its body was writhing with the contractions of transformation. Ripples waved across the ghoul's features, distorting them. Bedford cocked his head to one side. It was changing. Right before his eyes, the creature was taking on the shape of the dead man he was consuming. Its posture was still hunched forward, still monstrous, but the ghoul was taking the dead man's likeness onto his bubbling skin.

More German voices behind him.

The ghoul looked up then and spotted him.

Oh no, he thought. Bedford was stuck. He couldn't go forward, and he couldn't go back. The voices were getting closer, and now the ghoul was standing upright, hopping toward him. He had to get out of here.

Bedford ran toward the voices until he spotted one of the cutouts in the trench wall. German trenches sometimes had these short storage tunnels. They were used to keep ammunition and supplies out of the rain. They rarely went more than five feet, but he had nowhere else left to run. This would have to do.

He crawled inside the tunnel. The closeness of it didn't bother him. It actually felt welcoming, like an embrace, and for the first time in days, he found he could breathe freely.

He sniffed the air.

Something was dead in here.

That made him pause, but only for a second. The German soldiers were still back there, and their voices were getting louder, closer.

He clawed his way forward, surprised that the tunnel kept going. This was far longer than any German tunnel he'd ever seen, and yet he wasn't scared. If anything, the feeling of comfortable closeness grew within him, warmed him, and he felt at ease, even when the first bones crunched beneath his weight.

Bedford finally stopped.

He shook himself.

This wasn't right. Why was he pretending that it was?

There were piles and piles of bones down here. Some were still recognizable as a hand or a section of a leg, bits of meat still clinging to them, the marrow still packed inside the hollows. But others were old, powdery old and brittle. Years and years old. They were all jumbled together down here.

These bones, he realized, were the refuse of a scavenger.

What had he wandered into?

The answer was obvious at once. This tunnel through the old churchyard. The ghoul feeding up and down the trench. The bones.

Oh God, this was its home.

A sickening dread wormed its way through his gut. What a stupid fool he was. He had gone and delivered himself into that creature's den.

Bedford began to back up. He was terrified but moved with deliberate speed, pushing himself along in reverse on his belly, dragging the weapon along in front of him by its strap.

It was then he heard the sound of that ghoul calling into the tunnel.

Yes, Bedford thought, shocked. That's what it was doing. It was calling into the tunnel. He could hear the same sound spoken again and again, and from the tone, it sounded like a question.

Bedford rolled onto his side, as much as the confines of the tunnel would allow, and screwed his head around so that he could look behind him. He knew there was no way he should be able to see anything, but he thought he could see a form working its way quickly through the darkness.

"No!"

Moving as fast as he could, he lunged forward, pulling himself along the length of the tunnel. The creature was behind him, gaining on him. He had to move faster. He had to get away. He couldn't be caught down here, crammed up in here like this. The thing would overwhelm him in a heartbeat.

It would feed on him.

That thought made him sick with revulsion. He thought of the dead out there in the trenches, their bodies torn apart, first by bullets and then by ghouls, and he wanted none of it. He found the idea of being eaten so horrifying it nearly caused his mind to shut down. It took great control, but he managed to scramble faster through the tunnel, no longer paying attention to how it curved and branched off. Fear and horror had flooded his senses, and he pushed on with all his strength, oblivious to his fingernails tearing against the rocky earth and the dirt streaming into his eyes.

He pushed on, moving quickly until the tunnel suddenly narrowed. Here his arms were pinned in close to his body. He couldn't rise up onto his knees as he had been doing. The ceiling was only inches above his back. But his fear drove him forward until the dirt beneath him turned to rotten wood. There were more bones here, and it was so cramped he couldn't move his arms. Neither could he turn to see the ghastly form closing on him. Frantic with fear, he threw rabbit punches at the wood that blocked his way forward. It felt soggy against his knuckles, but it didn't give.

And then the realization hit him. He knew where he was. The tunnel beneath the graveyard. Oh God. He was inside an empty coffin.

He sniffed.

The air had filled with a charnel stench. The noises he'd heard earlier, so much like speech, were back. He knew then that the ghoul was behind him, waiting in the wider section of the tunnel.

But what was it waiting for? Why wasn't it attacking him? He'd seen how strong the thing was. It could easily grab him by the heel of his boots and pull him out. Or with that snout, it could simply start eating him from the feet up.

Bedford groaned.

He was to be eaten alive. Dead was bad enough, but to feel it coming, to know that one's self was disappearing down the gullet of such a vile thing. What must that pain feel like?

Then the sound came again, that sound that so closely resembled language yet consisted of nothing more than meaningless pops and cough-like noises.

In horror, Bedford realized the ghoul was speaking to him. It was calling to him.

He tensed, and waited for the thing to attack.

But it didn't. It stayed back there, coughing and popping at him, as though he could understand.

Bedford closed his eyes and made a decision. He wasn't going to die like this. Perhaps the thing would eat him, but it would have to kill him first. It would have to work for its supper.

That was, he realized, the best he could do.

He backed out of the coffin, moving like an eel through the narrow confines until suddenly the ceiling opened up above him.

He rolled over and found himself face-to-face with the ghoul, side by side, like lovers. The ghoul had a piece of meat in its hand, a section of what looked like a cracked femur sticking out of it.

It pushed the meat towards Bedford, like an offering.

"I don't want it," Bedford whined.

But he did. His mouth was watering, his resolve crumbling. He was so hungry, so terribly hungry.

"No," Bedford said. "Please don't."

The ghoul pressed the rotten piece of leg into his lips. Bedford, unable to resist any longer, opened his mouth and sank his teeth into the meat.

His eyes popped open.

Lightning flashed in his mind. He was flooded with the knowledge of who he was, of what he was. This human form, it was a lie. It was not him. Long ago, his kind had developed the power to change into what they fed upon. It was their best defense as they scavenged the old graveyards on the edges of human settlements.

Memories flooded into him. He remembered a British rifle team surrounding him, horrified at his appearance, ready to kill him until they themselves were killed by an artillery shell.

He had found himself amid the remains of two dozen men.

There'd been so much food. He had gorged upon their corpses. He'd been unable to control the change.

But now, all that was past.

He was home, in his mate's arms, and with all this food around, he'd never be hungry again.

THE CANDLE AND THE DARKNESS

Aric Sundquist

1. The darkness comes at dawn.

Megan watched her mother grip the wristwatch. She tightened the winder as far as it would go, then handed the watch over, dangling it from the leather band like a pendulum.

Megan plucked the watch out of the air. Although the item was small, it still felt heavy in her hands. But it also felt comforting, like a miniature heartbeat. It felt alive.

"Make sure it never stops," her mother warned. "And wind it every morning."

"Okay."

"So tell me again... How long do you have to wait here?"

"Three days."

"Right. And how many hours is that?"

Megan counted on her fingers. "Seventy-two," she answered proudly.

"Smart girl." Her mother hugged Megan and didn't let go for a long time. "You're going to get hungry, Megan. And thirsty. But you have to fight it, okay? You have to stay here no matter what. And never leave the safety of the light."

"I won't."

"I mean it."

Megan nodded.

"Now I have to go find your dad." Her mother stood up from the tile floor and crept to the edge of the candlelight. "I promised I would never leave him again."

The kitchen was gone, consumed by a darkness that churned and roiled like thick storm clouds. Megan had seen pictures of black holes in her science book. She knew they were powerful enough to swallow whole planets and moons. There was no doubt in her mind that this darkness could do the same thing, and eat them both up. Maybe the entire house itself.

Her mother stopped at the edge of the light and turned to Megan. “I love you,” she said. “I’ll go find dad and we’ll all be together again soon. I promise.”

Her mother blew a kiss. Then she stepped inside the darkness and was gone.

2. Luckily she saved the candle.

Megan’s mother had received the candle as a confirmation gift when she was just a young girl. It was a thick candle, crimson in color, with a squat silver base. Megan knew her mother wasn’t religious anymore, because the church people did mean things to her growing up. Megan often wondered why her mom kept the candle at all. It must have reminded her of something good.

A little over a year before, the power had gone out all across the city. The batteries in their flashlight were dead, so Megan had helped her mother rummage around in the closet. Eventually they found the candle in a chest full of old yearbooks and high-school tennis medals. This was the first time Megan had ever seen the candle. Then her mother set the candle in the center of the kitchen table and said it matched perfectly with the cherry wood top. She lit the wick with some matches and was surprised that it still held a flame after so many years.

Megan’s father came home shortly afterward from his afternoon shift. A month before he hadn’t come home at all. He stayed in a hotel and called them on the phone. Megan’s mother had said that they just needed some time alone and that he would be back very soon. But they seemed to be getting along better now, and he was home again. That made Megan feel good.

That night the three of them sat around the flame and played Go-fish and Crazy Eights and ate popsicles that had started to melt. Megan liked the orange ones the best, her mother liked purple, and her dad liked banana, so everything was rationed off with ease. After two hours the power sputtered back on. But then her dad crept away and flipped the circuit breaker off, saying the power had gone out again. Megan knew it was him, but didn't say anything because she was having so much fun.

They played cards by candlelight until well after her bedtime. And ever since that night, the candle remained on the table, unlit.

3. The father crosses first.

Three days before her tenth birthday, Megan heard something in her closet. It sounded like fingernails scratching across wood. At first she thought of opening it up, but when she got closer, she heard voices whispering on the other side. They told her to open the door. When she didn't comply, they said mean things. So Megan woke up her dad instead. He was tough and would deal with it properly.

He listened to her story while throwing on his robe, telling her they would go take a look. He lifted her up on his shoulders like a backpack and carried her to her room, telling her she could watch Saturday morning cartoons in an hour or so. He had tucked her in bed and was just ready to flick off the lights when he heard the voices too.

Megan had never seen her dad look scared. His whole body froze for a moment, fingers on the light switch. Then he lifted her chair over his head like a club and twisted the doorknob. The door exploded outward and the darkness had him. It melted over him like dark syrup and he dropped the weapon, grabbing the sides of the doorway with his hands. The darkness closed around him like a blanket, enveloping him. And then he was gone.

His severed arms fell to the floor.

Megan knew she had to get out of her room. She opened the shades and thought about pushing out the screen and jumping down onto the lawn, but she froze. There was no morning sunshine cresting the horizon, no blue clouds, no birds singing. There were abandoned cars and people scurrying about and no sun at all. Black fog crept through the alleyways and streets. She heard people screaming.

She jumped off her bed and ran out of her room just as her night-light flickered and went out. Overhead, the light bulbs along the hallway exploded and rained shards in her hair. Groping around in the dark, she missed the first step and stumbled down the hallway steps.

Downstairs, her mother lit the candle and asked why she was running around so early in the morning. Then she saw the blackness shift and swirl and race toward them like a chaotic tidal wave. The darkness hit the candlelight and stopped.

"The candle is keeping it away," her mother said after some time, holding her daughter tightly.

"Why?" Megan asked, crying. "What's happening?"

"I think it's the Three Days of Darkness. It's from the Bible, Megan. From what I remember, Hell is unleashed on the world for three days, claiming all nonbelievers. We're safe here, though, as long as the candle is lit. The only thing that keeps the darkness at bay is a blessed candle. Nothing else will stop it."

Her mother cupped the candle and walked slowly from the table toward the kitchen sink. Megan held her mother's sweatshirt. They stopped right where the sink was supposed to be, but there was nothing left, just an empty void.

Then they began hearing the voices.

4. The son is not blessed.

Megan had gone to school for four years with a boy named Robert Mullins. Then one day he hung himself in his closet. A letter was found in his pocket, a list of people who had hurt him in school. Nothing more, just thirty names. The list contained the entire third-grade class, all except Megan and two others.

Megan hated bullies. She treated everyone with respect. If people were mean, she tried her best to ignore them. So when Robert started sitting near her in the cafeteria, she told him to ignore all the other kids. Usually they made fun of his clothes. His family was poor and couldn't afford new things. Robert always answered with an "Okay" and blushed heavily. Sometimes he gave her some Skittles. She accepted just one (orange flavored, of course) because Skittles were hard to stop eating once you started.

Then this past spring Megan found herself sneaking upstairs to her locker during recess. She had to get a lunch ticket she owed to one of her friends. She saw Robert sitting by himself in the cafeteria, waiting patiently for the bell to ring. She never saw him outside with the other kids anymore. He was teased pretty badly, so he must have stopped going outside altogether.

Megan crept up closer to the side of the door and waved. But he didn't see her, just kept glancing up at the clock and pushing food around on his tray and waiting for the bell to ring. She decided right then and there to help him find a friend. It would be her mission before school was over. For some reason she now had power over the boys in her class. She could tell them to do something and they would argue a little, but eventually they always did what she asked. It was pretty strange.

When his body was found that same evening, school was canceled for the remainder of the week. Megan stayed in her room for two days. She didn't want to talk to anyone. Although she hadn't known him all that well, she wanted to go to the funeral. She felt it was the right thing to do.

The funeral hall smelled of flowers and chemicals. People were dressed in black, and they all stood in a long line to see Robert in his casket. He wore new clothes—a nice black suit. But he still looked sad to her, even in death. People cried and hugged and argued. Robert's mother was religious, a devout Catholic, and kept saying that her baby was damned for eternity. Megan didn't know why anyone would think that, so she decided to ask her mother when she got home.

"His family believes that when you kill yourself, it's an unpardonable sin."

"Oh. What does unpardonable mean?"

"You know what pardon means, right?"

"Yes. Like when you're in jail for a long time, and then you're forgiven for being bad so they let you out."

"That's right. Unpardonable is the opposite. It means it can't be forgiven. Not ever."

"What if the person is really nice but just feels kind of lonely and sad?"

"It doesn't matter if the person is good or evil, Megan. That's not how the Bible works. Suicide is against God's will, so the person goes to Hell. There's no gray area. There's only light and dark."

5. A ghost in the shadows.

On the second morning, Megan realized the candle wasn't going to last the entire Three Days of Darkness. Her mother had told her that it was a special candle, made of pure beeswax, which burned really slow. It was labeled "Three Day Devotional Candle." But they had lit the candle the night the power went out. From what Megan could remember, they had played cards for four hours. So she needed a way to extend the life of the candle at least that long. It might be tricky, but she could figure it out.

"I don't know if you can do it," Robert said from the shadows.

She could see him vaguely in the dimness, swinging back and forth on a noose like a clock ticking in perfect rhythm. He had started talking to her an hour before. At first she ignored him, covered her ears and sang every song she could think of from the radio. But as time went on, she grew tired and eventually listened to him talk.

"It can't be done, Megan. The candle has a day left, at best. You can't make it last long enough. Just like you couldn't help me."

She had already apologized to him twice for not helping him. So Megan ignored him and thought about her predicament.

She was starving and dehydrated at this point, lips cracked and starting to hurt. It was becoming harder to think clearly. Sometimes her vision blurred and she had to close her eyes until everything returned to normal. Her body felt heavy and slow.

She hobbled over to the candle, knelt down, and began pressing the sides of the wax toward the center, as if building up a sandcastle on the beach. Hopefully it would cause the wick to burn slower. But she had to be extra careful—one quick move and the candle would go out.

"That won't work," Robert said.

"It might if I keep doing it."

"No, it won't. You have to start thinking outside the box."

"Like how?"

"It's your birthday tomorrow, right?"

Megan forgot all about her birthday. She would turn ten tomorrow. Her mother had a chocolate cake wrapped in tinfoil hidden away in the freezer, labeled "Lasagna." It was funny because Megan wasn't a little kid anymore. The trick wasn't fooling anyone.

Then Megan thought of all the frosting and sugar and her mouth began watering. Two days without food was hard. Three days would be unbearable. She tried not to think about food at all. She had other things to ponder.

"Haven't you ever made a birthday wish?" Robert asked.

"Yes, many times."

"Why don't you make a wish?"

She was tired. She put her head down and decided to sleep. "I'll think about it." She held the watch close to her ear, listening to it tick away. Her mother always wore that particular watch. It still smelled like her.

Megan drifted off to sleep.

6. The Morning Star.

Megan awoke from strange dreams and realized her right hand was missing. Her arm didn't hurt at all. There was just a stump of flesh that felt smooth to the touch. Somewhere out in the dark, she could hear her mother's watch ticking like a mechanical insect, taunting her, buzzing closer, fading.

Megan cried.

"What's wrong?" Robert asked from the dark. He still swung back and forth on the noose, but now he moved faster, and the sounds of the rope were louder.

She tried to answer him, but she couldn't talk. Sobs wracked her. She motioned to her missing hand.

"Looks like the flame tipped too far to one side while you were sleeping," he said. "And then it looks like the melting wax created a blind spot. You should be glad it didn't take your head."

Megan wiped the tears from her eyes and checked on the candle. Robert was right: the candle had melted to one side and the flame was almost extinguished. The other side of the candle was a tower of wax.

"What now?" Robert asked.

"Do you think making a wish to God will work?"

"It would be praying, not wishing. But you aren't Christian, so I'm not sure. Are you baptized?"

"No."

"Then it won't work. God only likes people who are baptized."

"I could try making a wish. It is my birthday."

"That's what I would do. Like when you wish on a falling star."

"Right."

"Did you know that the name "Lucifer" means "light bearer" in Latin? It was a name given to the Morning Star. Funny how they change little things around like that."

Megan tried her best to ignore him. His conversations had become much stranger and darker. She decided to concentrate on the task at hand.

She sat and thought for a long time. She knew she couldn't make the candle last for another day. Her watch was gone. And she wouldn't last much longer without food and water. So after much thought on the matter, she decided to take the initiative.

She closed her eyes and made her wish.

"What did you wish for?" Robert asked.

"I can't tell."

"Oh, that's right. Because if you tell, then it won't come true, right?"

"Right."

"Now blow out the candle to seal the deal."

Megan nodded and blew out the candle. As soon as she did it, she realized her mistake.

Robert's laughter filled the void.

The darkness slammed her to the ground. It spread her legs open until tendons snapped and ligaments ripped. She screamed and the darkness spilled into her mouth, burning like hot oil slipping down her throat, deep into her lungs.

Then she was falling.

When she landed, she didn't hit the ground. A long stake drove up between her legs and out her mouth. Her broken limbs flopped uselessly at her sides as she choked on blood and charred wood.

It was at that moment, her body broken and slipping down the stake an inch at a time, when Megan realized her wish had come true. She had wanted more than anything to be with her mother and father again.

They were impaled right next to her.

THE LULLABY MAN

John McNee

There were no doors in the Muddle House. Only endless crawlspace opening into crooked corridors and rooms filled with smoke and sawdust. Jenny scrambled on her hands and knees between splintered wood and cobwebs, pausing only briefly to peel off her coat when it snagged on an exposed nail. She had to keep moving, if only to prevent a collapse into useless panic. Do that and it was all over. She knew there was no escape. She knew, eventually, he would find her.

"Seven, eight," he called with an ever-so-relaxed lilt in his voice. "Lay them straight..." His words could be heard in every passageway and corner. "Nine, ten. A big fat hen..."

"He's real, isn't he?" Jenny said.

Heather froze in mid-step, head turning back, listening over her shoulder, as though waiting for her to say it again.

She did.

"He's real." Jenny feared the champagne glass in her hand might shatter at any moment and wished she'd never picked it up. The drink had left her mouth tasting like battery acid. All around the gallery, the chatter continued—buyers and sellers, creators and their critics filled the space between piano notes with their noise. But here there was silence, and Jenny felt it acutely as she waited for Heather to respond.

Jenny felt foolish, blurting it out the way she had, all dressed up for the occasion, high heel shoes and lipstick smeared on the rim of her glass. And Heather, too obviously the artist, wearing paint-flecked denim in a crowd of suits and skirts, her pierced eyebrows and bad dye job—non-conformist by committee.

After the passing of far too many seconds, Heather finally turned, fixed Jenny with a narrow gaze, with the slightest twitch of a smile on her lips, and answered: "Yes. He is."

Hours later, the smell of oil paints and white spirit burned her nostrils as she sat on an old wooden bench. She could still taste the cheap champagne, even after trying to wash it away with the beer Heather had offered when inviting her into the studio. The can in her hand was still half full, but the beer inside was warm and flat. She didn't want to ask for another.

Heather, meanwhile, had just cracked open her sixth.

"I don't know for how long," she said. "Weeks, maybe, we just played games, told jokes, sang songs. The sort of things little kids do. And then one night, when he asked me if I wanted to go with him to visit his house, of course I said yes. When he asked how much, I said 'Very much.' And so we went."

"To the Muddle House," Jenny said, half statement, half question.

Heather nodded. "The instant we arrived, he changed. No more fun and games. At least...not for me. I couldn't go home, no matter how hard I wished. I couldn't...couldn't keep his hands off me, no matter..." She closed her eyes. Took a breath. "I begged him not to kill me. And he promised he wouldn't, if I pleased him." She opened her eyes and stared down at her drink, then shrugged. "So I pleased him."

Jenny stole a glance at the fresh canvas on the easel, trying hard not to let her emotions show. The painting called to mind a work by another, much younger artist she knew—overly-large circles for eyes. Big triangle grin.

"It felt like days," Heather said. "Weeks, I don't know. But when he took me back home, when I woke up in bed...it was the same evening. The same hour." She nodded. "He can do that. That's one of the things he can do."

Silence passed between them for a moment. Jenny found her hand slipping absently into her coat pocket and she quickly withdrew it. “What about after?” she said.

“After?” Heather looked up. “I forgot all about it. Or repressed, or whatever you want to call it. Then...years later...I would’ve been about fifteen. I went to a party and convinced a boy to let me give him a blowjob. And when he put it in my mouth...I tried to bite it off.” Another sip and a dismissive wave of the hand. “He was fine,” she said. “They sewed him up pretty good. I was sent for therapy. It only took four sessions before it all flooded back. Vivid. Like someone switched on the light.”

“Yes,” said Jenny.

Heather glanced around the room at the portraits on the walls. “That’s where all this started. A couple years ago someone saw one, asked how much; it all snowballed from there. My agent says she wishes I’d paint something else. I don’t know how to tell her...I’ve tried. I can’t.” She drained the last of the can, crushed and tossed it. “Anyway, how did you find out about tonight? You on the gallery’s mailing list?”

Jenny shook her head, eyes on the floor. “I typed the words Lullaby Man into a search engine,” she stated blankly. “Your paintings were the first thing to come up.”

Heather laughed and reached over the side of the bed to grab another beer from the cooler. “Whatever the hell possessed you to do a thing like that?”

There were no clocks in the Muddle House. Such things were of no use. There were, however, parts of clocks. Mechanical entrails, liberated from their glass and copper houses, littered the floor among torn scraps of clothing and crumpled newspapers. It was like some terrible attempt at wit. Some kind of metaphorical middle finger to the laws of reality and that Other Place where seconds ticked by in an orderly fashion, somewhere beyond the murky limbo he had created for himself and his victims.

To Jenny, the cogs also called to mind what Heather had said about the house’s layout, the way its levels twisted on dials and rooms shifted position in clockwork complicity with his demands.

This was his maze. His geography. His own Rubik's Cube. She could run for days and still arrive back in the same room. Maybe that's what the cogs on the floor meant. A reminder. All the time in the world and no way out.

"Thirteen, fourteen. Draw the curtain..." His whisper shook the walls around her.

"There's not a paint in the world," Heather said, "not in the whole world...that gets the whites of his eyes, the brilliance of his teeth. That smile: it's like burning magnesium, and there's nothing…I can never…I'll never be able to convey that." Her head was propped up with one hand, eyes squeezed shut. The words kept spilling out in a relentless stream. "In the dark…the darkness…when you can't see your own hand in front of your face…you could still see his eyes, his grin. Like a fucking cartoon. That's what he is. And I made him."

One eye flickered open and rolled around towards Jenny, checking to make sure she was still listening. "It took me a long time to get to that point," she continued. "Where I could finally admit what he was. We're talking years. They tried for so long to find someone to pin it on, my...trauma. And I said: 'Nooo, it was the Lullaby Man. He took me to a place where time doesn't exist and, when he was all done, put me back to bed.' Eventually, I realized that which the doctors could never conceive."

"What?" said Jenny, casting a furtive glance at the clock on the wall. 11:24 p.m.

Heather tapped a finger against her temple. "He started up here," she said. "And grew. I made him, but never controlled him. I created something so powerful…" She said it with a kind of pride. "Even with all the pain he brought, I'd wanted him. I still did. I do."

Jenny nodded, doubting every word.

"When I went to bed that night," Heather said, "I lay down, closed my eyes, and told the darkness: 'I want you. I want you to come back. Very much.' "

"And did he?"

Heather shut her eyes and nodded. "Only this time it was more…tender. Like we finally understood each other. I forgave him. I mean…I had to. He's a part of me, and I love him. For all the things he does and all that he's capable of...he's mine." When Heather opened her eyes, she wasn't looking at Jenny. "You want to meet him, don't you?"

Jenny's breath caught in her throat. "Yes," she whispered.

"How much?" she asked, still not looking her in the eye.

Jenny's hand slid back into her coat pocket. Her fingers traced the knife's blade. "Very much," she answered.

Heather nodded. She was looking past Jenny, over her shoulder, into the corner of the room.

"Why?" Jenny said.

Without averting her gaze, Heather took one last swig from the can, then answered. "Because he's standing right there."

"Hark, hark, the dogs do bark,
My wife is coming in.
With rogues and jades
And roaring blades,
They make a devilish din…"

Damp and rot pricked at her flesh. Death, decomposition, dust. They were heavy in the air, soaking her skin. Already she was afraid to breathe and only half awake.

"Jenny, we're here. Wake up, Jenny. Jenny. We're here..."

Knowing she shouldn't, Jenny opened her eyes. Gray wisps of vapor curled slowly upwards through the gloom. The wall was brown cork, with a thin film of grease on the skirting boards.

Jenny was lying on her front, left cheek pressed to the floor. She could feel the gentle rumble of hidden mechanisms above and below. She could hear the faraway echo of tinny chimes, like piano hammers tapping on empty bottles. She could smell the lingering scents of old fires and old blood. It was all so painfully, frighteningly familiar.

"Come on," Heather said, hooking a hand under her arm, pulling her up. "You'll feel better when you're on your feet."

"Christ," Jenny whispered, sitting up, staring down the dank corridor.

"I did what you wanted," said Heather. She was grinning. Her eyes blinked slowly, lids weighted from the alcohol. "Now come on. He'll be waiting."

Jenny threw her hand out to the wall, letting the uneven timber prop her up. Her throat was tight. "I can't," she croaked. "Please don't make me." Shaking. She was actually shaking. Her mission momentarily forgotten.

Heather cocked her head to one side, looked her companion up and down. "I didn't think you'd be like this," she sighed. "I thought you'd be one of the eager ones. It's disappointing."

Jenny's breath was shallow. She hugged herself and tried to stand up straight. "What…what do you mean?"

Heather turned and started walking slowly down the passageway. "There's always two kinds," she said. "I meet lots of hungry young boys and girls who are oh-so-desperate to have their flesh abused and souls corrupted. Like they think it'll make 'em more interesting at parties…"

"Worked for you, didn't it?" Jenny snapped, then instantly hated herself for saying it.

Heather didn't seem to mind. She laughed, continuing amiably down the crooked hallway, heel to toe to heel to toe. "The point is, you get the ones who say they're after corruption and mean it. And you get the ones who talk the talk, but as soon as they're in it's all tears and screams and begging to take it all back." She turned back and fixed Jenny with a very serious glare. "Of course, by then, it's much too late to say no."

Jenny was moving at last, still leaning on the wall, but dragging her feet across the floor. They were like lead weights. She blinked, willing her eyes to adjust to the gloom. They refused. "What are you saying?" she hissed. "How many others have you brought here? How many have you offered him?"

Heather halted and turned to her left. There was an opening. Soft amber light. She shook her head. "That's the wrong question," she said. "You should be asking how many survived." She stepped forward, into the next room, and disappeared from sight.

Oh good, Jenny said to herself. *She is a psycho after all...*

Then came the voice:

"Jenny, Jenny, skin so fair,
Pretty flowers in her hair,
Would that any man could snare,
The beating heart of Jenny fair…"

For a few moments, his voice was in and around everything. It permeated every molecule in the air and bubbled in Jenny's skull. Not loud, just everywhere. Then silence fell like the blade of a guillotine and Jenny feared she might die. She thought her heart might stop beating, lungs might burst, blood might freeze, thought she would scream, weep or piss herself and collapse into a gibbering wreck on the floor.

Instead, she closed her eyes and reminded herself—very clearly—why she was there. Pink little girl with pigtails, tall stick figure in black. Then she took a few very deep breaths and followed the same routine she always employed ahead of any important meeting—she ran a hand through her hair, brushed down the front of her dress, and walked into the room.

Jenny could hardly see him at first. Just a dark smear, like a burn on her cornea. Then the edges began to sharpen and became a shadow with burning eyes, coiling itself around Heather, thin limbs pressed tight to her skin. Then the smile, glinting white and cold. He bled his way into her vision with convivial ease.

This was a rare privilege. The Lullaby Man wasn't meant to be seen by grown-ups.

The two "lovers" stood on a raised platform in the center of a round room, four exits into intersecting tunnels. The ceiling was frosted glass and, beyond that, golden liquid. It shimmered, coloring the room below—and people within—a sickly sepia shade.

He kept his eyes on Jenny as Heather embraced him, then spun her round, keeping a firm clutch on her body, to face the newcomer.

"Jenny, Jenny, can it be?" he breathed. "Pretty Jenny, all for me. How you've grown."

Jenny, standing in the archway, could say nothing yet. The terror was too strong. She had to force it down, pummel it into submission through action. Clenching her jaw to keep her teeth from chattering, she forced her foot to take a step forward and reminded herself why she was here.

"He knows your name," Heather laughed, running her fingers over his polished features. "How does he know your name?" It was a genuine question that, as soon as she'd said it, transformed into a genuine fear. "How does he know your name?"

"Because," Jenny said through gritted teeth, "we've met before."

The Lullaby Man's grin widened. A grotesque caricature of a smile. Too many teeth. He had hundreds and hundreds of teeth.

"You're crazy," Heather said grimly. "That's impossible."

"I was eight," said Jenny, spitting the words out as if they were poisoned. "The first time. That's five years before your introduction," she added, to save Heather the trouble of doing the math. "I thought he was magical…at first." She kept moving slowly forward as they spoke, pushing on towards the stage, staring straight at him.

His fiercely bright eyes stayed focused on Jenny, shivering black pupils trained on hers, almost as though he'd forgotten about Heather, even as his arms drew her closer.

Jenny continued: "There have been hundreds. Thousands. The ones he likes he sends home with their minds stained and memories buried deep. Only sometimes, something sets them loose and they remember. It happened to you, and it happened to me."

The Lullaby Man leaned forward. "And I know why..." he purred. His voice, lush and soothing, never mean, echoed in her head, swirling like brandy in the bottom of a glass. It made her want to vomit. He pawed at Heather, sliding one white-gloved hand between her breasts, the other slipping under her shirt, rubbing across her midriff. "But she's so pure," he said. "So young and much too beautiful. I couldn't resist."

"Leave her alone." Jenny felt tears welling up in her eyes.

Heather smiled, biting her lip and tilting her head back, eyes closed in a parody of ecstasy. “But I don’t want him to—”

“We’re not talking about you!” Jenny snapped, emotion cracking in her voice. She was just a few feet away from them now. She only had to push herself a little closer.

Heather stared at her coldly. “I don’t understand any of this,” she said.

Another step closer. And another. Jenny felt the tears begin to roll down her cheeks as she pointed at Heather and told the Lullaby Man: “Will you tell her, already? She thinks she invented you. Thinks you belong to her. Thinks she dreamed you up. She doesn’t have a fucking clue! Won’t you just tell her?” *Listen to you*, she said to herself. *Barking orders at a murderous abomination.*

His grin shrank a little, eyes narrowing, and he finally turned to look at Heather. “You didn’t make me,” he told her. Simple as that. She stared back, still not comprehending. “Nobody made me.”

Jenny was close enough now. She had to act. Knew she had to act. While he wasn’t looking at her, do it now, while he was focused on Heather, do it now, before he turned back, do it now, do it now, do it, do it, DO IT!

She thrust her hand into the pocket of her coat and grasped—nothing. It was gone.

“No,” Heather whispered. “Don’t...”

The Lullaby Man raised his right hand, and Jenny saw it there. The knife. Her knife. It shone golden in the liquid’s light, the hands of one embedded timepiece glinting between his fingers.

“I made myself,” he said. “I can do that. That’s one of the things I can do.” He pulled Heather towards him and plunged the blade into her chest. It sank through her breastplate with a wet snap.

Jenny screamed, already staggering backward towards the exit.

He drew the blade out, casting an arc of blood into the air, then stabbed again, this time driving the knife into her belly and twisting it. Heather bent forward and opened her mouth to cry out, but only frothing blood spilled from her lips. Her hands went to the wound at her stomach, curling around the knife as she stumbled over the side of the stage.

He let her topple, granting her a few claps by way of applause, then spun back to Jenny. "Did you think you'd smuggle that past me?" he said. "That's cheating. I don't care for games with weapons. Let's play something else, shall we?"

Jenny turned and bolted into the corridor, hurling herself down the passageway and into the clockwork maze.

"Hide and seek," he said. "That's good. You go hide." Still grinning, he placed his hands over his eyes. "One, two, buckle my shoe..."

There was no hope in the Muddle House. Nothing of the kind.

As a child, Jenny had sprinted unthinkingly down these hallways, wriggled through every narrow crevice and sought out every concealed nook. She had been slow to learn that there was nowhere to hide. No place could she go where the Lullaby Man wouldn't find her. She now feared this was true of the outside world as well.

"Three, four, knock at the door..."

At eight years of age, it had been fear that had driven Jenny deeper, ever deeper into the maze, desperate to find an escape. Twenty-five years later, a new fear had brought her back, her own terror driving her to seek him out. Not revenge. Never that. She hadn't known Heather would lead her straight to him. Couldn't have known. Just a hunch. Just enough to justify the purchase of a knife.

She'd carefully considered what kind of weapon could hurt him, if anything could. She'd found what she was looking for in a display case with a thousand-dollar price tag—the Huntsman's Companion. Sharp enough to slice open a rhino, with a compass studded into the handle. She'd asked the craftsman if he could swap the compass for a watch, then: "Actually, think you could fit three or four?"

She'd put her faith in the knife. Without it, there wasn't a chance.

"Five, six, pick up sticks…"

She couldn't hide. He'd find her sooner that way. To keep ahead of him, she had to keep moving. Even if the constant shifting and reshaping of the architecture turned her around a dozen times, she had to keep moving.

"Nine, ten, a big fat hen…"

The heels came off, then the coat. Soon she was down to the cocktail dress and shredded pantyhose, crawling on hands and knees through tunnels lined with fairy lights and burnt matchsticks, face slick with sweat and filth. Nothing to use against him now but her fists.

"Thirteen, fourteen, draw the curtain…"

She began to weep, stepping awkwardly across floors littered with cogs and pins, occasionally stumbling upon items other victims had brought in and discarded—a ribbon, spectacles, a small blood-spattered slipper. Objects alien to the Muddle House were always easy to spot. They shone with a kind of newness.

"Fifteen, sixteen, maids in the kitchen…"

He wouldn't play the game like she expected him to. Not now. He'd kept Heather like a pet all these years, feeding him bloody entertainments. This time she had brought an assassin and so had to die. But he wouldn't be happy about that. He'd keep counting, letting Jenny run, wear herself out, but he wouldn't waste any of his own energy hunting for her. When he reached twenty he'd just close the book.

"It's like a default mechanism," Heather had said. This was still on her third beer. "He just snaps his fingers and the whole thing reassembles, all the corridors lining up and locking into place. Then..." She had pressed the heels of her hands one to the other, fingers out, like she was holding up an invisible chalice, then slowly drew her palms together. "Like a book, see? And everything rolls downhill...to him."

"Seventeen, eighteen, she's in waiting..."

Jenny still had the image of Heather in her mind, hands clasped as if in prayer, as she stepped out into another corridor and felt dampness under the soles of her feet. She looked down. Even in this gray light she could see it was blood.

It trailed in a long, thick line and she followed it, just a few steps along the hallway, to where a frail form lay crumpled in the shadows. Jenny lowered herself onto one knee, squinting through the darkness, and recognized Heather.

She had died slowly. For a time there had been enough strength in her limbs to drag herself out of the round room and into this hallway—wherever that was now in this geographical jumble—but her heart had long since stopped.

Jenny looked away from Heather's face to her outstretched arm and stained index finger, which seemed to point to a bloody marking on the floorboards. For a moment, Jenny hoped the symbol might be some clue to aid in her escape. Then she recognized it: two bloody circles for eyes and a bloody crescent smile. He really had been all she could paint.

"Nineteen, twenty, my belly's empty..."

His words echoed everywhere, but Jenny didn't hear them. Her total concentration was focused on Heather's body, her eyes having only just fallen on the wound in her stomach. On the gleaming handle of the knife, protruding from her cold flesh.

Scarcely believing it was real, Jenny reached out her hand towards the blade, brushing her fingers against the surface of the handle. The clock faces, she saw, were all frozen at 11:24 p.m. A noise like the snap of a spring-loaded jaw sounded in her skull.

The book closed.

The Muddle House sprang instantly into a new configuration; the corridor became a chimney into darkness, and Jenny fell along with Heather's body, tumbling down, over and over, down and down and down.

They plummeted for a time through air, then through honey-colored water. Turning madly, spinning together through liquid churned into foam, their limbs entwined, and for a moment Jenny feared that Heather's corpse would drag her down to her death.

At last she broke free and swam up to the surface, gasping for air and thrashing desperately with one hand, trying to find something to hold on to. Bitter water in her eyes, she kicked her way blindly to the edge of the pool. Exhausted, still breathless, she laid her head down, left arm outstretched, gripping the floor.

Behind her, the detritus of his world continued to rain down, splashing and quickly sinking into the brimming trough.

Jenny could feel him gazing down at her before he spoke.

"Ladybird, ladybird, fly away home. Your house is on fire. Your children are gone."

She opened her eyes, blinking away tears of golden water.

He crouched low, leaning towards her ear as he breathed: "All except one, and that's little Anne. And she has crept under the warming pan."

Green lines for grass. Blue for sky.

He lifted her head in his hands and turned her face towards him. "You know, I'd hardly even started with her," he said. "Only a few songs and games. Nothing more. But you needn't worry. I'll take good care of Anne."

His candy-colored lips peeled back and Jenny saw her own haggard face, reflected in his teeth. Teeth like razors. Big, big, *big* grin.

Her right arm shot up out of the water, fist clenched. He glanced sideways and caught the slightest glimpse of the blade before it sank deep into his neck. The tip emerged from the other side, driven through to the hilt.

His eyes continued to look down for a moment, as though he could see the clock-studded handle. Then he looked to Jenny as blood trickled thinly from both wounds, meeting at his chest to form a crimson necklace.

Jenny stared back, anticipating that same eager expression, ready for him to laugh, decry her as a fool for ever thinking a creature like him could be killed. Yet all she saw, all his burning eyes conveyed, was fear.

The watches in the handle sprung to life—she could feel them beneath her palm—quickening in time to his ebbing pulse as his life poured in a thick stream from his throat.

Tick, tick, tick, tick…

The walls of the Muddle House shuddered—a prelude to total collapse.

He moved then, jerking back as though to save himself, but Jenny turned the blade toward herself as blood spurted up her arm, putting her free hand on the back of his neck and pulling him close, tugging him into the water.

As his hands cradled her head and hers clutched his, they sank together into the darkening depths, the light from his smile flickering fast. The water blossomed red all around.

When she opened her eyes, his grin was the first thing she saw. He was looming over her, mad pupils gazing into hers.

She scuttled back, halfway across the room, before realizing it was just a painting. Heather's latest portrait, sitting on the easel.

She was back in the studio. Alone. Still wearing the sodden dress, her body caked in filth and blood. The clock on the wall read 11:25 p.m.

Jenny rose, shakily, to her feet, still dizzy, still in pain. She gazed about the room, trying to assemble her thoughts. The knife was gone. Heather was gone. The Lullaby Man…

Yet here Jenny was. Against the odds… but not the rules.

Well, then. That was that.

Following a brief analysis, she limped into Heather's bathroom and showered. Then she sought out some clothes, dressed, gathered her bag, and went out into the street, where she caught a cab to the airport.

The plane returned her home the following morning. Still a little woozy but feeling generally okay, she picked up her car from the lot and drove to the house. It was a warm, sunny morning, and, walking up the drive, she could hear the kids playing in the yard out back.

Her husband met her in the kitchen, greeting her with a kiss and asking how the trip had been. "Fine," she said. "Tiring," she added, then smiled and went to the refrigerator to pour a glass of orange juice.

Closing the door, her eye was drawn again to the crayon picture pinned there with a daisy-shaped magnet. Green lines for grass, blue for sky. A pink little girl with pigtails was holding hands with a tall stick figure, drawn all in black. Overly-large circles for eyes. Big triangle grin. An arrow pointing to the girl read "ME." The second, pointing to the black, taller figure, read: "THE LULBY MAN." The signature in the corner: "ANNE."

Jenny stayed there for a while, just looking.

Then, with a kind of serene care, she lifted the magnet and took the drawing down. She folded it three times, dropped it in the trash, and went outside to join her children.

THE FINAL ONE PERCENT

Desmond Warzel

Genius is one percent inspiration, ninety-nine percent perspiration.
–Thomas Edison

In the room are two female personages: one, an ordinary woman; the other, something much more.

The woman fancies herself a playwright. A month ago, she was a poet; in the months preceding, a novelist, an essayist, a screenwriter. She suffers no shortage of ideas; half-filled pages litter the room in veritable snowdrifts, each bearing a few typed or handwritten lines as a memorial to an idea readily conceived but ultimately stillborn. Their strata, if excavated, would describe a sequential history of her short-lived literary obsessions, but taken as a whole, they are silent testament to her shortcomings: though not unintelligent, she is dismissive—a page, once set aside, will never be taken up again—and unreflective, abandoning each unsuccessful piece with no consideration of *why* it has failed.

Of late, her search for inspiration has her imitating her betters: she has begun this session with a spoken invocation of the Muses, cobbled together from Homer, Dante, Chaucer, and Shakespeare. Her fingertips have no sooner come to rest on the dusty keyboard than a sudden sensation of being watched suggests to her that this simple affectation has actually succeeded where other tactics—writing exercises, people-watching, meditation, drugs—have fallen short.

When she turns in her chair, the newcomer is there: a female form, perhaps the ideal female form, in a flowing garment of preternaturally pure white. She occupies the one bare place in the room, a roughly circular bit of wood floor showing through the carpet of papers. She does not speak, and her expression is unreadable.

This is a Muse in the divine flesh; of that the woman is certain, even if she has no idea which one it is (the nine names and spheres of influence have fled her memory). But the mystery of the goddess's identity is secondary to that of her presence in this place. The woman has always imagined the attentions of the Muses to manifest themselves indirectly: a stray sunbeam illuminating an ordinary object in an unusual way, or a snatch of peculiar conversation overheard by chance—intangible inspirations to be whimsically ascribed to a metaphorical deity. But this is no metaphor.

It may have been the woman's invocation; perhaps she has accidentally hit upon the precise wording and tone to best attract the Muse's notice and interest. It may be the mounds of discarded pages; perhaps the unfulfilled potential of all the false starts thereon inscribed, continually tugging at the edges of the Muse's attention, has finally attained a critical mass that warrants direct intervention.

Whatever the cause, the perplexity that suddenly inhabits the Muse's face, the cocked eyebrow forming a flawless arch, suggests that she is not accustomed to visibility to the eyes of mortals.

The woman springs to her feet, knocking over her chair. If there is protocol that applies here, she does not know it. All she can think to do is put forth her best work, on the notion that the Muse helps those who help themselves, and so she looks around desperately for a page to serve as the exemplar of her literary output. A few interminable seconds pass. Finally, with crushing regret at the negligence she has shown her abandoned compositions, she gathers up an armload of papers at random and displays them before her visitor. It is a tentative gesture, part offering, part supplication.

The Muse has no need of it. Mediocrity pervades the room and everything in it like stale cigarette smoke, to a degree that offends her rarefied senses. That its author has laid eyes on her, by whatever agency, compounds the affront. The Muse will give her assessment with awful honesty.

In the past, the woman has placed her work before a parade of friends, colleagues, lovers, relations, the odd stranger. She has endured unconvincing flattery, polite dismissal, puzzled incredulity, and derisive laughter, and she has easily dismissed them all, if indeed she truly heard them.

But nothing can compare with the scorn of a genuine goddess. The Muse's withering stare pins her against the worn lip of her desk, stripping away the barriers she has erected against the world's mockery. It penetrates her to the core of her being, forces the breath from her body, scours the very thoughts from her mind. Her heart strains to beat against the pressure of that Olympian gaze. The pages she was holding drift to the floor.

The Muse's dissection of her, the laying out of her inadequacies before all the cosmos, continues for a full minute. It is the longest minute the woman will ever know.

The ordeal ends when the Muse withdraws her frightful attentions, not out of mercy but out of simple disdain. She has made her point.

In a minute or so, the burning in the woman's chest grows insistent enough to penetrate the smothering emptiness inside her, and she remembers to breathe once more.

She pushes herself upward until she is standing once more, and—soaked in sweat, hands shaking, leaning on the desk for support—stares the Muse in the eye, at once bold and pathetic. The Muse's lesson, it seems, has been wasted. Her contempt has receded, and it is the work of a moment for the woman to remake that which was swept away.

"Fine," she says. The word leaves her throat reluctantly; she has not spoken aloud since she cloistered herself in this room two days ago. "My work is pedestrian. Derivative. Uninspired. But that only means you've been neglecting your duty, doesn't it?"

(Her defiance would serve her well if only it were coupled with talent.)

The Muse is perfectly capable of responding in English, but she will not sully her tongue by doing so. She answers the brazen charges with a single, insultingly simple image, which elbows its way effortlessly into the woman's thoughts: a great, Niagara-like torrent, and a child's outstretched hand bearing an empty cup hardly bigger than a thimble. The cup has only to touch the water and it is ripped from the tiny fingers and lost forever. The message is clear: *My inspiration is for those with strength enough to endure it, and talent enough to contain it.*

This frank assessment has reached the woman in a way that past criticisms have not done; it takes over her entire consciousness, leaving no room for dissenting thoughts. When it finally passes, her confidence and certainty do not return. She sags against the desk, eyes cast downward. Her only comfort is that the Muse is done with her, that she is alone again; but when she looks up once more, she is denied even this consolation.

The Muse has not departed; her singular expression—divine consternation is quite a thing to behold—suggests that she *cannot* depart. She is evidently confined to the circle of bare floor where she has been standing; in attempting to cross this boundary, she resembles almost exactly a mime trapped in an invisible box. The discarded papers forming the circumference of her prison apparently function in the manner of Faust's infamous pentagram, binding her within—or so it seems to the woman. She will never actually know, but she is certain of one thing: the comical tableau before her has dissipated whatever remaining awe she may have felt at keeping company with the goddess.

The tide thus turned, the woman addresses her captive. "Inspire me, and I'll break the circle." Once again she sees the raging waters in her mind, but the image has lost its potency. "I'll take my chances. Inspire me."

The Muse makes no further response; she is immortal, and patience will prevail.

Emboldened by the shift in circumstances and the realization that immortality does not imply invulnerability, the woman considers how she might take that which the Muse will not give.

She tests the circle with an outstretched foot, careful not to disturb the papers which make up its edge, and discovers that she can enter and leave the Muse's prison unimpeded. As the woman advances, the goddess retreats, not in fear but in distaste at a mortal daring such proximity, until her back rests against the invisible barrier. When the woman reaches out and grasps her by the arm, she does not resist—a vulgar scuffle does not become her—but remains defiantly passive. For the woman's part, she is unsure how to proceed now that the Muse is in her clutches.

Simple perseverance assures the Muse's eventual escape. Papers decay; buildings fall. The circle *will* be broken, and the Muse has, quite literally, all the time in the world. Therein lies the woman's conundrum: she cannot hope to outplay her captive in the waiting game. She must act, immediately and decisively. But how to draw forth that which she desires, that intangible treasure bound up in the Muse's very essence?

The phrasing of the question itself precipitates a possible solution, and the woman leaves her home for the first time in days.

When she returns, she half-expects the room to be empty, but the Muse is still there. *What*, she wonders, *does a Muse think about, left to herself?*

She attacks in one quick motion, stepping into the circle, seizing the Muse's arm once more (noting in passing how coarse her palm feels against that smooth, cool skin), searching for a vein.

There is no reason the Muse's anatomy should mirror that of human beings, and no reason it should not. In any case, the vein is there; the woman draws a syringe (unwrapped outside for purposes of stealth) from her coat pocket, pierces the vein, draws the plunger outward. The blood emerges: a bright, clear red. The Muse will not dignify this imposition by reacting to it.

The woman places a single drop of the blood on her fingertip and rubs it with her thumb; rather than smearing, it remains whole, like a bead of mercury. Its fragrance is floral, not metallic; it is sweet to the taste. But when she inserts the needle into her own arm and pushes the plunger home, it is as if she has pressed a hot iron to the spot.

She is sure she has poisoned herself, but the piercing heat in her limb quickly diffuses throughout her body, diluted to a pleasant, tingling warmth. She is considering repeating the procedure when suddenly the efficacy of a single dose demonstrates its sufficiency.

It is as though a great mass has collided with her mind and jarred it free of some impediment: her consciousness, in the space of an instant, expands to nearly infinite breadth and depth. Her vocabulary—now increased a hundredfold—is no longer a set of child's blocks, to be clumsily rearranged without thought; words suddenly have color, pitch, texture, and scent, and their proper, organic relationships have become obvious to her. Stray tatters of thought, once consigned to oblivion, now join together into vital, original concepts. Insight piles upon insight, with geometrically increasing complexity. It is a state of pure inspiration.

It is not the overwhelming surge she was expecting but a gentle, insistent pressure within her, whose relief will come only through expression. She must write.

She makes a mad dash for her desk but is immediately stopped short. At first she thinks the Muse is somehow hindering her, but a frantic probing reveals that the circle is barring her progress.

Courtesy of her newly acquired powers of discernment, understanding comes at once. In taking the Muse's substance into herself, she has altered her own essence irrevocably. She and the goddess are now of like natures, and whatever force has imprisoned the one, now imprisons both.

When the barrier fails to yield to her fists, she rams it halfheartedly with her shoulder instead, but as the pointlessness of the exercise makes itself evident, she sinks wearily to the floor. A single, desperate hope—that she may have acquired the Muse's immortality along with her blood—flickers into existence and is abruptly extinguished; the ache in her hands and shoulder, and the hunger pangs that until now she has ignored, are all too human.

With trepidation she gazes up at the Muse's countenance, hoping to see an expression of commiseration, or at least pity, but there is only a devastatingly spiteful smile.

It is a small, but real, mercy that thirst takes the woman before she is driven mad by the continuous onslaught of ideas that she can never purge. Her landlord discovers her body. An unimaginative sort, he cannot see the other personage standing nearby; his experience of the Muse is limited to an uncanny, elusive sensation worrying at the outer edges of his awareness. The feeling persists until he disturbs the circle, whereupon it vanishes as though it had never been and is soon forgotten.

THE PHILOSOPHER'S GROVE

Brad C. Hodson

I attended the Academy for a while. I know what you're thinking. A drunkard like myself in those hallowed halls of philosophers? No doubt they'd have a brute like me thrown from the Cimonian Wall, eh? Listen, and I'll let you in on a little secret: no man drowns in wine as much as a philosopher.

There are exceptions. Zeno the Stoic is averse to anything that smells like living, as is Xenocrates these days. But when we were all young men, before our hair ran away from us and our joints creaked, we embraced life. Aristotle, tutor to that Macedonian tyrant preening around in his oriental dress, had been the worst of the lot. "Put your sisters under lock and key. Aristotle's coming tonight." That was our little joke before a party. What would those starry-eyed brats at the Lyceum think of that?

There was one night in particular where Aristotle revealed what he was made of. Prometheus's liver, was that a night I've often wished I could forget. I haven't spoken of this in years.

Ah, what the hell. These lungs aren't getting any better. I'll be dead by the Olympiad.

I was very young. Demosthenes had coerced the men into allowing me at their evening gatherings. The Academy was very exclusive in those days, even more so than now, but the old boys would allow certain citizens to attend the later salons as probationary members. Many, like myself and my cousin, would never join the Academy, but used this as a way around Speusippus, who had taken over as scholarch after Plato's death. He was cold and a stickler for the rules. Until his stroke, Xenocrates made jokes at his expense. After the stroke, Xeno took over and felt pity for the old wretch.

Dem, high on the renown he had gained through his tirades against Phillip, wormed himself in and invited me to tag along. Most evenings we simply drank and argued philosophy or politics. This particular evening promised to be the same. It was winter; snow dusted Athena's sacred olive grove as we lounged deep in our cups. Huddled in our furs, surrounded by roaring braziers, we yelled at one another over whether there was an afterlife or some other ridiculous shit. Whatever it was, the topic came around to demons.

"The demon," Aristotle said, belching so loud that souls in Tartarus must have heard, "is a part of each of us. It's a divine shred that nurtures and guides us. Any evil we do is our own decision, which is what makes it so tragic. We ignore the noble part of ourselves."

The playwright Menander laughed and shook his head. Wine flew from his red beard. "No, no, no. We are base creatures, little more than animals. We eat, we fuck, we shit, and that's about it."

Aristotle flew off the bench, thick legs almost propelling him into the air. He was a wrestling champion, awarded the laurel three times in his life, and could have pummeled any one of us into submission. Menander froze, his cup to his lips, and Dem and I nearly fell to the floor laughing.

"If that's all we are, then how do you explain Pericles or Leonidas? Homer? Fucking Socrates? Or even your own plays, that miserable mess of words you shit onto the page?"

"I thought you liked *The Farmer's Wife*?"

"I loved it, but I'm a man of exceedingly poor taste."

Xenocrates leaned against the wall and sighed. The mist of his breath hung in the air like a spirit. Aristotle stumbled over to him.

"And what does that mean?" Aristotle asked.

"You're both wrong." Xeno's eyes were black as pitch. I heard Plato had refused to make eye contact with him during his lectures lest he stutter. "And right, in a way."

Dem nudged me in the ribs. "Watch Menander now," he whispered. "He'd lick Xeno's ass for a kind word."

Menander leaned forward. "I was thinking something similar."

Xeno ignored him. "We are animals, in our way, but the demon is a spirit that has the ability to guide us to noble things. Socrates claimed to be spoken to by a demon, you know."

Aristotle beamed.

"But the demon can be corrupted," Xeno went on. "It can be a petty and spiteful thing that pushes us towards disaster."

"It could be argued," Dem said, "that Socrates' demon did just that."

"Bullshit." Aristotle grabbed the amphora and filled his cup. "Socrates will be remembered for a thousand years. His demon pushed him toward greatness, no matter how he ended. If the way we died determined things, all those heroes whose demons swirl about their shrines would be disgraced. Instead their noble essence remains here to help guide us. They are divine. There is no corruption." Aristotle had been depressed all that year. He felt he was destined for greatness, even then, but never seemed to rise in the Academy's ranks. He constantly went on about Socrates, and you could tell he fancied himself the man's successor in a way. Yet at that point he'd come up with no great advances himself and it looked as though he were destined for obscurity.

"Perhaps you're right." Xeno said, shrugging. "You know, there's a shrine hidden in the olive grove there. Dedicated to Theseus and said to house his demon."

"They say," Demosthenes said, "that the demons at shrines can tell your future."

"Do they?" Aristotle tapped a finger against the rim of his cup.

"Yes. They also say that a shrine-demon can help guide you toward greatness."

We all stared out at the olive trees; their ice-encrusted bark shone in the moonlight.

"Fuck it," said Aristotle, throwing his cup. He pulled his furs tight and stomped across the courtyard.

"Where's he going?" I asked.

Menander laughed. "To wake the dead."

Xeno lit a lantern, and we made our way through that ancient grove; Menander muttered an apology to Athena every time a twig snapped underfoot. Frost crunched and the wind stabbed us even through our furs. The moon, so full and bright from the courtyard, now struggled to find us. We wandered around for what felt like half the night before finding Aristotle on his ass in a small clearing, his back against a tree. He held out a hand as we approached, and Dem hauled him to his feet.

"I tripped," he said.

Xeno smiled. "And this tree was too comfortable to get up from, I see. The shrine's over there."

A stone jutted from the ground—about the height of a whore on her knees—an alcove carved into it. A stained copper bowl rested inside, a small scattering of bones and soot circling it.

"This is the shrine to Thesues?" I said, waddling over to it. "Looks like a piss pot."

Dem smacked the back of my head so hard my ears rang. "Show some respect, Manacles." Dem always called me by that nickname, earned from a dozen incarcerations.

Aristotle kneeled and eyed the shrine. "Xeno, tell me. Is the demon here corrupted?"

"Many are these days. They are becoming foul and base. As for this one, you'd have to ask him yourself."

"All right, I will. How do you summon a demon?"

We all stood there like mutes, rubbing our beards and pretending to think of anything but the cold.

"Maybe you can bleed into that bowl," Menander said. "Didn't Odysseus do something like that?"

There were grunts of agreement.

"None of us brought a knife," I said.

Aristotle raised his hand and bit deep into the webbing between thumb and forefinger. Making a fist over the bowl, he squeezed blood into it. Steam rose into the night air.

"What now?"

"Are there words?" Dem asked.

Xeno cleared his throat. "Theseus, by this offering we call to you."

The wind whistled through the olive trees. Somewhere a dog barked.

"Are you sure those were the right words?"

"I don't know," Xeno said. "I just made them up."

We waited in the cold, urging Aristotle to give up and come back to the Academy, but he refused. When the man had an idea in his head, he wouldn't abandon it until he could see its conclusion.

The smell of burning trash drifted in from the direction of the Areopagus.

"They're going to set the entire hill on fire," I said.

Xeno cradled himself and shook his head. "I don't like that smell."

"We'd worry about you if you did," Menander said. "Whoever's burning that had better be careful. They'll be executed."

I should say now that, to the best of my knowledge, there were no fires that night. We asked around the next day, and no one had seen or even smelled trash burning. Keep in mind we were six stadia from the city, and, for that smell to reach us, the cloud of trash-smoke would have had to hover over all of Athens. Yet only the five of us in that grove could smell it.

"Well, gentlemen," Dem said, "the cold and the smell have done what King Phillip could not. I am defeated."

Menander laughed. "Let's go, then."

"I'll stay awhile." Aristotle stared into the black alcove.

Xeno pleaded with him, but it was no use. Stubborn as Xerxes, that one.

We marched back up to the Academy. Xeno made a big show of swinging the lantern around to remind Aristotle he'd have to find his way back in the dark.

Menander had sobered by the time we crested the hill, and he bid us good night. Dem required a few splashes of cold water on his face before riding off. He asked me to come with, but I worried about Aristotle and said I'd go back into the grove and retrieve him.

"Persephone could have used a fellow like you, Manacles." Dem patted my shoulder and left me and Xeno in the courtyard.

"Well," I said, "I guess we should fetch him."

"Let him stew in his melancholy a bit, eh?" Xeno went to work getting a new fire going and poured wine into a pot over it. We had another cup or two, and I asked him how long he planned to leave his friend out there in cold.

"Aristotle's not like us," he said.

"What do you mean?"

"There's something missing in that one. The fact that he's simply another brother here and not a scholarch drags him down. He's a hero in his own mind, sitting around brooding about how he's not a legend."

"Not every man can be a Socrates or a Plato."

Xeno nodded. "Right? But try to tell him that and he'll tear you to pieces."

"Reminds me of a lad I grew up with. His father named him Pericles and it went to his head. Thought he was another Achilles in the making. Went around all the time with his fists clenched and ready for a brawl. Got himself killed fighting some sailors at a brothel one night. Like my father used to say, pride is a virtue—"

"But hubris is a vice. Try telling Aristotle that."

At that, the man himself stumbled into the courtyard, cloaked in shadow.

I laughed. "There he is. Tell us: did the great hero show himself?"

"He needs more," he said and stumbled into the light. His arms were painted with blood.

"Athena save us." Xeno jumped to his feet and helped Aristotle sit. I ran inside and woke two young slave boys to come look after him.

Aristotle rocked back and forth on the bench, eyes fixed on some distant sight. The boys rinsed his wounds while Xeno tried to get him to talk, but it was useless. He wasn't there.

When his arms were clean, we could see his wounds. Bite marks covered him.

Xeno grabbed his jaw and opened his lips. Aristotle's teeth were stained red, and his beard was sticky with the stuff. "What in the name of Olympus have you been doing?"

"He's been…gnawing on himself," I said.

Aristotle smacked Xeno's hand away. "You don't understand. He needs more."

"What?"

"More blood."

"You drunken fool."

Aristotle grabbed Xeno's arm. "It's not the wine, damn you." His eyes burned, and it seemed his wits had rushed back to him. "It's Theseus. His form is there. I can feel it. It spoke to me, Xeno. Damn it, it spoke to me."

The night had grown colder. I shivered inside my furs.

"All it needs is to change. It needs an agent of change. It needs blood, more than I can give it."

"Shhh," Xeno said, taking a knee. He grasped his friend's hand. "It's late, brother, and you were dark and cold and not in the best frame of mind. The night has played tricks on your senses. We'll fetch you some henbane and you can sleep. Tomorrow we'll talk about what you think you heard."

I followed Xeno to the pantry, where he grabbed the plant and began crushing it into powder.

"Has he lost his mind?"

The philosopher nodded. "He'll be fine. Dionysus has him, is all. He'll sober up after a good night's sleep and feel like the fool he is for what he's done to himself."

"Did you see his arms?"

"Of course I saw his fucking arms."

"That's not just the drink, Xeno. He's been out there biting his arms open and bleeding out for…for what?"

He snorted. "For his destiny."

When we returned to the courtyard, Aristotle was gone, as were the slaves.

"Gods be damned. Grab a lantern," Xeno said, snatching his from the ground. I pulled one down from the entrance and lit it from one of the braziers. We marched into the grove.

The smell of burnt trash was overwhelming. It scorched the inside of my nostrils and I had to pull one of my furs around my face to keep from gagging. Years later I'd smell the dead burning at Chaeronea and recognize the stench of the grove that night.

Xeno pushed on without pausing. He knew something more than he was saying; I could tell by the resoluteness in his shoulders.

When we stepped into the clearing, we saw the shadow of the man crouched before the shrine. Xeno pressed a hand against my chest. "Aristotle. What are you doing, running off like that?"

There was a rustling of grass and a sound like wet air pressed from a wineskin. We stepped closer, the orange glow of our lanterns creeping over him.

He was on his knees, one of the slave boys draped across his lap. A large rock sat to one side. The boy twitched and shook, one leg kicking out into the grass, his arm flopping against Aristotle's chest. His eyes were wide and vacant; the wet sound we heard became a feeble screech pushed through bloody lips. His scalp had been split, the copper bowl placed under his skull. Aristotle tilted the boy's head over it, peeling away gory strips of flesh to let more out. Blood sloshed over the sides of the bowl and into the grass, steam reaching like fingers toward the philosopher's red-speckled face.

"Dear Gods…" I said, stumbling back.

Xeno stepped forward. "Brother. What madness is this?"

Aristotle looked up and smiled. "Shhh. Listen."

The cold and foul-smelling wind picked up, lashing our faces and hands, churning our stomachs. I could have sworn I saw the figure of a man standing behind the shrine. The lantern shook in my hand, and I was tempted to raise it and look, but I must be honest: I was frightened that there might be someone there.

The rustling of the grass grew louder even as the boy's thrashing stilled. It sounded like words. Aristotle cocked his head to one side, listening. Whatever spoke, it spoke to him alone.

The color was gone from Xeno's face. "Brother?"

Aristotle waved us away, his concentration fixed on the rustling. He nodded and mumbled.

"Manacles, help me." Xeno bent over his friend and, like a mother trying to keep from waking a newborn, gently raised the body of the slave. I grabbed the legs, and we pulled the boy away. His skin was still warm and his limbs still twitched.

Aristotle sat as though the boy still leaned over his lap and filled the bowl at his side. Tears streaked his face.

Xeno kneeled and met his friend's eyes. He held his face and whispered to him. I wasn't close enough to hear what he said, but when he had finished, Aristotle nodded. Xeno kissed his forehead and helped him to his feet.

"I can't go on like this." Aristotle leaned against his fellow philosopher and fought to get his feet under him.

"It's all right."

"No, Xeno. No." He shoved himself away. "I can't fade away, I can't. He said a gift of blood would bring me what I needed."

"Brother…"

Aristotle stumbled over and kicked the bowl. Blood arced through the air, and the bowl clattered away into the dark. "I thought he'd tell me… I thought…" He fell to his knees. "What have I done?"

"Let's get you into the warmth, brother." Xeno helped him to his feet again.

"What about the slaves?" I asked.

"Help me get him inside. We'll grab this boy and find the other after."

Aristotle was quiet the rest of the way. He trembled and sniffed every now and then. I'm sure he wept, though I couldn't bring myself to look at him. Once inside, he let us place him in bed with little fuss. Xeno gave him the henbane and we locked him in his room.

"He's mad, Xeno."

"I know."

"What was he saying?"

"He craves it so much, this idea of greatness of his. Whatever he summoned out there took advantage of that. He thought he was being pushed on to a noble destiny, but all he did was shame himself."

We were quiet, both of us certain that something had come to him in that grove, had urged him to feed it blood. Call us superstitious, but we knew.

We waited until Apollo pulled his chariot over the horizon to creep back down into the grove. The dull light of morning changed the place. It was absurd to imagine the sinister proceedings of the night before while walking between the olive trees. I almost joked about it.

But then we stepped into the clearing.

I had been right the night before. There was a figure behind the shrine. The other slave boy, his arms wedged into the tree limbs. His face and neck were a savage mosaic of bite marks. Blood was frozen on his jaw and chest. It coated the shrine. His digits were missing, as was his manhood. Aristotle had not had a knife the night before, and I still lie awake at night, shuddering at the implication of that fact.

Xeno and I took the bodies by cart to the sea and dumped them in. We tried to keep the entire mess quiet, but somehow word got back to Speusippus. From what I heard, he almost beat Aristotle to death with his cane. The incident ruined Aristotle at the Academy, though they did close ranks and keep word from spreading outside the walls. Speusippus expelled him, banished him from the Academy. The philosopher had called down his own fears.

Of an interesting note to any who might doubt my story, Xenocrates took the now-expelled Aristotle to visit their friend Hermias in Asia Minor, hoping to raise Aristotle's spirits. It was on this trip that Aristotle married Hermias' daughter, Pythias, and was introduced to King Phillip. Phillip would later invite Aristotle to come tutor his son Alexander the Great. This chain of events led to Aristotle founding the Lyceum and becoming the most famous philosopher of our day. If you ask me, Xeno had been wrong. The demon had set Aristotle on a path to greatness that night. If he hadn't committed those horrid blasphemies in that grove, he might still be wasting away at the Academy.

You can believe me or not. I don't care. Xeno and Aristotle will both deny it if asked. But I will say this one final thing. From that day on, Xeno took up Plato's idea of evil demons and pushed it in his writings. No doubt that, generations from now, they won't even realize we once revered demons as good and noble. Demons are real, you see, and they can be corrupted. And the most frightening part of all of this to me?

The demon in that shrine, whether Theseus or not, was once a man. Aristotle was right on that account.

We all have a demon inside of us.

THE UNBELIEVER

Brian Lumley

Mercenary? You don't know the meaning of the word.

It was in '74. A certain film had been released and was doing the rounds of the cinemas. Crowds were coming away stunned, riveted by an alarmingly violent and nauseous supernatural adventure. A story of possession by a demon. There have been others since, but this was the one.

Personally, my interest was marginal. I was a soldier. Soldiers live by their ability to move fast, think quickly, and, in real terms, hit the target every time and not get hit. Occasionally, because of the nature of certain jobs certain soldiers are called upon to do, the world sees them as mercenaries. Their uniforms are different, and they're working in foreign parts, and they may be French and German and British and American all thrown together, but if they're soldiers first, that's okay. Then you get the other sort of mercenary: a bully boy who doesn't know one end of a bayonet from the other, who goes for the money and usually doesn't come back. I've no time for them.

Me, I've been a mercenary. The right sort. And when it's devil-take-the-hindmost…well, I'm still alive. The devil has not taken me.

But he very nearly did.

Above all things (at that time, anyway), I was a realist. And a materialist. Does that sound like an ambiguity? A military materialist? It depends on your material needs. Put it this way: I was getting what I wanted. And I knew what could hurt me. So, a realist and a materialist, the unreal held no special terrors for me. Horrors I had already experienced made mincemeat of those of trick photography. I was wary of weapons, not of weirds. Some of my very best friends were now ghosts. In short, I was an unbeliever.

Brandy was my tipple, women my pleasure, the pits and nets and slippery poles of a timed assault course my only enemies. No EOKA in England, no bombers (or damned few) in Chichester, no terrorists taking hostages, and no reds skulking in their black watchtowers. And I was getting older.

What do you do with a man who is way past thirty? A man with just a few useful years left in him, who still has the skills but lacks the anger? A man whom sergeants and sergeants major hated, who has now grown into one of them himself, who is now hated in turn by his subordinates because he's rough as a badger's arse and has been everywhere and done everything? I wouldn't fit behind a desk, for sure.

The answer was simple: send him on a drill course. Make him into a pig. Hell, he's halfway there already! Let those spit-'n'-polish bastards at Purbright work on him, shine him up, take some of the pride out of him, give him his anger back. Even if it's just parade-ground anger. At least he'll have something to shout about. Then send him to a training camp, put him on a square, let him mark out his territory, and give him a lot of little recruits to terrify. And watch all the timid little boys in uniform go tick-tock, tick-tock, tick-tock until they're just like him and grown into men. And when his time's up, retire him, and the ones he's taught will take his place. His and the places of all the others like him.

That's what they did to me.

But I wasn't bitter—don't think it. I merely mention it as another reason why I didn't believe in things…

So there I was in Purbright, and after the first week the world hadn't caved in on me, and after the second it dawned on me that perhaps the pigs (the drill instructors, if you like) were just a bit intimidated by me! They couldn't read me. I brooded, or seemed to brood. They didn't know what was going on in my mind, how I'd react. Maybe, if they shouted a bit too loud, maybe then I'd explode. And I hadn't come to them with the sweetest reputation. And so I grinned to myself, and in the third week got drunk and fought and generally tore the arse out of it and nearly got myself thrown off the course. Or into the guardroom.

So on that third Friday, when one of the blokes (a tough midget with Para wings on his shoulders) said, "Let's simmer down a bit and go see this bloody picture they're all talking about," I agreed.

There were six of us, as hairy a bunch as you could imagine. I'll call us Jim, Joe, Dave, Ted, Jack, and me—Bill—because those weren't our names. And we went to see this picture (this "movie," as Joe, the Yank, insisted). But how in the hell do you frighten blokes like us, eh?

Joe, black as the pit and big as a house, seconded to the SAS because of his "specialist knowledge" (because he was a killer born) and now shoved off to a drill square while waiting for recall back to his American unit. And Jim, a tiny Para with scars you can't buy at Heidelberg. And Dave, who'd done so much close protection on oil sheiks that he could smell a gun a mile away and know which way it was pointing. And Ted, whose job it was to lift fuses out of boobied bombs. And Jack, whose number is at the top of the list whenever they're looking for a knock-'em-dead sniper. And me.

Dave and Ted, because they were into weird stuff and read a lot of it, were impressed by the film. Jack and Jim were more interested in a pair of young ladies in the row in front; they changed their seats during the show and disappeared afterward until the next morning. Joe and me, we chortled all the way through.

Back in Sergeants' Mess, Dave got out a deck of cards. "Did you notice the Ouija board scene?" he asked. We sat there at a small, round table, pints in our big hands, and stared at him.

"What?" Joe rumbled, his American accent thick as a plank. "Lissen, bro',we gone play some poker, o' call up devils? Ain't no tarot deck, y'know."

Ted said: "No, listen. Dave's right. You can use a pack of cards just like a Ouija."

"You all shit," said Joe.

"Let 'em be," I told him. "Kids will be kids."

"Okay," said Dave, his color rising fast. "Let's see." He put the deck down, tapped it, and asked Ted to cut the cards. Then he picked up the deck and held it in his hands, both of them. He closed his eyes tight and asked of no one: "Who's here?" He dealt three cards face up in the middle of the table: a jack, an ace, and an eight.

"There you go," said Ted. "Joe is here, sure enough." He grinned at him.

Joe frowned. "Hey! I see the J and the E," he said, "but—"

"Ace is high-low," said Dave. "It's not only top card, it's also a one…"

(Of course, those weren't the three cards he actually dealt, since Joe's real name wasn't Joe. But you get the idea.)

"Try me," said Ted.

Dave put the cards down for me to cut. Then he took them up, held them tight, closed his eyes, and said: "Is Ted here?"

He dealt three cards: a ten, an eight, and a two.

"Tet?" Joe grinned.

"No," I said, suddenly interested. "The two is a deuce…"

Joe's jaw dropped.

I was sitting to the left of Dave. I looked at him. "Try yourself," I said.

He let Joe cut, closed his eyes, and said: "And who is this guy?" He dealt one card, face down this time, to himself. Then he stood up and made for the bar with his empty glass. "You and Joe owe Ted and me a couple of pints," he said casually over his shoulder.

"What?" I turned up the card. It was a joker!

"Bastard!" Joe yelled, laughing like a madman. He tore across the mess and wrestled with Dave a little at the bar, swapping playful punches. Both of them were laughing.

"Hey!" Joe said, sitting on a bar stool. "And I was gonna play poker witchoo guys!" We didn't play poker. We filled up with beer until the bar closed. It's funny how you make friends, funny how quickly you discover people. I had made friends that night. And later…later I would lose one.

I remember that from then until closing time the beers went down much too fast. I'm a brandy man, as I've said, but couldn't afford it just then. Beer fills me up. And it gets me drunk far too quickly.

Joe and me, we argued with Dave and Ted. We beat them down, but it wasn't easy. Card tricks aside, those two were convinced—they really did believe—that there were big and nasty things "out yonder." Joe had been in 'Nam, and I'd been places, too, and we were much of a sort, I'd guess. We *knew* there were nasty things out yonder; we didn't call them demons, that's all. We called them hot lead, napalm, jelly, gas.

And Dave a CP man, and Ted with bomb disposal. How can you figure it? Didn't their lives have enough horrors without they should want to believe in others?

Well, Joe got dangerously drunk, and the barman didn't like it. Also, there was a crowd of stiffs in the mess who didn't like blacks, period. Any more trouble and I was out, so…

I bought him a big, big whiskey, just to make sure he'd stay down, threw him over my shoulders, and climbed the stairs. It was late in the year and cold outside. I stretched Joe out on his bed, tossed a blanket over him, and closed his window. Before I left the room he sat up.

"Hey, Bill," he said, his eyes not really seeing me. "All that…that shee-*it!* Make anything of it?"

"Not me, friend. The last demons I saw blasted themselves back to hell with their own bombs."

"Damn straight!" he said. "Next one I see, I'll *eat* the mother. An' I hope he's white. You white mothers all the same!" And he fell back on his bed, rolled up his big brown eyes, and went out like a light.

I staggered out of there, feeling the booze working in me, and headed for my own room. We were all on the same floor. Dave and Ted had adjacent rooms. Right then I could hear their drunken voices. They were showering in the bathroom, still babbling on about ghosts and ghoulies.

Drunk myself and beginning to feel wobbly, I grinned as a notion swam up out of the beer. Their rooms were where the corridor turned at a right angle. Mine was around the corner. I went to my room, stripped down, laid back my covers, and waited for them to finish showering. When I heard them say their goodnights and enter their rooms, I gave them a couple seconds, then ducked back out into the corridor and put out the lights. The whole floor was in darkness. No lights showed from beneath the doors. I tiptoed to Dave's and Ted's doors, put a hand on each one, and raked my nails slowly and loudly down the panels.

Dave's coughing and Ted's rustling of bedclothes stopped instantly. I rattled both doorknobs simultaneously, then quickly fled to my own room, pulled the door shut quietly behind me, lay down on my bed, and yanked up the covers. I faked a snore.

The door burst open a second later, and the light blazed in my eyes. "You mother!" said Ted, white-faced. "You scared the steaming stickies out of us there!"

"Listen," said Dave over the other's shoulder. "No more games. I might be scared of the dark side, but I'm not scared of you. One more like that, Copper, and I bust your lip!"

I blinked my eyes at them, tried to look innocent, gave it up, and grinned. "Something bothering you boys?" I asked. "You little devils, you?"

They went, slamming the door behind them.

Now I was hot. I got up, unsteady as hell, and opened the window wide. It was a cold, bright night. Stars like beacons. I got into bed and put my hands behind my head. I knew that if the room began revolving I'd throw up. I willed it to stand still, commanded it, as if the room were out there on the drill square. "Stand still, you bloody, silly little room, you!"

It did as it was told.

Eight, nine pints. Too much for little old brandy drinker me. Then I remembered something, got up again, and turned the key in the lock of my door. And at last I fell into bed. Then I thought about it. About what I'd done.

Now why had I locked the door? Christ, I *never* locked my door! Lord pity the man I catch in my room without good reason for being there. So why now? Did I fear a playful little visit from Dave and Ted? No? From who, then? Had those two bastards gotten through to me with all their mumbo jumbo?

Shit!

"Hey, you out there!" I snarled at the open window. "You hear me? If you're really out there—if there's any goddamed thing *really* out there—just you come on in and try it on with little old Bill. Why, there's devils in me would crush you down, pour milk on your skull, and listen to it go snap, crackle, and pop. See, I don't believe. I just *don't*. So do your fucking worst, baby!"

And then I went to sleep.

We were three stories up. I'd like to make that plain. A long way to the ground. The windows were maybe ten or twelve feet apart. No balconies. Outside my window was air. And I was on the corner of the building. A cold and drafty space. The ground below and the starry sky above.

And I dreamed.

Dreamed? It was a nightmare!

Something came. Something big. Awesome strength. It stank. It burned. It crouched on the sill of my open window. Big and black, it came in. The night came with it.

My bedclothes went haywire and flapped about in a sort of torment. The room rocked. I tried to sit up, but Something put a great black hand on my chest and pinned me down. The pressure was enormous. I could feel the bed's steel springs straining. But those old army beds were indestructible!

UNBELIEVER? Something said without speaking.

"Not me, uh, friend," I gasped. Or, if I didn't answer out loud, certainly I said it inside. "Not me. Oh, I believe. Seeing is believing!"

NOW YOU BELIEVE. BUT YOU CALLED. YOU CHALLENGED…

"What, me?" Are you sure? Hell no, that wasn't me. That was Joe, down the hall. He's the one who doesn't believe."

JOE?

"You can't miss him. Why, he's blacker than you!"

The weight was gone from my chest. Something crouched on the window sill and was gone in a rush of stinking, foul air, a blast of rotten darkness. I got up, almost fell, and banged my head on something. The room seemed topsy-turvy. I couldn't find the light switch. Then my legs hit the bed, and I fell into it. And I stayed there…

~

Next morning…Lord, it was like waking up into a different world! Thank God it was Saturday. I had forgotten about the dream, but what those lousy bastards had done to my room…!

A barrack bunk, even a senior rank's room, is tiny. If you don't have a big chest, there's room to breathe. A room in a Sergeant's Mess is something like a nest. Room for just one bird at a time. That's why you keep it neat and tidy. Get something out of place, and there's no room left for you. Well, something—many somethings—were out of place.

The bed was sideways. The wardrobe was open and my clothes and uniforms were strewn everywhere. My sheets and blankets were knotted together in a big ball. And…someone had wet in my dirty linen basket. The room stank of urine. Five or six pints of alcohol-free beer vented pressure from someone's big pink willy. But whose?

The key was still in the door. I turned it, yanked the door open, and staggered out into the corridor. Silence. No, someone snoring. Gently. The bastards!

I went to smash in Dave's door and barely stopped myself. No, this wasn't the way. Whoever the culprit was, sooner or later he—or they—would give themselves away.

I dumped my dirty linens, shirts, underpants, et cetera, into a bath and soaked them through with hot water. Then I drained it, added soap powder, and pounded the hell out of the mess until soap suds were everywhere. That got rid of the anger but did nothing for my hangover.

I went back to my room, washed, shaved, and climbed into civvies. Thank God (again) for Saturdays. A tiny breakfast, lots of coffee, a couple of Alka-Seltzers—and Dave and Ted coming into the dining hall looking miserable. I promised myself that they'd look a sight worse later.

"Morning," I said, forcing a smile.

"Is it?" Ted asked. He fingered chin stubble. "What are you made of, Copper? How can you look so good when I feel so bad? Was I defusing a bomb last night and did something go wrong? I feel like death!"

Dave said: "Death would be preferable. At least it's quicker."

I said, "Maybe my conscience is clear, eh?" Then: "Why don't you both sit down and I'll order more coffee—and a couple of big plates of beans and greasy bacon!"

"Jesus H.—" Dave began.

"You must be *iron*!" Ted finished.

By now I'd worked out what must have happened, what they'd done and how they'd done it. They had taken the duty clerk's spare key to my room. They'd used it to push my key out of the lock. Then they had come in and quietly worked my room over. Finally they'd passed a rope through the tiny fanlight over my door. Dave had gone out, taking the spare key with him. Ted had locked my door from the inside. Dave had anchored the rope while Ted climbed down from the window, then Ted had yanked on the rope till it fell, and he'd coiled it up and walked away with it. They'd probably done it at an early hour, maybe first light or just before. This hangover thing was just an act. But a good one.

I "accidentally" pushed my used plates off the edge of the table. They hit the floor and shattered loudly, echoing throughout the mess. Ted and Dave went rigid and white, moaning softly to themselves. A hell of a good act.

"Seen Joe?" I asked as a steward came tut-tutting to clear away the debris.

"Not since last night," said Dave dully. "I remember there were two of him, both arguing like hell against the existence of dark forces. Two of you, too. And then your stupid practical joke and our desire to brain you."

I couldn't play this game any longer. "Well, you paid me back for that. You boys surely wrecked my room. Which is okay—but when I find out which one of you leaked in my linen basket, boy, he's in the shit."

They looked at me blankly.

Just then, Jim and Jack came in. Unshaven, they wore smug expressions and eye-bags. No need to ask where they'd been or what they'd been doing all night. But give them their due, they didn't boast about it.

My chest was aching. And suddenly I remembered my dream. My nightmare. Not all of it, just something that had leaned on my chest. An awesome strength…

I spotted the duty clerk heading out of the diner with a plate of steaming something. He would be going for breakfast before signing off for the day. I went after him, stopped him as he reached his desk in the foyer, and asked him:

"Who borrowed the spare key for 311 last night?"

"311? That's your room, isn't it?"

"Right. Who took the key?"

"Nobody. Impossible. No spare key. An Irish Guardsman lost it three months ago. We had another cut and he lost that, too. There's only one. Don't tell me you've bloody lost it!...er…sir!"

"No, I didn't lose it…" I frowned, shook my head and let him go. "Thanks."

I crossed to the full-length mirror the boys use before they go out to play soldiers on the square. I opened my shirt. There was a big leaf-like bruise slap in the middle of my chest. I don't bruise easily.

I walked unsteadily back into the diner, went over to the table, and sat. They were talking, the four, recovering from the booze, the girls, from weeks of bullshit and drill. Thanking God it was Saturday. I could hear them, but dimly. Things weren't adding up. My flesh was tingling. No, creeping. My dream was vivid.

I had wrecked my room? *I* had pissed my own stuff? I'd never done anything like that before, not even drunk out of my mind. And I hadn't been *that* drunk. But if not me, who?

Lots of other guys were eating now. A sort of late breakfast, early lunch. Brunch. They clattered their plates, slurped their coffee, mumbled, and chattered. Through it all, I distinctly heard a cleaning lady say to the cook behind his service bar: "It's red and it drips. Must be coming from the third floor."

"See 'Arry on the desk," cookie answered. "Get 'im ter call the duty plumber, love."

As she passed our table, I asked: "What drips?"

She smiled at me. We were her boys. Older women love soldiers. The older and uglier they are, the more they love the soldier boys. She held out her hand. "Paint, I reckons."

It wasn't paint.

"Show me," I said.

The others had seen my face. They came with us. We went up to the second floor to a broom closet. She showed us. The ceiling was one big, dripping patch of red. I crossed to the window, which was tiny, and managed to stick my head out. It took a second or two to orient myself. The room up above was Joe's.

I went up the stairs three at a time on legs like jelly. Why they didn't crumple up I'll never know. At Joe's door I skidded to a halt, and the others, puffing and panting, piled into me from behind.

"What is it, Bill?" asked Dave.

"Are you okay, Copper?" Ted was frightened.

"What's up?" asked Jack.

"Hey!" said Jim, pointing to the red stain seeping out from under the door.

I turned the knob, took a deep breath, shoved the door open, and walked in.

They came in behind me, then went out again. At least two of them were throwing up in the corridor.

The room looked something like mine had earlier, but a great deal worse. There was shit everywhere, but not human shit. Everything was layered with shredded sheets and blankets and feathers from ruptured pillows. The bed was in the center of the floor, stripped down. Its tight lattice of crossed wires and springs were a dull black. Not shiny, steely bright, but black. Or red turning black. There was a reason…

Now give me a little time and I'll go on. Christ, I'm hardened to it now, but it's still not a nice thing to remember. See, I've asked myself about it a thousand times. In the dead of night I ask myself. And, of course, others asked me about it too. But…hell, I'm Military Fuzz! Or I was. Jesus, they knew it wasn't me! They knew it wasn't anybody…human.

Now I'm over the top, junked. But the old instincts are still there, just as they were that night. A soldier—especially one who gets involved in the more unpleasant, less obvious side of the game—learns to think and act fast. And sometimes to talk fast if there's no other way out. He has to. Survival is simply this: not getting hit. Even if you have to duck behind somebody else. Sure, I have regrets, but I'm still here, still in one piece.

I still drink a little, sometimes a lot, and I still enjoy a girl now and then, but I don't play cards. Can't stand a deck near me. And I don't issue or accept challenges. Not ever. Fighting doesn't interest me. There's always someone bigger, better—or worse.

And I don't sleep much.

The tight lattice of wires that formed the platform of Joe's bed—that chicken wire of springs and steel strands—was black with dried or drying blood. Some of the wires had snapped, but not many. Those old army beds are indestructible. His body lay beneath, black criss-crossed with red. Some of the outer columns of flesh had toppled over or slid to one side, but the greater mass of him had hung together remarkably well, considering that something had shoved him through the wires.

Just thinking about it, I feel again that weight on my chest, that awesome strength.

What was it Joe had said? "You white bastards are all the same…"

Yes, and you black bastards, too—only some of you are bigger, and trace your roots to darker places than Africa.

Mercenary? You don't know the meaning of the word.

THE TRUE WORTH OF ORTHOGRAPHY

Lisa Morton

The magician took a seat at a table in the rear of the coffeehouse, flipped open a leather-bound journal, and began to write. His instrument was a pen with a fat, square, sponge nib; the ink flowed in perfect dark lines that occasionally spun off into flourishes. His thick brows drew together; the furrows in his sand-colored skin formed like cracks in mud brick after a storm.

He didn't look up as a young woman approached. Holding a grande Frappuccino in one hand and a laptop computer in the other, she pushed aside long blonde hair to find an empty table near the magician. She sat down, opened the laptop, sipped from her drink, waited for the machine to fire up, sipped from her drink, stared for a while at an empty word-processing screen, sipped from her drink, and finally glanced up.

After a few seconds of watching the magician at work, she leaned forward and said, "God, your writing's so beautiful."

When the magician didn't respond, she went on. "It's not a screenplay, is it? I mean, I think that'd make you the only person here who's not working on a screenplay. Me included. Course I haven't gotten very far yet—"

Without looking up, the magician spoke, cutting her off; he had a faint trace of accent. "If you please, I need to concentrate."

The young woman nodded, held up a hand apologetically and leaned back. "Oh, right, sorry." She went back to her computer screen, halfheartedly typed two words, then laughed at herself. "Jesus, that's pathetic. 'Fade in' is all I've managed so far."

The magician's strokes grew bolder, the ink lines thicker.

"Everybody makes it seem so easy. You know, you buy these books like *How to Write a Screenplay in a Two Days*, but…"

His frown and focus deepened.

"Maybe I should try acting instead."

The magician drew his hand across the page with a final, definitive curl, twisting his hand.

"My mom said—"

The young woman vanished.

The magician smiled to himself, capped his pen, closed his journal and stood. His gaze turned from the laptop that still glowed on the table and the half-empty Frappuccino to another man who stood on the far side of the coffeehouse, watching, his mouth agape in open astonishment.

No one else had noticed.

The magician picked up the laptop, snapped it shut, and walked across the room to the staring middle-aged man. He extended the computer. "Would you like this? As a souvenir? I of course can't abide the damn things."

The man dumbly accepted the offered machine, holding it gingerly as if it might start shrieking any second, screeching out accusations of murder. "I don't...would they be able to trace her through this...?"

The magician's smile broadened. "I still have much to teach you."

"I don't understand."

"No, they won't be able to trace her, because she never existed. At least where the rest of the world is concerned."

The magician walked out of the coffee house, leaving the man alone. After a few seconds, he opened the laptop and looked down at the glowing word-processor screen.

It was empty. He'd seen the woman type something onto it, but her words had vanished along with the rest of her. She'd never existed.

Feeling both terrified and saddened, the man closed the laptop and followed the magician out of the coffeehouse.

The magician's library was exquisite.

The middle-aged man, who was a writer named Marshall Watts, scanned the volumes on the sixteen-foot-high book cases, some hidden behind rolling brass ladders. Most of the books looked old—many were bound in nondescript sixteenth-century tan vellum, some had elaborate metal hinges and ornamentation, some were not even really books but actually tall, custom-made folios housing millennium-old scrolls and manuscripts.

Marshall, who had once written a highly-regarded (but little-read) novel based on the life of the early-twentieth-century occultist Aleister Crowley, spotted a volume bearing his subject's name and the title *The Collected Works*. Curious, he pulled it down and felt his heart stutter when he saw that not only was it signed and inscribed by Crowley ("To my dear Frater Alexander"), but Crowley had annotated it throughout with handwritten comments. "My God, this must be worth a fortune."

Alexander—the magician—shrugged. "Undoubtedly. But it has greater value to me than that provided by money."

"Of course." Marshall carefully replaced the volume and turned to his host, pondering the "greater value" comment. Crowley had died in 1947, but Alexander didn't look a day over forty; surely he wasn't suggesting that he was the Alexander to whom Crowley had inscribed the book?

"Aleister, sadly, was unable to master the techniques I tried to teach him. He'd still be alive if he had."

Marshall restrained an urge to laugh. It wasn't the first time that Alexander Nabu had left Marshall torn between disbelief and fascination. Marshall's agent had arranged their first meeting, yesterday; he said Nabu needed a ghost writer for a project that would come with a six-figure advance. Marshall had an ex-wife, two children, a teaching job that had tenure but continual budget cuts, a mortgage he was falling behind on, a drinking problem, and a last novel that had failed to find more than a thousand readers.

Yesterday, Nabu had told him the book was about magic; today, Nabu had shown him magic, first with the blonde woman, and now here, in his house. When they'd approached on a popular street in one of the Hollywood Hills canyons, Alexander couldn't shake the notion that he'd driven past this lot just a week ago and that it had been vacant; now a classic 1920s-style Mediterranean home surrounded by tall hedges sprawled here.

"You still haven't told me about your project," Marshall ventured.

Nabu gestured at a large, comfortable couch, and Marshall sat. "Yes. Well, perhaps it's better if I show you." He opened the leather notebook he'd used at the coffeehouse, and set it on an elegant table before Marshall. Beside the notebook, he laid down the pen with the thick nib. "I used these at the coffeehouse. Please examine the last sentence."

Marshall squinted; the writing was so elegant and ornate it took a few seconds to read:

The young blonde woman vanishes. The final "s" trailed off in a swirl of ebon ink.

"So…you…wished her away, is that it?"

"You know that Crowley spoke of the 'True Will,' of finding one's ultimate purpose in life…? I discovered my purpose when I was quite young: I could affect my will through writing. And I don't mean 'writing' as in what you do, Marshall; I mean the actual art of the rebus, of finding a visual representation for the sounds we make to communicate."

"Orthography, in other words."

Nabu smiled, pleased. "Yes, precisely. Orthography—the way we write down our language. If you think on it, writing is an astonishing act; when we read, we are incapable of other thought, and so writing allows one man to enforce his thoughts on another without the use of verbal means. This is nearly the definition of magic as well."

Marshall glanced at the page again, at the beautifully rendered letters. "So writing is magic…"

"When done properly, yes. But it's an extremely difficult art to perfect; only a handful of magicians have ever used orthography properly, and none have achieved my level."

Marshall thought back to the blonde woman, looking for a flaw, for the trick, the scam. A concealed mirror, a trap door, a distraction. He couldn't find it but was sure it had been there. "Why should I believe you?"

"Would you like another demonstration?"

"Please."

Nabu retrieved the notebook and pen, positioned them carefully on his knees. "What would you like to see?"

Marshall thought for a moment, trying to imagine something that Nabu would have no familiarity with, something he couldn't possibly know about. The teacher who'd first told him he had a gift for stories, whom he'd wished for forty years now that he could go back and thank.… "My second-grade teacher, Mrs. Woods."

Nabu's pen flowed across the page, his wrist moving in practiced precision. He wrote for several seconds—

An elderly woman with a stout figure, 1960s-era floral-print dress, and coiffed white hair stood in the library with them. Marshall openly gasped; he'd forgotten so much about her—the glasses with the tortoise-shell rims, the glittery peacock broach she liked to wear. Her warm, patient smile.

"Mrs. Woods…"

He half rose, and she simply ceased to be.

A choked sob caught in Marshall's throat. He still hadn't had time to say what he'd wanted to her. "I thought she was dead all these years…"

Nabu closed his journal. "She is. I did not summon her from the living."

Marshall's blood froze. He had to swallow down an impulse to run, back to the world he knew, where the dead didn't reappear because of a line of careful writing.

"What…what do you want me for?" Marshall heard his voice reduced to a croak by fear and didn't care.

"Rest easy, sir—you have nothing to fear from me. If you dislike my proposal, you are free to leave here, and you will not remember me within the hour."

Or will I be the one who is no longer remembered? Marshall wondered.

"Go ahead," he said.

"I have reached a point beyond which I cannot pass," Nabu said, rising to pace as he spoke. "I want the abilities of the ancient Egyptians, the scribes of whom communicated directly with their gods. Or the ancient Chinese calligraphers, who summoned dragons for their emperors. I am adept in those language forms as well—in fact I believe the Egyptian hieroglyphics to be the most beautiful writing—but I remain unable to reach beyond. There is a divine realm I can sense, but not truly penetrate. And I believe the reason for this is that my writing is transcendent, but my words are dull. I need to meld my talents with those of an author. I need you to create what I write."

"So you want to hire me to…what, create spells?"

"Essentially, yes."

Marshall looked away, stunned. When he could muster speech again, he asked, "Spells to…do what?"

"As I said—I want to converse with gods. I want to know the unknowable, to attain higher power."

Marshall thought about a girl who had just vanished. And Nabu's expression as he'd looked up at Marshall. Smug. Regardless.

"Why do you think I have the talent you need?"

Nabu shrugged. "You obviously have some interest in this area already. And you're a gifted author."

"You've read my books?"

"Yes. Impressive."

When Marshall didn't respond, Nabu continued, "I know it may still not work, but I assure you—you will be paid for your efforts."

Marshall wondered how much Robert Oppenheimer had been paid for his work on the Manhattan Project. What was it Oppenheimer had later said about his part in the creation of the atomic bomb? *Now, I am become Death, the destroyer of worlds.*

Would I be giving Nabu the ability to destroy worlds? he thought.

"I need some time to think about."

"Of course. Take what you need. I have nothing but time."

Marshall peered at Nabu's face again—the skin a shade darker than his own, the heavy brows, dark brown eyes—and realized he couldn't begin to guess the man's age. "How old are you, exactly?"

Nabu smiled. "Look up my name when you return home."

Marshall did.

Nabu was the Babylonian god of writing. The first god of the written word, when writing had been not letters or pictures, but wedges pressed into clay.

Marshall called him when he found that online. "Is 'Nabu' your real name?"

"No, but I think it more appropriate. Don't you?"

Marshall didn't answer.

Marshall spent two days contemplating, drinking, weighing alternatives.

He went to the best used-book store in Los Angeles and looked at books that reproduced early illuminated manuscripts; he wondered if the monks who had drafted them in the first millennium had called up devils or angels. He wondered if any of them had been Nabu. He looked at books on magic, and on the history of writing, and on Aleister Crowley (and grimaced when he saw his novel shelved in the non-fiction section). He looked at books on Babylonian mythology and saw carvings of Nabu, the patron god of scribes, bearing scrolls. He wondered what would have been contained in those scrolls.

What he finally concluded: If he didn't help Nabu, the magician would find someone else; authors were plentiful in Los Angeles.

If he agreed, he stood to meet God along with Nabu.

So he agreed. And hoped this was his choice, not something that Nabu had majicked into him.

"Where do I start?"

They were together in Nabu's library, Marshall's own laptop (he'd kept the blonde woman's but had been unable to bring himself to use it) set up before him.

Something skittered at the far end of the room, where the shadows gathered even in early afternoon. Marshall stared, trying to penetrate the gloom, feeling a shiver ripple across his back.

"Describe how you would reach Heaven."

Marshall caught a glimpse of golden eyes flashing in the darkness, and a whiff of something rotten.

"Are you sure it's Heaven you're after?"

Nabu frowned and followed his gaze. Marshall heard a distinctive, sibilant hiss from whatever lurked at the end of the library.

"My apologies," muttered Nabu, picking up a brush and bending down over a sheaf of parchment. "An experiment that I thought I'd finished."

Marshall heard the soft sound of brush strokes on paper; he held his breath, straining to hear anything else. Nabu finished his work, and Marshall relaxed as he felt a chill leave the room. "What was that?"

"It doesn't matter now. We were saying…"

"We were talking about what I'm going to write. It's going to take some time."

"As I told you before, Marshall—I have time."

Marshall closed the laptop and left.

Marshall soon realized that he'd always had far more experience with Hell than Heaven.

He had no idea where to begin. He typed a dozen opening sentences, then deleted them all. He looked at books, films, works of art. He walked through restaurants and shopping malls, seeking inspiration. But he had always been inclined to notice and comment on imperfections. He was more interested in corruption than sainthood, in evil than good.

He finally realized Nabu was as well.

He began to write.

Nabu gazed at the printout that Marshall had handed him. After a few moments, he sagged into a chair, still scanning the text that filled two single-spaced pages.

"Well…?" Marshall asked when he could stand waiting no longer.

"It's not what I expected."

"Will it work?"

Nabu read again, then pointed at a line halfway down the first page. "This line—'The eternal ladder that ascends also rests far below, in primordial mud and blood, the ladder twists as it rises and evolves, as it leaves chaos and dark for order and light'—this I can make work. Think of how the lines will look when written, not how they appear on this screen. This—" he said, flinging a dismissive hand at the screen, "—means nothing."

Marshall nodded. "Then it might be helpful if I had some of your writing, so I could get a sense of which letters to emphasize…"

Nabu handed the pages he'd just written to Marshall. "Of course. Take these."

Marshall glanced down at the last sentences, and saw, in Nabu's spidery hand: "I send you back to the hand of your maker, Tiamat. Leave this world."

He remembered a line he'd read in a Babylonian creation myth, about how the furious mother god Tiamat had declared war on her own divine children and had created scorpion-men to carry out her will.

He wondered if scorpion-men had golden eyes that glowed from the darkness.

When he returned to his own home, he turned on every light and tried not to think about the shadows.

"Yes," Nabu said, nodding as he read the new pages he'd just been handed. "Yes! This is better. Yes."

He took the typed pages and sat down at a writing desk. He chose a metal nib, inserted it into an exquisite jade pen, dipped it in ink, and began to write. After a few seconds he turned to Marshall, who stood nearby.

"You may go."

Marshall didn't question the command. He left.

Marshall sat at home that night, lights turned up, drinking scotch. He wondered if he would know—if everyone would know—

whether Nabu had succeeded. Would the monstrous armies of long-forgotten goddesses suddenly appear, rampaging down modern city streets? Would all light wink out, replaced by the permanent void?

No, Marshall thought. I can't do this. I won't sit here drinking, wondering if I've condemned my world.

He staggered to his feet, set the bottle aside, and picked up Nabu's hand-written leaves. He cleared space on his kitchen table—his own work desk was cluttered with computer supplies and equipment—and found a black marking pen that was the closest thing he had to one of Nabu's writing utensils. He grabbed the top sheet from a stack of clean, white pages, laid it before him, and began to write as neatly as he could.

He decided he would test himself with something small, so he wrote about a single sheet of paper catching fire, bursting into luminosity when its own inherent energy was released in one explosive outpouring. He wrote for hours, trying to pour himself into his moving hand, referring to Nabu's work, trying to copy the magician's style and beauty.

Nothing happened. The paper did not burst into flame, it didn't glow or tremble.

At some point Marshall set down the pen and clutched at his head in despair. Why had he thought he could master in a few short hours what Nabu had studied for years, decades, centuries? It was ridiculous, of course. It was like expecting a child to play Beethoven perfectly. He could never hope to copy Nabu's work—

He suddenly stopped as an idea struck him. He remembered a friend, Clark, who was adept at graphic design on his computer…he remembered a drunken afternoon spent designing new business cards that Marshall had never actually printed up…

An hour later, Marshall's phone rang. He was almost shocked to hear Nabu's voice, sounding normal, mortal, carried across the 4G waves. "It almost worked," Nabu told him. "I could feel energy moving through the room, gathering…but I couldn't quite direct it. Just one more rewrite, I think."

Nabu gave him suggestions, then hung up.

Marshall laughed to himself: Even this assignment comes with new drafts.

~

When Nabu called the next morning, Marshall asked for a few more days.

At the end of the week, he told Nabu he had something for him. They met in the library, and once again Marshall had his laptop. He opened it, brought it out of hibernation, and turned it carefully to face him, away from Nabu. He tried not to shake as he readied his fingers over the keys.

"What do you have for me?" Nabu asked anxiously. The library felt different. It looked different—somehow less solid and real, as if the last attempt at their merged spell had begun to strip away layers of the border around reality. Marshall tried not to imagine a wall now thinner, the things that prowled just beyond growing more excited, their stinger-tipped tails quivering in anticipation of sinking into flesh…

"Give me a moment," Marshall said, gathering focus. He took a breath to steady himself (wishing he had a drink), typed a few last words, stood while juggling the laptop, and hit the ENTER button.

Nabu was gone, as was the library.

Marshall stood in a vacant lot, weeds pushing up through cracks in old, crumbling concrete; at the edge of the concrete, the thick, brown growth of Southern California's wildlife encroached. He stood for a few seconds, stunned by his own success, staring down at the words on his computer screen:

The magician, Alexander Nabu, is only a creation in the life work of Marshall Watts. As a character owned by Watts, Nabu's entire existence is controlled by the author. When Watts decides that he's finished with the character, he completes Nabu's arc by hitting the computer key labeled "ENTER".

Of course Marshall knew it wasn't the words that had given him victory, but the font, made from a scan of Nabu's own writing by his friend Clark, who possessed superb font-creation software.

Marshall exited the word-processing program, choosing not to save the document he'd just typed; no point in tempting fate, not when he'd deleted Nabu and possibly saved the world.

But he still possessed Nabu's font.

He figured he had plenty of time to decide how he'd use it.

FALLING PAST THESSALY

Christopher Hawkins

"Get your ass in gear, pledge. She's gonna show!"

It wasn't a request; it was an order. Brian wasn't moving fast enough for the three Neanderthals upstairs, and maybe part of that was on purpose. *Let them get their own damn beer*, he thought. *Let them walk down here and get it, assuming any of them still can walk. Even money says they fall down the stairs or forget where they were going and end up pissing in the fridge.*

Another bellow came from the top floor. "I do not *hear* the sounds of *beer*!" That was Brother Clash, dusting off what had to be his favorite phrase. The others laughed as if they hadn't heard him say it at least a dozen other times that day, but Brian just shook his head. None of them could see him, or he wouldn't have risked the gesture. Pledges did not raise their eyes to upperclassmen, nor did they speak unless spoken to, and at Theta Omega, retribution was swift and humiliating.

The house was empty, its long hallways dark and quiet but for the hooting and cackling of his three keepers. Brian didn't know their real names any more than they knew his. Fully-initiated brothers had names bestowed on them by the group. As a pledge, his own name was irrelevant. He wanted to shout that name to the empty walls just to prove he could still remember what it was. After five weeks in this place, he wasn't so sure that he could.

Once again, he caught himself wondering why he hadn't just said no to pledging the frat: his legacy, the house where his father had left his mark so long ago. If the old man had been able to look past his own memories, he might have seen the house for what it was, recognized the desperate caricatures within, the complete rejection of anything that involved the use of one's brains, and known that this was not the place for his son. If he could have looked ahead to see his son, his honor student, playing Stepin Fetchit for a bunch of half-stoned apes, he would never have suggested it in the first place.

He pulled a fresh supply of bottles from the fridge, three in each hand, two for each of the brothers upstairs. *That should keep them busy a good ten minutes*, he thought, making a point to clink the bottles together as he moved. *Hear that, Brother Shithead*?

He double-timed it up the steps and made it into the room just as Clash was throwing his head back to yell his favorite phrase again. He promptly forgot all about it when he saw the bottles in Brian's hands and made a lurching grab for them. The other two followed and, like a magic trick, he was empty-handed again. Clash twisted the top off one of the bottles and downed half of it without stopping to breathe.

"Faster next time, pledge," he said, wiping his mouth, "or we will wash you out."

"Wash you out like a skid mark in your underwear," chimed in Brother Lardo, his chins disappearing into the bulk at his chest.

Wash you out. It was the worst threat in their arsenal, one they had used so often that it no longer meant anything. Brian wished that it did mean something, that they would give him the excuse he needed to leave this place once and for all. But they lost interest almost before they got started. Tonight was a night for other pleasures, other torments.

Their eyes were all fixed on the computer screen. Brother Clash hunched over the keyboard, practically salivating. Brian's eyes went there too.

On the screen, in a small window, was the image of a woman.

She wore a dress of white linen that plunged low and gathered at her chest. Even with the extra material, Brian could see the curves of her body, the pleasant fullness that suggested maturity but defied age. Her arms were bare, and poised at a keyboard just out of the frame. His eyes followed those arms up, to the soft curve of her shoulders, to the pale skin of her neck and on upward to—

Nothing. The image ended there, electronically decapitated by the top edge of the window. Then the picture winked as another one took its place, the same as the first but shifted a little, the barest adjustment to the posture, a slight movement of the arms, but still the same woman.

A live picture.

"What the hell are you looking at, pledge!" Brother Lardo had caught him staring at the screen and pulled himself forward with as much menace as his weight would allow.

Brian immediately cast his eyes to the floor and let his shoulders take on a submissive hunch. *Go ahead,* he thought. *Three more days of this crap and you'll never push me around again. Three more days or wash me out right now. It's all the same to me.*

"Oh, just let him watch." This from Brother Attila, who sat at the far end of the desk, looking eager but relaxed as he sipped his beer. He gave Brian a conspiratorial wink. "Maybe the little slug will learn something he can take to his girlfriend back home."

Lardo's nostrils flared, but he was outranked on this one, and there was nothing he could do about it. "All right," he said. "But you will keep your eyes open and your mouth closed! I will not tolerate one word from you! Do you understand me, pledge?"

Brian wasn't going to take the bait and open his mouth. He just stared down at his feet as the upperclassman's cheeks burned red. Out of all of them, Brother Lardo was his worst tormentor, and the only one Brian felt truly sorry for. Three months of pledging last year only to be saddled with the name "Lardo" for the rest of his college life. The big guy took it in stride, but how much of that was because he didn't have a choice? After a moment, Lardo let out a derisive snort, and sank back into his seat.

"Watch and learn, maggot," Clash called over his shoulder. The image shifted again, and this time one of the girl's arms was upraised, as if to run her fingers through her hair.

"Lardo met this girl the other night in a chat room," Attila explained. "Now we're going to see what she's got to show us."

The image shifted again, and in a box beneath it, a question appeared.

DO YOU REALLY THINK I'M PRETTY?

Brian wondered how she could ask that question, how there could be any doubt at all in her mind. In the sunlight that surrounded her, he could see the curve of her hip as she sat just a little to the side, the way her breasts lay round and firm beneath the folds of her dress. The light made shadows on her bare shoulders from the ringlets of her hair. She was the kind of woman that they made sculptures of, the kind that men fought over in the old stories he'd devoured in high school. Brian thought that he had never seen anything so beautiful in his life.

"She's from Turkey or Italy or something," said Lardo. "Still thinks I'm the only one on this end of the line." Clash laughed at this, and Attila just smiled.

"Almost got her worn down, too," Clash said, taking another swig from his bottle.

Clash said the words aloud as he typed. "Of course I think you're pretty. You have a great body. I want to see more."

Lardo almost spit the beer all over himself. "Dude, don't say that, you're going to lose her." But it was too late. Clash had already hit the "ENTER" key. When the image refreshed itself, she seemed to have stiffened a little in her seat.

Brother Attila bolstered himself with another hit of his own drink and rolled his chair closer to the screen. "All right, move aside, you amateurs. Let the pro show you how it's done." That was Brother Attila. Attila the conqueror. Attila the collector of broken hearts. Attila the date-rapist, acquitted thanks to his family's money and influence. He shouldered Clash out of the way and began to type. "I only mean that I really like talking to you."

The image refreshed again, and her body seemed to relax. Brian's eyes followed the ringed shadows of her hair down her shoulders and into the depths of her cleavage. He felt his face go flush with a mix of excitement and shame—excitement because he wanted to see the same thing those three grinning monkeys wanted to see, and shame because it made him more like them.

When her words came back on the screen, he imagined the voice that went with them. It was soft, and kind, and full of innocence.

DO YOU MEAN IT?

Brother Attila looked around at the others and smiled, the undisputed lord and master of the moment. Brian saw the smile, and just for an instant, wanted to smash it in. "Of course I mean it." Attila typed. "You seem really nice."

Lardo snorted a laugh, and Clash rolled his eyes. The image on the screen shifted again, and this time one of her hands was at her chest, fingering the white cloth that ran up to her shoulder. The three brothers of Theta Omega crowded closer to the screen, their mouths gaping.

The image refreshed once more, and suddenly Brian was seized by the idea that something about it was wrong. It was more than just the situation, that they were all watching this girl, watching her when she thought she was talking one-on-one. No, there was something specific in that image that disturbed him, that made his stomach turn in lazy little loops.

He thought of those half-remembered stories once more. He thought of the goddess Diana, how she had punished a man who had stumbled upon her when she was bathing. She'd turned him into a stag and set her dogs loose on him. They had tore him to shreds while she watched, and as he recalled the story, Brian wondered if perhaps she had let herself be seen on purpose, just to have a reason.

With a dry mouth, Brian spoke. "How come she doesn't show her face?"

Lardo's head swiveled around, cold anger in his eyes.

Crap, I spoke out of turn, Brian thought. *Go ahead, then. Wash me out. Wash me out and maybe I won't feel so dirty right now.*

But the others were still glued to the screen, and Lardo didn't dare keep his eyes off it for long. "Who cares about her face," Clash said. "I want to see her tits!"

"Maybe she's got a butter face," Lardo said.

Clash looked confused and asked, "What's a butter face?"

"It's where everything looks good but her face."

The two of them threw back their heads and laughed through their high-fives. The image shifted again. Now her hands were at the keyboard. As if she had somehow heard Brian's question, she answered with one of her own.

DO YOU REALLY WANT TO SEE ME?

Something inside Brian urged him to cry out. He didn't want to see her face or any part of her. He didn't want to watch anymore. He wanted to run from that room as fast as his legs would take him. He never really wanted to be here, anyway—here in this house full of sociopaths, trying to belong. Only he didn't belong, not here, not with them.

The image shifted. The shadows had changed and she was typing again.

ALL OF ME?

"I'm going to get some more beer," Brian said. He did his best to keep his voice level, but to his own ears, it sounded tinged with fright. The others didn't turn to look at him.

"Make it snappy this time," Clash said. "I'm timing you." But he didn't take his eyes off the shifting image on the screen. Next to him, Attila was typing. Brian didn't wait to find out the words.

Outside the room, the air seemed lighter, less cold. He let out his breath, and suddenly he was aware of how fast his heart was beating. It was more than lust that had made it run so fast, lust and fear of that woman on the screen. The absurdity of it hit him at once, and he let out a nervous little laugh.

Stupid, he thought as he descended the stairs. *She's just a picture on the screen. What could she possibly do that I should be afraid of?* Behind him came another burst of laughter. One of them—Clash? Lardo? He couldn't tell—cried out. "Don't tell her you want to see her face! Tell her to take off the dress!"

Brian came to the last step and froze. He thought once more about the shadows on her shoulders, and in that moment he understood why he'd been so afraid. Again, in his head, he heard the girl speaking the words she typed on the screen, only this time, the gentle innocence had twisted into croaking menace.

DO YOU REALLY WANT TO SEE ME?

Those shadows, the ringlets of her hair. They fell on her shoulders in wide loops, shadows that were thick, and solid, and dark. And as the picture refreshed again and again and again, those shadows were moving. It wasn't just the wind blowing through them. They moved like they had a will all their own. They moved like something alive and angry and full of malice.

They moved like snakes.

"Oh great! Now she's moving the camera!"

Again the voice came to him, cold and hollow, like a mouthful of dead leaves.

ALL OF ME?

Then, everything fell silent.

Brian turned on the stair, and cast a wary glance over his shoulder. He could see the room through the open doorway, the shadows cast in the darkness by the light of the monitor. The shadows were stone still, and the only sound in the house was that of his own heartbeat.

He put a foot on the next step, willing himself to stop there. He felt the pull of his own dark curiosity, his desire to see what had silenced the brothers so completely. More than that, he wanted to see the image on the screen, to bask in its horrible beauty once more. He took one step, then another, drawn forward as if led by the hand, unable to stop, unwilling to stop, until he knew.

Then something cracked in the room above him. He felt the impact of something heavy carried along the floorboards and heard the slow, wobbling roll before it came to rest somewhere in the shadows.

He burst through the front door without stopping to put on his shoes and didn't look back. As he ran, he imagined he could hear the call of hounds close at his heels.

SLEEP GRINS

Chad McKee

The pressure on its skull was frightening. Its heartbeat ramped up and it pelted the walls with what little it possessed for arms. They were not very strong and the force against it did not subside with the effort. It resumed the fight anyway, in desperation. There was little enough pain but much discomfort. Ordinarily it would like tight spaces but this was too tight. Its skull felt soft and the pressure made it move, the bones shifting around with alarming popping sounds. It screamed, but nothing came from its mouth.

Janis's shrill laughter sounded like a scream: Aaaaahhhh! It stretched on. When it stopped, she belted out another phrase in Spanish: "*Me gustan tus pompis!*"

This was directed at Daniel, whose bemused look expressed everything before he even opened his mouth. "What did she say?"

Nita, at hearing her native tongue, shook her head. "It is not worth repeating."

The others laughed and nodded their heads; an obvious conclusion.

Jude did not laugh, not really, a sort of half smile and throwaway chuckle. He was white-knuckling a bottle of beer but not drinking it.

No one seemed to notice but Lydia. She transferred her grip to the arm not holding the beer and felt tension there as well.

"And that's only after two weeks! Just imagine what I'll know in two months!" Janis said.

There were speculative murmurs as their little circle closed in on itself, not wanting the rest of the party to hear. It was an instinctive gesture, like a mother protecting a baby or, perhaps more appropriately, buffalo herding together to keep the lions out.

"I've been able to write with my left hand," Daniel revealed. He tried to keep his voice down but the alcohol was getting to him. He always got wasted at his own parties. "Could hardly hold a pencil in it a week ago, I swear."

Faces looked to Jude. "Well?" Janis asked. "Is it possible?"

Jude shrugged and made a little sigh as if to say, *Who knows these things?* "If the drug works the way it's supposed to, then changes in motor control are possible. Very possible, in fact…"

Lydia felt her husband's body language become more favourable as he discussed their little pharmaceutical venture. He tended to relax in his lecturing mode. She entered the conversation: "How about you, Jessica? Any interesting changes? Tom?"

Tom said nothing, but his wife Jessica piped up cheerfully. "Is it supposed to increase blood flow to the head?"

Jude nodded. "It can enhance circulation in the brain."

Jessica smiled mischievously. "How 'bout in the other head? Since last week, that's what's been doing all the talking in this household!"

Janis let loose a peal of screeching laughter, and the rest of their circle laughed too, even Jude, as Tom stood there in awkward silence. A smile touched his lips, but he seemed elsewhere.

Pushing, then kicking. Its arms were bottled up at its sides, so keeping its legs in motion was now the only option. Even so, they moved slowly, as if caught in an undertow. Finding footing was difficult; its feet met with slickness all around. Still, to move was to possess some sort of control. Now that its head had been crushed, it felt that things could only get better.

"Did you see Jude? He looked awful."

Tom did not bother to make small talk with his wife, especially during sex. He repositioned his wife over the bathroom sink and kept in rhythm. Although he was not particularly aroused, he felt an odd comfort, a security almost, as he stayed inside her.

He concentrated on holding that feeling as firmly as he was holding his wife's ass, staving off the finish.

The sounds of the party were muted here on the second floor. They had found Daniel and Nita's bathroom. Tom had not actually suggested it—in fact, he had said only a few words all night—but she sensed that he was horny. She didn't know why or how that she knew. Maybe she had been given extrasensory perception by the drug. It sounded ridiculous, but then again people didn't just start using their non-dominant hand to write with or learn a language in two weeks. Or part of one. That Janis, what a mouth she had on her. Always talk, talk, talk. Jessica actually enjoyed her husband's change in demeanour. Strong and silent, the cliché was actually true. She literally bit back a scream herself as she climaxed, using the flesh of his hand like a muzzle.

The bite left red, semicircular indentions in the top and bottom of his left hand. Jessica felt a twinge of guilt, but Tom stepped back without comment, although his lips formed a small frown, a sort of childish pout. His eyes remained distant, so she never said the "sorry" that formed at the end of her tongue.

She began putting herself back together, wondering at how Tom could be so good in bed and so suddenly lousy at conversation.

"Why don't you talk with Jude," she suggested. "He's a good friend of yours and he seems down tonight." She flashed that mischievous grin again. "And anyway, he's the only one who can get more of this drug."

Quite suddenly it was all over. The pressure was gone. The frantic punching and kicking were done. There was irritating pain in its eyes, and much worse was occurring at the back of its skull. It made sounds—or thought it did—but the pain didn't subside. For a time that seemed to last as long as the painful escape, no one came to its aid. Then, a sharp thump to its back.

It opened its eyes. Mucous on its cornea filtered light into a fishbowl effect, adding to the discomfort. It felt disoriented. It felt pain. But it was free. In a crude, primitive way it experienced joy.

But also anger. And the bloom of some infantile petulance. It wanted to strike out.

Ventura parties were always the same: the revellers came late and with wine, always white and never from Napa. The homes were of the Ventura plan, with the master bedroom on the first floor and a pyramidal shape whose second floor opened onto the blue expanse of the Pacific. A large reception room tended to occupy its heart, where self-absorbed chatter hung in the air alongside tastefully framed prints of William Wendt and Paul Darrow.

Jude found himself slipping into depression again. His partners in conversation droned on about their support for the Oakland Occupiers even though they secretly voted Republican. Political gossip bored him; unfortunately, it filtered into half of every conversation on the West Coast. He extracted himself from it while also prying himself free of Lydia. She had been glued to his arm all night, no doubt concerned about him.

No matter. He stole his way to Daniel's study, passing through the kitchen and its lingering aroma of quesadillas. Despite his discretion, a shadow passed in front of him as he went to draw the parlour doors.

"Tom?"

"Can we speak, Jude?"

Reluctantly, Jude let Tom pass, and the two of them stood momentarily in the center of the room without a word passing. "What's on your mind, Tom?"

"What's on yours?" Tom countered. "You've been tense all night. Everybody has noticed."

It was odd to hear this from Tom, with his blank stares and sudden mood swings. Lydia joked that he must be entering menopause. Jude wondered how closely it matched his own recent black tempers. He felt an irrational envy of his friends' newfound abilities, even if they were limited in use and dubious in likelihood.

Jude had studied them tonight. Daniel, for example, continued to use his right hand predominately despite his claim otherwise. The insufferable Janis and her pidgin Spanish. And Jessica's newfound sexual voraciousness. He doubted that Tom was initiating things on his end. He knew that it was the inclination of every psychoanalyst to attribute physical phenomena to changes in mental state, but Jude had convinced himself that these so-called talents were the mind's trick on its owner.

Or perhaps his own lack of response to the drug was inherent to his own analytical personality. Maybe he possessed too little imagination.

"Tom, are you taking the drug?"

"Daily."

"And what have you felt in response? Do you feel as though you can do something that was previously beyond your ability? Or felt in some way different from before taking it?"

For a time, Tom only answered Jude's questions with a stony, empty gaze. Did the question anger him? Jude looked for the narrowing of eyes or the tightening of the lips that might reveal such an emotion. But finally Tom shook his head. "No," he said.

Jude nodded as if this were the answer he was looking for. "I think this drug is a failure."

"I don't know about that. But I did have a question for you."

"Of course."

"Do you remember what it was like to be born?

It did not know where it was. Many hands touched it, probed it. It felt resentful, particularly as it could not see or hear well. It could feel. Its flesh was soft and yielding and bruised easily in the exchange of possessors. It often felt cold, much like the acrid concoction it was fed to quell its hunger. It slept alone in a plastic box. And no one came to comfort it.

Nita was blindfolded but felt confident nonetheless. She held the pole—actually a croquet mallet—firmly in her hands, left over right, so tight that she felt her engagement ring digging into her skin. There was not enough light through the blindfold to zero in on her target, but she felt something—intuition?—as she moved forward, swinging the mallet down with a force she wouldn't have dared to use on another day.

The head of the mallet landed home, smashing her target with a satisfying thud and spilling its contents onto her face. Something hard bounced off her lip and she uttered a surprised little "Oh!" while the onlookers laughed. "Should have been George Bush's face!"

"*Muy bien*!" she heard Janis cry out. "Well done!"

There was general laughter and clapping. She ripped off the bandana and saw that she had nearly decapitated the donkey's head with the blow.

She beamed. "I could have never done that a few weeks ago," she said to Lydia in a voice not loud enough for the rest of the party to hear. Then: "Drink up!" The piñata had been filled with little bottles of liquor.

Daniel gave her a hug and a sloppy kiss on the lips. "Way to go, babe."

Jude and Tom had emerged from the study only seconds before Nita assaulted the papier-mâché animal. As the birthday girl, she was given first strike, but nobody had expected the little latina woman to bust it open on the first swing, or perhaps even to hit it. This despite two men at the end of a pulley who had been jerking it up and down, side to side, as if the piñata was blowing wild in an *El Niño* wind.

A birthday cake followed, but a round of tequila shots put everybody off eating it for the time being. The women were in the mood to dance, and the DJ alternated between disco and salsa. The party was turning into a good one.

Eventually, like the ocean tide, the energy waned as the moon began to fall. Attendees joined a gradually building exodus in the early hours of the morning, leaving only the hosts and a few guests who didn't have to return to children or the warmth of their own beds.

"Jessica, Tom, stay," said Daniel. He was drunk on Corona and Don Julio.

"Yes, stay, please," said Nita, only a degree more sober. "Don't drive tonight; the cops are out all over town."

"How about the rest of your friends?"

"They're from work," she said dismissively with a wave of her hand, and Jessica laughed.

Neither Jude nor Tom even smiled, though the latter had a faraway look that wasn't necessarily unpleasant. He looked stoned.

"So, Jude, can you believe I knocked the head off of the donkey?"

"You should have tried out for the Dodgers."

"I think it's those pills, *sí*."

Jude's smile was sour. "If that's what you believe, then maybe."

Lydia was back on his shoulder, squeezing. His arm felt sore from all the attention she had been giving it. "So, guys," she began, looking at her husband and Tom. "What have you felt on the drugs?"

"A headache," said Jude, hoping to avoid the subject.

"Sleep grins," said Tom. His voice carried a touch of satisfaction with it.

"Sleep grins?" said Jessica, her face screwing up into a doubtful grimace. Then a thought struck her. "Oh, those little faces you make before we make love in the middle of the night! That's your lust waking you from sleep."

Nita laughed. "Is that what you meant, Tom?"

"I put the idea into his head," said Jude. "He thinks the drug has given him flashbacks to his birth."

"Oh, shit!" said Daniel. "That's crazy! Like those guys who took LSD in the sixties and started reliving it twenty years later." He momentarily looked concerned. "Jude, that wouldn't really happen, right?"

Jude shook his head. "Flashbacks are frightening but usually very temporary things. If Tom is having them—and who can know that but Tom?—then they should be no more than impressions."

"And the grins?"

"They're what babies do when they are responding to stimuli for the first time."

"You're reliving your infant years?" Daniel couldn't resist a laugh. "Ha! I thought becoming ambidextrous was weird."

"That's why he's been on my tits all the time," announced Jessica. She, too, had drunk herself into a mild delirium.

Tom just smiled. It was his first true smile of the night.

"I need to get home," said Jude. "I'm beat." Lydia followed him out, worried about the bleak expression on his face. Others followed in a stream to the dark, early-morning roads.

Before long, everyone staying had been given a bed, and the house was quiet in the hours before dawn.

Life in the light was confusing. It could see nothing but what was immediately in front of it. Its only real vantage was of two things: slowly moving block-like objects that dangled in the space above, and at times a face. A hard, gaunt face with dark, unreadable eyes. They regarded each other uncertainly in their occasional encounters. It wanted to be held, but when the face held it, pain resulted. It was perhaps not intentional—it had an intuition that the face was new to this—but perhaps it was. Or became. Neither knew what the other one thought. But there was suspicion on both sides. And it cried and continued to cry. After a time, it was left alone and the face did not trouble it. Nor did anyone else for a long time.

Tom made love with his wife again when they went to bed. The sex, as always, was intense but patient. To Jessica, he seemed to be forcing himself as deeply into her as he could. She did not complain, as it only heightened her passion, but there was more concentration, more determination in his face, his body language. He wanted to be part of her, for their bodies to fuse into one unit. It was an incredible sensation; she tried to steady herself in kind, to provide a vessel for all of that thirst, but it was difficult.

They thrashed in the covers, intertwining themselves in sheets, which became second skins on their bodies. Despite the cool night temperatures, the doors were tightly shuttered; the room locked in their friction, incubating them. Tom continued unabated, and for Jessica there was no real escape. She was his prisoner.

Finally, as it all came to the end, they were so tightly wrapped in the blankets that she could no longer stand it.

"Tom, let me out of the covers. I can't breathe."

Tom was panting as well. Choking sounds emanated from his throat, and his face was arranged in an angry contortion. He seemed to resent her struggle out of the cocoon-like nest of linen. She wriggled from the sheets anyway, pushing off of him and to the floor at the foot of the bed. Cold air rushed into their warm pocket and Tom gasped. Bringing the sheets back around his neck was not enough to recapture the warmth and he slithered, snake-like, onto the floor next to her. She moved away, a little stunned by the shocking coldness of her naked buttocks on the floor and the strange wheezing from his sternum.

She couldn't properly see his eyes in the dim moonlight that was able to penetrate through the gauzy curtains. It made his eye sockets look like dark holes and he reached out for her clumsily as if they no longer worked. She grunted and looked for her panties, her bra, a shirt, something to cover herself. Not finding anything, she made her way along the wall, hoping to run into a light switch. Tom continued to writhe on the floor, inching his way towards her.

Jessica considered calling out his name but restrained herself. She didn't want to be found. He didn't look like her husband but like a grey changeling making horrible mewling sounds. She found the bathroom door and quickly searched for the light. She couldn't remember its location in this room; she had never slept in it. Where was the goddamned light?

Her fingers found it and yellow fluorescence stabbed in to the area where the grey, eyeless version of her husband should have been but was no longer.

It lay for days before anyone found it. It was almost dead, having been without food or water for so long, but tenacious life still burned, ember-like, in its tiny body. When it was found, medical personnel had been called upon to intervene. There were many appalled faces but also some astonished ones as well. Despite its ordeal, the little thing seemed, at least mentally, to be in a better place. It smiled endearingly, impishly in its sleep.

~

Daniel woke and went into the kitchen and found Tom already there. He was sitting at the table, a glass of last night's leftover wine in a jelly glass.

"Christ, how can you drink that this early in the morning? I always thought that 'hair of the dog' stuff was complete bullshit."

He readied the coffee maker with a filter and scooped in some new grounds. Only when the machine began to percolate did he turn back to Tom, his eyes red rimmed. Empty glasses littered the room, seat cushions were askew, and the detritus of the piñata had merely been pushed to the side of the room.

"What a mess," he commented. He pushed through busted donkey corpse for a moment. "Where's the croquet mallet? Well, it will turn up."

He sat down at the table with Tom after pouring a cup of coffee, not bothering with cream or sugar.

"What's with the grin? You look like you're still drunk."

The other man shook his head. "Not drunk. But celebrating."

"Celebrating what?"

"My birth."

"Huh? What are you talking about, Smith?"

"Did I ever tell you that I was an orphan?"

Its sleep was not peaceful. It was bombarded with images of the face with the dark, hard eyes hovering over it, which then vanished into the nebulous background of dreams. Its eyes were pinballs in their sockets, a dry tongue sucked at the roof of its mouth, and unsettled sounds emanated from there, sharp squeaks and grunts. Finally, it came to a conclusion, which was subsequently filed somewhere buried deep in its brain, and the sleep became restful. When it was roused by others with their probing instruments and bright lights, it held onto its smile for just a moment longer before unleashing a wail of anguish. The bubble of anger that caused that scream to surface gradually became smaller, then smaller still, finally diminishing to something it could not access with its conscious mind. But never went away.

~

Jude fell asleep contemplating causes and effects. Truths and consequences. Patterns of behavior. Typical thoughts of a psychiatrist, and they followed him into his dreams, at first easing him into REM sleep and then trapping him into a nightmare where he was pulled from a warm, comfortable place and handled by cold, foreign hands. Crying in confusion at first, then from dark, unrestrained anger.

His eyes shot open the instant that feeling rushed through his body. His gaze fell upon Lydia, and for a frozen moment he wanted to hit her, to lash out. He gripped the iron bars of the headboard instead, panting. His body shook for a long time in great, wracking tremors, and he was silently thankful that the alcohol kept Lydia asleep. In time he steadied himself, but his hands still shook. He had not experienced such a vivid dream in years. Or...a memory. Was that what it had been? A memory. He tried to shake off the absurdity of the idea, but it felt primordial; it felt correct. Could it be that it was possible to relive the instant that you were born? The drug opened up dormant areas of the brain; could it also open up repressed memories—events that were forgotten for a reason? Dredge up the traumatic event of birth from your subconscious and put it on display before your rational adult ego? The experience would be frightening, even if afterwards the infant is thrust immediately into the hands of a loving parent. However, what would happen if there was no such person? Perhaps the vessel that has expelled you, like refuse, does not want you. Thoughts of revenge, perhaps. That was what Tom Smith had hinted at. Maybe the man had been drunk. Or perhaps the drug had awoken some dormant disturbance from deep within. Sleep grins and childish violence. It was a puzzle.

However, when he received a hysterical phone call from Daniel minutes later, he thought he knew the answer.

THE LADY WITH TEETH LIKE KNIVES

Mark C. Scioneaux

"Cheer up, buddy. You've barely touched your steak, and that bourbon cost me sixty dollars a glass."

Jack Kraven wasn't hungry. He hadn't been hungry in days. Not since running the old lady down.

"I can't enjoy this," Jack said to his lawyer-buddy, Dirk.

The pair was seated at the best table in the most expensive steak house in town. It was supposed to be a celebration dinner, as Dirk had weaved a technicality—and a few rounds of golf with the local judge—to reduce Jack's charges of vehicular homicide to a simple "accident." Jack being a fellow lawyer as well didn't hurt either. Dirk was able to spin the sympathy card of a hard-working, public defender that let his guard down for just one moment, and an elderly woman paid the price for it.

"This is supposed to be a celebration of my hard work, but you are really making it a drag," Dirk said, sipping his bourbon and shoveling a piece of rare prime tenderloin into his mouth. He chewed noisily and the sounds made Jack's stomach rumble.

"I appreciate it, Dirk. You know I do. But I still have a conscience. You weren't there. You didn't see it."

Jack was right. Dirk hadn't seen the carnage that unfolded when Jack decided to put his head down for a moment, texting his girlfriend, and running through a stop sign in the process. His head had been swirling from a three-martini lunch with a few of his lawyer friends, and he was heading home for an afternoon delight with his girlfriend. He never saw the old lady cross, but she had. He heard a horrible thump followed by the crack of a fragile skull against the windshield. Her dead eyes stared into his, a trail of blood made its way down the splintered glass.

Jack remembered screaming, and then heaving his lunch onto the leather seats of his sports car. When he had collected his senses, the first person he called was Dirk, not the police. A resident of one of the houses had called the police for him. As he waited for Dirk, he could hear the sirens, and panic set in. His career was finished, toast. Hell, his life was over. Until Dirk arrived. Dirk worked his magic, a mix of legal mumbo-jumbo, to persuade the cops not to field test for alcohol. At the trial, so much evidence had been compromised that the entire thing was thrown out. Jack had to pay a fine for running a stop sign. $150 for the price of a grandmother's life.

"Look, I'm going to head home. Thea is waiting for me, and I'm just not in the mood for this."

"Well hitch a cab back. I'm not done here," Dirk said, eyeing a pretty blonde drinking at the bar alone.

"You're a real pal," Jack said, pushing away from the table. He didn't offer to pay for his share.

"I don't see why you hang out with that creep," Thea said, taking Jack's coat from his hands as he entered the spacious condo.

"That creep made sure I didn't see the inside of a jail cell for the rest of my life."

"Oh, you're right. I forgot what a great guy he is."

They had been fighting every day since the accident, though Thea knew it was no accident. She had been texting him back, short explicit messages to get Jack fired up and home fast. She felt just as responsible as he did, if not more. She thought about leaving him every day, and tonight all the stars were aligned. Tears rolled down her cheeks as she plopped into an overstuffed leather chair and began to sob. Jack placed a comforting hand on her shoulder, but she pulled away. His touch didn't do it for her anymore. She was touching a murderer.

"Will you cut the shit," Jack said. "You act like you killed someone."

That was the final straw.

“You asshole!” Thea said, jumping from the chair. Her face was red and her eyes puffy and wet with tears. “I did kill someone! I played my part, just as you did.”

A moment of clarity came over her, like a wave of reassurance. Things were so clear. She knew what needed to be done.

“I’m leaving,” she said.

“Fine. Go cool off and we can talk when you come back.”

“I’m not coming back. I’m going to my mother’s, and I’ll come get my things tomorrow when you are at work. I can’t do this anymore. I can’t look at you anymore. Hell, I can barely look at myself.”

Jack said nothing and, in doing so, said everything. She left the room, threw a few items into a small suitcase, and left. Jack sighed, walked over to the bar, and poured himself a glass of scotch. He downed it. Then another. And another. A wave of nausea slapped him, and he ran to the bathroom. The expensive tenderloin rushed up to greet him. For a moment he felt happy that Dirk had spent his money on the steak. He showered, feeling the hot water work its magic on his tired, aching body. His stress lifted, and a feeling of relief overcame him. Thea was gone, but so what? He would have sent her packing in a month anyway, and there would be plenty of Theas. Plenty of women like her ready to spread for a young lawyer with time and money to burn.

“I’m going to bed, and when I wake up I’m starting my life over,” he said as the hot water ran down his face.

He toweled off and climbed into bed, not bothering to put on a pair of boxers. The cool sheets soothed him, and soon Jack was fading into unconsciousness. As time passed, he was starting to convince himself that it had just been an accident after all. Thea’s weepy attitude had made it impossible for him to move on and forgive himself. But now that she was gone, the healing could begin. The world went dark as sleep cradled him.

He was in the car. The woman’s face was pressed against the glass. Her eyes, blue eyes, were staring at him accusingly. Then she blinked, and her eyes turned red. Blood red. Jack couldn’t move.

He felt trapped, pinned down. The old woman smiled, revealing a mouthful of teeth that resembled daggers. Teeth like knives.

Jack woke up screaming. He was relieved to see he was in his bedroom, safe. There was no car. No woman. No teeth.

He took a deep breath. Just then, a shadow moved across the room. It made a path from the foot of his bed to the bedroom door and then was gone.

Jack rubbed his eyes and attributed the alcohol to him seeing things. He tried to get back to sleep, but he never did.

"Thea left you? She was a cunt anyway." Dirk raised his finger to tell the bartender he needed another bourbon. "So how have things been going? I haven't talked to you in a few days. By the way, totally sealed the deal with that blonde."

So much had happened since their last dinner, and Jack wanted to tell him, but he was sure Dirk would have him committed. Still, he had to try. "Things have been, well…not good."

"What do you mean?"

"I mean there is something going on in my house. I don't know how to say this, so I just will. I'm being haunted, and I think it's the woman I killed."

"Jesus, keep your voice down," Dirk said, making sure no one was eavesdropping on their conversation. "What's happening?"

"All kinds of crazy shit. Shadows moving in the condo. Crap moved around. I've even heard a scream or two. The first one scared the hell out of me. My dreams are the worst. She's in every single one of them, and it's always the same dream."

"Buddy, sounds like you need to cut back on the drinking."

"It's the only way I can sleep now. I've already burned through all my vacation time after the accident. I can't work like this. I can barely live like this!"

"I don't know what to say, because I don't believe any of that crap. Sounds like a combination of alcohol and guilt."

"Thea was right about you. You are an asshole."

"Yeah, well go home and cry to her. Oh, wait…"

"I'm out of here," Jack said, angry. He threw his money on the bar and stormed out. Dirk didn't try to stop him.

~

Jack polished off an entire bottle of vodka when he got home. Drunk, he stumbled through his condo.

"Where are you!" he screamed, ordering the fiend to reveal itself. But it didn't. Not on his terms, anyway.

He made his way through each room, shouting and breaking whatever was in his way. He felt the urge to vomit coming again and didn't bother making it to the bathroom in time. He dropped to his knees, and a puddle of vodka-soaked mush settled into the carpet. Wiping away the remaining chunks that clung to his face, Jack got up and made it to the bathroom. The cold water splashing on his face felt good, but when he stared into the mirror, there she was.

Her eyes burned with hellfire, with vengeance. Dried blood caked her face. Her nose was gone, replaced with a tattered hole, and her forehead was dented in like a tin can that had tumbled from the top shelf. But it was those teeth. A mouth full of daggers smiled menacingly at him. Suddenly, a hand came through the glass and gripped his throat. He could feel the sharp nails dig into his flesh. He screamed, swatted the ghostly appendage away, and ran.

His legs became entwined in a pair of slacks that were crumpled on the floor. He pitched forward and landed on the bed. Small specks of blood dotted the sheets from the tiny holes on his neck. His head was spinning, and for a moment he felt he might lose consciousness. Then he heard the breathing.

It was ragged and wet, the sound of dead lungs struggling for air. He spun around and there she was, standing at the foot of his bed. Raising a boney finger, she pointed it at him in an accusing fashion. He knew who she was.

"It was an accident! An accident!"

"No. No accident," the horrifying specter said. "No justice. No peace." Her voice was cracked, as if she was speaking with a throat full of glass. She opened her large mouth, and Jack could see the light reflect off her teeth with a metallic sheen.

"No! I'm sorry!" Jack pleaded, but his cries fell on deaf ears. Vengeance had to be taken, and it would tonight.

He felt a pressure on his heart, as if it had been seized by an invisible hand. He was falling, spiraling into her mouth, into the blackness. Into eternity. He felt the teeth graze him and let out a cry of pain. He could see his ceiling fan, spinning fast, and the cream-colored ceiling. They'd be the last things he ever saw. She closed her mouth, and he was gone.

"I don't know what could have happened," Dirk told the police officer, who recorded his statement. "He liked to drink, but an entire bottle of vodka isn't like him."

He glanced over at the bed where Jack lay on his back. His eyes were wide with fright and his mouth twisted in a final scream. His hands were frozen like he had been defending himself. It was a horrible sight to see. Poor guy, he thought. Maybe now he can find some peace.

"Wasn't this the guy who mowed down that old lady a week ago?" he overheard a cop say. The officer near him grunted a reply.

"Guess he got what he deserved. Karma's a real bitch!" A few of the cops chuckled as the coroner snapped pictures.

"So, Derrick..."

"It's Dirk. Dirk. And he was my friend."

"Well, we have your statement, so you are free to go."

Dirk took one last look at his friend, wiped a tear from his eyes, and left the condo.

Judy Banks should have been celebrating. Her husband, Howard Banks, the real-estate mogul, was dead. The poison had worked perfectly. Completely untraceable, just as advertised. The coroner ruled the death a heart attack, and the court ruled all of Howard's possessions to be transferred to Judy.

"Come back to bed, baby," the voice of her lover called. "There's more champagne, and I want to screw again while staring at that picture of your asshole husband."

She didn't answer him. She couldn't. She was too busy trembling as she looked into the mirror and into the face of a man with teeth like knives.

THE BINDING

Daniel O'Connor

Soon.

There were three bullets. 9mm. They lay at the bottom of a stainless-steel soup ladle. It was lowered into a large, black cauldron containing what appeared to be too little water for such an ample container. But it was enough liquid to submerge the ammo. His hand left the ladle, and a mumbled prayer escaped his taut lips.

The benediction, and rite, of a novice.

A Catholic, a Jew, a Hindu, and an atheist walked into a bar.

Not at the exact same time, but in they walked as they had every Thursday evening for nearly four years. They had been coming since the night of the four visions, or dreams. Call them what you like.

On each of the fifth sunsets, be gathered within the out door, apart the cashless society, where the silver becomes the gold.

Curtis Massey, the Catholic, was the first to arrive this evening. He entered to the stink of smoke, but it wasn't the usual cigarette choke. A white man in a whiter hat sat at the bar burning a piece of notebook paper.

Bartender Grant accepted payment from a rosy-cheeked regular with a thick leather wallet as he spotted Massey heading for his usual table. It was round, wooden, and aged. It wasn't far from the old jukebox—a machine filled not with computer files or even compact discs but 45-rpm vinyl records. A prostitute leaned against it and dropped in some change. A portly old black fellow known as Knuckles halted the ragtime tune he'd been pounding out on the dusty upright piano. He played when the jukebox wasn't. He'd then resume his job of tidying up the bar. But he never dusted that piano. It was a lot like Knuckles: slightly out of tune but loaded with character. He nodded at Massey as he picked up a chair, toppled by a drunk who'd been cut off and shown the door. Knuckles never showed much affection, but he had a bond with Massey because they were frequently the only African Americans in the place.

There were two other ladies present, seated at opposite ends of the bar. One was a call girl, from the same stable as the woman at the jukebox. The other had been twice mistaken for a hooker today. Quite irksome. She had come alone after a dispute with her boyfriend and was drowning her troubles. Not much different from the fellow burning the note, but nobody had offered him money for sex.

"A change is gonna come."

That's what Sam Cooke assured from the jukebox speakers. The hookers hated that there was no current music on there, but they'd grown fond of Cooke's soothing voice. They found it sexy, and they were sure he was delivering a positive message.

The sun was almost gone, and it was time for Knuckles to plug in the longstanding neon sign atop the establishment, which stood alone by a stretch of road just off Interstate 15. Surrounded by desert and mountains, this was a place that was mainly supported by locals but also welcomed the many driving between California and Las Vegas. It was just minutes from the border, on the Golden State side. The sign hummed as it flickered to life.

The Out Door Inn.

When each of them awoke, their first thoughts were that they'd had a dream. The most lucid and comprehensible dream imaginable, but just a dream. They had been spoken to and given detailed instructions by something that appeared to be the sun.

Befriend the law. Though not rife with belief, rife with purity of heart.

That was part of it, along with the stuff about the cashless society and the fifth sunset. It was very real yet still confusing. But then, very quickly, things became quite clear. The four men who had had this vision did not know each other and were miles apart when it came over them.

Sunburn.

Each of them awoke with a blistering rash that had overtaken them as they slept, even Massey, whose ebony shell had never been torched this way. Each of them got into their respective vehicles and drove instinctively, without map or GPS, toward the desert. They arrived within minutes of each other, standing in the shade of a mountain, dust at their feet. That was the day they first met. Brought together that morning in the middle of nowhere by something they could not understand. They talked about their visions. Each one identical. They learned about each other. None of them shared the same religious beliefs. Each lived alone. All in their mid-thirties. To the east stood a lone structure, small, ringed by cactus, brushed by tumbleweed, and touched by the shadow of a Yucca palm, or, as many say, a Joshua tree.

The Out Door Inn.

They knew that was where it was to be. Whatever and whenever *it* was. They reasoned that "where the silver becomes the gold" must refer to the nearby border between the Silver and Golden states. They discussed more of this riddle—this mission, perhaps—for which they had been chosen. The four men got in their cars and drove to the inn. Naturally, it was closed this early in the day. A lizard scattered as Massey read a sign in the window.

Cash Only.

That took care of the "apart the cashless society" puzzle. In time they determined the "fifth sunsets" to mean Thursday nights. Simple math.

They bitched to each other about why this divine vision couldn't just cut the crap and be straightforward. Why the theatrical conundrum?

Then they stopped laughing, got in their cars, and drove to a CVS for some skin cream.

~

Curtis Massey hadn't waited more than a few minutes before the rest of them arrived. First came Stephen, the Jewish businessman who owned three inexpensive but successful shops in the lower-end casinos in Vegas. Right behind him was Vir, an Indian doctor with Hindu beliefs. The last to enter the bar was McKenna, a small-town deputy from thirty miles deeper into California. He was still in uniform, as always, with a Stetson atop his curly blond mat. He wore a vintage California Angels baseball jacket over his police duds. Deputy McKenna didn't believe in God.

Here they were again on another Thursday evening at the Out Door Inn. It was the 204th consecutive Thursday. Even Thanksgivings were spent at the bar. Despite the fierce protestations of the others, McKenna had missed three of the gatherings, but the others had been to every one, through weather, sickness, or family tragedy. They couldn't tell you why, but they knew they had to be there. The time and the reason would come.

...and that no man might buy or sell, save that he had the mark, or the name of the beast...

There had been a number of times when doubt would arise in one or another of them.

"Why us?"

"Why do we keep coming here when nothing ever happens?"

One time McKenna drank too much and was puking in the men's room. Massy spent those same moments in the face of a doubtful Stephen, telling him in no uncertain terms that it was all a test. If they could come every week for years on end with nothing to show for it, they'd prove themselves worthy. Another time it was Stephen who had to bring Massey to his senses. It was one of the nights without McKenna. He'd been stuck on a police matter. Massey was sure that "mark of the beast" referred to a tattoo that a group of rowdy bikers had on their foreheads. They came roaring into the bar, loud and strong, taking command of the jukebox and dartboard. Some took to the men's room with prostitutes. Massey tried to convince his friends that the time was at hand. He was sure this was the night of their calling, and McKenna wasn't even there. Stephen literally had to smack his bigger, stronger friend across the face while Vir got between them. It was all captured on Bartender Grant's rudimentary security camera, which was hooked into a rather primitive backroom VCR. He had viewed the tape and reminded them the following week that he wouldn't stand for violent behavior.

"When it is our time, we will *all* know!" Stephen shouted at Massey during the incident.

Massey came to his senses when he saw one of the bikers helping Knuckles repair a faulty piano key, right about the same time the leader of the gang bought drinks for everyone to apologize for their commotion. He personally carried a pitcher of beer to their table and asked them to tell him if they had any complaints about any member of his crew. Massey and Stephen had some of the beer, and Vir had a few sips. None of them drank much. Never had.

This night was no different. They'd ordered a pitcher; they had to or else risk blowing their cover. They'd mix in a few colas as well. Besides not wanting to cloud their minds, they just weren't drinkers. It was one of the traits that seemed to bind them. None of them had ever been married or had children. They were all far away from any real family. While McKenna had long thought nothing of religion, the others believed in a higher power but had never been extremely religious. In fact, they had each been almost shunned by their families for not practicing their religions with vigor.

But they were all good people.

Massey knew men who would never miss church on Sunday, only to beat their wives later that evening. Though he wasn't at the altar every weekend, Curtis Massey dedicated his time—both at work as a high school physical-education instructor and in his spare time working with orphaned children—to getting this generation off the computer and onto the playground. It saddened him to see today's children sitting on couches with French fries on their laps and greasy game controllers in their hands.

Stephen bucked the trend of tourist gouging, choosing to sell reasonably priced goods, and he shared his modest profits with numerous charities.

Nearly half of Vir's patients paid what they could or were seen for free.

McKenna drank more than the others and had no fear of God, but he treated everyone with dignity—even those he arrested. It said something for Deputy McKenna that he led a genuine life while believing that death held the same in store for both Mother Teresa and Adolf Hitler.

He considered his behavior a tribute to his late mother.

Thank God for Thursday Night Football. Massey, McKenna, and Stephen loved the games, and Vir had become a fan of late. They'd happily watch any contest on that small television that hung over the bar. The sound was always muted in deference to the jukebox or piano, but that was fine. A game would usually help the night pass quickly. They'd always leave at midnight, figuring that was the appropriate time to go as Thursday—or the fifth sunset—was officially over. They'd been given no specific instruction on when to leave.

The game would be a refreshing diversion from what had blanketed the airwaves of late. The presidential election was a week away, and between the ads, debates, and general mudslinging, most Americans were ready to just get it over with. The pregame show was just wrapping up with the logos of the Detroit Lions and New Orleans Saints carved into glowing pumpkins, because tonight was also Halloween.

"Come on!" grunted McKenna.

The network temporarily cut away from football coverage to present a talking head musing on the results of an election poll. Dead heat. The sound was down, but the graphic showed it all. Too close to call.

"Not interested in the election, Deputy?" said Stephen, smiling.

"Pick your poison," said McKenna as he removed the gun that had been strapped to his side all day. He discreetly ejected the magazine and the chambered bullet, then placed the empty weapon on the table in front of him and covered it with his Stetson. Same as he had each Thursday for the past two years. It took him the first couple of years to get comfortable enough with Massey, Stephen, and Vir to do so. By now he trusted them. He didn't like drinking with a loaded weapon strapped to his side. He tucked the ammo into the pocket of his Angels jacket.

The two presidential candidates were shown—split screen—on the TV. She had a pretty smile but a wild look in her eyes. Detractors said she'd have us in another war within her first year—if it took that long. He was relaxed but seemed to talk in riddles. He was motivational but not presidential. He had some extreme economic ideas that critics said would flush our economy and seal the toilet lid behind it.

It looked like a choice between World War III and Great Depression II.

Too close to call. Independent voters waited for a tipping point.

"The Lions got this one," said McKenna.

"My money's on the Saints," replied Massey.

Over at the bar, the man in the white hat put a match to another note from his former love and let it burn in the ashtray.

In came a noisy group of college kids. This happened many a night, but it always seemed to be a different bunch of students. As they jostled up next to the note burner, Bartender Grant spoke.

"Gonna need IDs."

Each and every student produced a device, slightly larger than a standard cell phone. They hit their touch screens, and their photos and pertinent info appeared along with a bar code.

"Give us a scan, bartender," said the smiling leader from under his knit cap.

"No *billows*. Regular picture IDs."

There was a shared whine as the students put down their billows and fumbled for traditional forms of identification.

"Old school," muttered one.

Saturday Night At The Movies.

That's what the Drifters were singing about through the old jukebox speakers.

The billow was an incredible creation. The "b" was never capitalized.

Curtis Massey tapped his fingers to the music as he eyed the college kids. He took careful note of everyone who entered the Out Door, as did Stephen and Vir. You'd think McKenna would as well, but after being on duty all day, this was his time to unwind and forgo his cop persona.

Satisfied with the IDs, Bartender Grant brought the drinks.

"I've got this round," offered one fresh-faced calculus major as he held out his billow for a payment scan. This would electronically transfer money from his bank account or lender of choice directly into the merchant's cyber coffer, which was off site and immune to the common stick-up artist.

Grant looked down at the sleek, glowing device. Each billow sported what had become the most famous logo on Earth: a fluffy cloud with the tip of the sun rising just behind it. This is where the merchant would produce his business billow and wave it over the customer's for a hassle-free scanned payment.

"Cash only," said Grant.

"You're kidding."

"Sign's on the front door."

The student turned to his friends and asked, "Anyone have money?"

Over at their table, McKenna felt a tap on the shoulder. It was Knuckles.

"Darts?" he asked.

Knuckles never said much, but he sure had a liking for McKenna, Massey, and the boys. Most Thursdays he'd be sure to fit in a dart game with McKenna. Bartender Grant was his boss, but he wasn't overly demanding, and he appreciated how Knuckles donated much of his time to his Baptist church. Whether he was passing the collection plate or doing handy work, they could always count on Knuckles. He was a good man, and Grant knew it.

"Sure, Knuckles. I owe you for what you did to me last week," smiled McKenna. Then he turned to his friends. "You know," he said, winking.

Translation: "Keep an eye on that gun under my hat. Someone stay at the table at all times."

"Yeah, yeah," said Massey.

The scorned woman who'd been sitting at the end of the bar in the aftermath of the boyfriend blowout stood and sauntered over toward the man in the white hat. She'd noticed some college boys ogling her and wanted no part of that. At least this guy was interesting. The final flame to consume his ashen note danced in the sooty tin receptacle.

"I'm Dorothy," she said.

As McKenna and Knuckles commenced their dartboard battle, Stephen produced his portable, magnetic chess set. He and Vir would often engage in a game. Massey never involved himself in any of that. He would watch some of whatever game was on TV, but mostly he'd just stare intently at the various patrons.

Especially first timers.

This would occasionally lead to conflict, but he could handle himself if apology failed. This was all much more important than a bloody nose.

"How was work this week?" Stephen asked Vir.

"The same. Not encouraging. Too many young people contracting diseases of the old."

"Sad."

"Sweet!" interrupted one of the college boys as he passed their table. "I'm a chess freak, dude. You guys really have one with the actual pieces? Ever try it on a billow? It's über cool. You can make the chessmen fight to the death."

"We have not," said Vir, smiling.

"In 3D."

The football game was finally starting. The election coverage ended with an image of Las Vegas on the screen. With the sound down and the digital grandmaster partially blocking his view of the television, Massey didn't get the connection.

"Did you see that?" Massey asked of his friends as the student moved on.

"What?"

"The election thing finished with a picture of Vegas. What's that all about?"

"Maybe a final campaign stop?" offered Vir while moving a pawn.

"Who knows what their think tanks have come up with," added Stephen. "Such a close race, and Nevada is up for grabs."

Massey excused himself from his chess-playing comrades and headed to the bar for a bag of peanuts. He did this every week because, though he wasn't really hungry, it gave him some sense of normalcy—almost tricking him into thinking he was there for pleasure.

"Good evening," said a smiling, attractive Asian woman who had arrived with the students.

"Hello," replied Massey, sensing more friendliness than flirtatiousness.

The woman's billow sat on a napkin atop the bar in front of her. Its screen was filled with small print that Massey couldn't read without his glasses.

"Doing some reading?" he asked.

"Midterms."

"This is no place to study."

"Not studying. Grading."

"Very sorry. You're a teacher?"

"College professor," she said. "So is he." She pointed at a colleague who was in conversation with students at the other end of the bar.

"Mixing with students at a bar?"

"Well, it's not *their* papers I'm grading."

Massey paid Grant for the nuts.

"Papers?" he said as he opened his snack bag. "I don't see any paper."

"Not a fan of technology, I'm guessing."

"Peanuts?" he offered

"No thanks."

"Technology is fine. I like it. Advances in medicine, solar power, and such."

"But?" she asked.

"I enjoy things like books, records, CDs, DVDs, Blu-rays. Things we can touch. There's a lot of character in physical media."

She took a sip of her cocktail. "All those things you mentioned: they eventually wind up in a landfill."

Massey shook a few nuts around in his fist.

"They only go to the landfill after somebody buys one of those," he answered, pointing a finger at her billow.

"Dang it!" shouted McKenna as Knuckles defeated him at darts.

"Another game?" asked Knuckles. McKenna agreed. The jukebox needle landed on a scratchy single, and Linda Ronstadt sang to a lover that they merely marched to the beat of a different drum.

"I believe in saving trees," said the professor. "Your physical books, though romanticized, devour forests. Not to mention that your leather-bound classics probably use calf skin."

Massey grinned as he shuffled more nuts around his palm.

"So are you picturing me as some pipe-toting, nineteenth century bibliophile? That's the right word, isn't it?"

She laughed as Massey went on. "You're envisioning me in my vast library with forty-foot-high shelving and a rolling ladder. Actually, when I do get the time to read, it's most likely a used paperback that I donate to the public library when I'm done. Not much falling timber there."

"Other than the initial printing," she replied.

"That billow thing you have, you ever read it at the lake, or by the pool?"

"Sure."

"Isn't that a waste of energy? You could be reading a book in that midday sun, but you're burning up a battery. Also, I'm guessing they use copper, gold, lead, zinc, crude oil, natural gas and who knows what else in manufacturing those things. Ever hear of the term 'persistent toxins'? If my book winds up in a landfill, it rots away. Those things last forever— and they go to the dump whenever version 'New.0' comes out."

"Well, you'll have to send an email—or write out a scroll in your case—to Joel Amator in protest. Maybe I will have some peanuts."

"An Amator fan, eh?"

"Who isn't?" she said as she popped a nut. "Probably the greatest genius the world has ever known. I don't think it would be overstating it to say that man is almost single-handedly saving our planet."

"Because he invented the billow?"

"That's part of it. But he has brought the world together. Changed the way people think. As soon as he announces his presidential endorsement, that candidate is guaranteed victory next Tuesday."

The tipping point.

As Massey downed his final peanut, every billow in the place began to vibrate and glow. Even the man in the white hat pulled his match away from another ill-fated love note so that he might read his billow.

"A mass email!" yelled one student.

"From Joel Amator to every billow user in the world!" howled another.

The female professor beside Massey clicked on her email, and it filled the screen.

"You can read mine," she said, tilting it toward him. He took his reading glasses from his pocket and leaned over.

Hello billowers! Joel here. Wanted 2 confirm 2 U all that the rumors R true. Excited 2 say I will be offering my support 2 a candidate 2morrow! Sry 2 keep U guessing, but watch my press conference @ Bellagio fountains Vegas 2morrow! On my way up 2 Vegas rite now!

"That's exciting," said the professor, looking at her screen. "By the way, my name's Hanna."

She glanced over at Curtis Massey, but he was gone.

Then, in an oddity for the Mojave Desert this time of year, it began to rain. Heavily.

An intense thunder clap opened the skies above the Out Door Inn.

Vir moved his bishop to g5.

"Stephen," said Massey as he rushed back to the table, "remember when we were talking about Amator's election endorsement?"

"Yes," he replied as he pondered his defense.

"What did you say he'd get out of it?"

"Said he'd be named to the Federal Reserve Board by the next president."

Lions 6, Saints 0.

Knuckles landed another dart in the bull's-eye.

Two dapper gentlemen scurried in from the rain. They went to the bar, were refused scan payment, had no cash, and quickly left with the two hookers who had been there all evening. The whores accepted billow.

Bartender Grant watched one of the students stick a pair of buds in his ears and scroll through the music on his billow. There was a song playing on the jukebox, but it wasn't to his liking. Fair enough. It sounded a little scratchy from years of play, but it *was* the entire song. What the student didn't know—or didn't care to know—was that the songs on his billow were compressed and clipped, shrunk into a tiny file that would allow for greater storage capacity. Portions of the recordings were discarded, and the dynamic range was squeezed together so that there was little difference between the loudest and quietest sections. Some cared about such things, but most did not.

All in the name of storage.

The billow users had all their music, along with their movies, books, documents, email, and just about everything else, stored on a *cloud*. They called it NINe. It's nice to picture the world's information lazily floating along the atmosphere in a fluffy cocoon, but this cloud was actually an army of gigantic computer servers that ran hot in any number of industrial areas throughout the world. Cloud enthusiasts were thrilled that they no longer had to care about physically storing items such as albums, books, and movies. Good riddance to those dust-collecting space fillers. Now they could just access these items through billow, and thanks to monthly subscription services, they needn't "own" any of them. They could watch, listen, and read on demand—all from NINe. Plus, there were multiple backups of their documents there. No worries about burglary or fire. It was all so safe.

McKenna had lost at darts again. The cop returned to the table to find Massey seated with his back to the television. Vir was packing up the chess game, and Stephen had gone to the men's room.

"Not watching the game?" asked McKenna.

Lions 6, Saints 3.

"Guess I found chess more exciting," replied Massey.

"Who won?"

"Nobody," said Vir. "We stopped."

McKenna sat and poured a glass from the warming beer pitcher. As was his habit, he picked up the edge of his Stetson just to be sure that his empty gun was still beneath it.

It was an involuntary reflex by now: lift hat, see gun, lower hat. McKenna almost did just that, but for the first time out of hundreds of inspections, things were different.

His gun was gone.

"Tell me someone is being funny," he pleaded. He lifted the hat to show Massey and Vir. Stephen opened the door from the bathroom and held it for the man with the white hat, who emerged behind him and returned to his seat at the bar. As Stephen reached their table, McKenna was bordering on panic.

"I have to search every asshole in this bar," he said, voice rising.

"What happened?" asked Stephen.

"Somebody's got my gun."

"You sure?"

"Of course, goddammit."

"Did you look under the table? Maybe it fell?"

"Yes. It didn't. I have to make sure nobody leaves the bar, and I'll have to call the station house to get some backup down here."

"Easy," said Vir. "Before you do all that and get yourself in trouble for losing a gun with a beer in your hand, let's put our heads together."

"Who came by this table?" asked McKenna. "Some students? I knew I should've kept it in the car. Some guys lock it under the seat, cuffing it to the frame."

"And then when the car is stolen?" asked Vir. "You did it right. Unloaded and nearby. I would never leave my medical bag in the car."

McKenna looked down at the leather bag by Vir's feet. Then he looked into his friend's eyes. Vir knew what was coming, so he offered: "You want to search my bag for your gun?"

McKenna rubbed his hand across his forehead, "Im sorry, Vir."

The doctor placed his bag on the table and took a key from his pocket. He unlocked the brass clasp and slid the bag over to the cop.

"Vir—"

"It's okay."

McKenna opened the bag. He tried to be gentle, but his mind was racing. He saw a stethoscope, then some syringes, tongue depressors, a blood-pressure cuff. There was a multitude of items in that bag, but no gun.

Massey stood up and said, "Well, you can now pat us all down or just go by the front door and check strangers as they leave."

"I'm sorry. You're right. I should concentrate on strangers. But you guys were supposed to watch it for me."

McKenna headed for the door.

"We *were* watching," said Vir.

Just as McKenna reached the door, thunder rattled the windows, and the billows lit up. Every one of them.

"No freaking way," gasped one female student as she read her glowing notification.

Then the door opened. The wind howled as it blew a spray of rain into the Out Door.

"A night not fit for man nor beast," a man said upon entering. "The roads are completely flooded. If not for these fellas, I'd be swimming toward Vegas!"

It was Joel Amator. Right there in the flesh.

He entered with two other men. Large ones. McKenna was momentarily star struck. He hadn't come across many famous people. He once got an autograph from Hall of Fame pitcher Nolan Ryan, and he and his late father had seen Joey Bishop in a restaurant decades before. But even they weren't this famous.

Hey, billowers! Joel here. I'm coming in! Get me a towel!

That's how his email read. Through his billow-track app, which only he had, Amator was able to connect with only those billowers in the Out Door. It was like a GPS that could identify nearby devices.

McKenna was surprised that the billionaire inventor wasn't in an expensive suit. Just a sweater and jeans. His two minders did wear suits.

The billows were in camera mode now, flashing away. Amator smiled and greeted the swarm around him. He signed autographs and posed for pictures with the students, faculty, and the man in the white hat.

"Since we'll be here until this storm passes, I guess drinks are on the rich guy," he laughed.

The patrons cheered.

"That's mighty kind of you, sir," interrupted Bartender Grant, "but, forgive me for being presumptuous, we can't accept electronic payments here. Cash only."

"Nothing wrong with cash," said Amator, smiling. "Big Jerry carries it." He pointed to one of his hulking assistants. "Who'd dare try and mug him?"

Most of the customers laughed as the guard dropped some crisp bills on the bar. He noticed a thick, worn, hardcover bartending guide lying near Grant's thick, worn hand. Stitch bound. Looked like a bible.

"You could probably have that on your billow and pull up any drink recipe with the touch of a finger," smiled Big Jerry

"Ain't opened that book in years," answered Grant. "It's there just in case."

Deputy McKenna scurried back to the table.

"We've *got* to find my gun. Now with this guy here? Bad situation."

"Stay calm," said Stephen.

"Look," added Vir, "see how many people are recording all this now?"

McKenna saw the glow of several billows as they documented Amator's pit stop.

"If we make some big announcement or start searching people for your gun, it might wind up on the national news. You want to be known the world over as 'The Cop Who Lost His Gun'?" asked Massey.

"Nobody will leave during this storm," said Stephen. "We have time. Plus, you still have all the bullets in your jacket, correct?"

"Yes," he replied, with a hand in his Angels pocket.

"It will all work out, I promise," said Massey, his arm around McKenna.

Over by the bar, the questions came quickly at Joel Amator.

"Who gets your endorsement?"

"When are you going to run for office yourself?"

"Is it true that the next-generation billow will be out on Black Friday?"

"Are you taking on any interns?"

Back at McKenna's table, the deputy was still uneasy. "We've got to do something. Can't just wait around," he said.

Massey looked at Stephen and Vir. They really felt for their friend.

"How about this?" asked Massey. "You start at that end, and we'll all branch out and discreetly ask about the gun. One person at a time, in whispers. If we spot anyone shaky, we'll notify you to question them."

"Well, at least it's something," answered McKenna. "Let's do it."

Massey exhaled as he locked eyes with Stephen and Vir. "You ready?" he asked.

They nodded.

"Then let us each say a silent prayer. You don't have to, Deputy."

They took a solemn, private moment. Not McKenna. Then they fanned out.

Lions 6, Saints 6.

Curtis Massey ambled to the bar. He wanted a closer look at Joel Amator, but he'd have to wait his turn. The genius was still besieged by questions and compliments. His two massive bodyguards were nearby but, under orders from their boss, quite relaxed and accommodating to the billowers. Photos and videos were being taken from all angles. The jukebox stylus landed on the final single released during Led Zeppelin's mighty career: *Fool in the Rain.*

Midway through the song, Massey pulled up beside Amator, who still held a Sharpie after signing about a dozen billows. Massey had a full glass in his hand. It looked like vodka.

"What, no billow to sign?" laughed Amator as he put a hand on Massey's shoulder.

"Not much of an autograph seeker, really," replied Massey. "Not a billow person either. Sorry."

"That's fine," he said, extending his hand. "I'm Joel."

"Curtis." He rested his glass on the bar and grasped Amator's hand. The billionaire had a firm grip, not the cold touch Massey had anticipated.

"Do you carry a cell phone, Curtis?"

"Yes. For emergencies."

"Well, the billow isn't much different," said Amator. "Just much better!" He smiled.

"I'm not much for all that extra stuff."

"Do you use social networks?"

"Nah."

"Try them. If you have friends or family spread across the world, it's almost like you can hang out with them the same way you used to. You can video chat—"

"Yeah, that does sound nice."

"So you *do* have an open mind? Not one of those 'technology is evil' people. Good!"

Joel Amator's hands rested on the bar, near his glass of diet cola. Curtis Massey's right hand passed over his own glass, knocking it on its side. The clear liquid splashed onto Amator's left hand, then dripped down onto Grant's voluminous bartending tome.

"So sorry," said Massey.

"No problem," answered Amator as he grabbed a napkin. Big Jerry took a step their way but stopped, sensing a simple accident. Bartender Grant headed over with his rag.

"Let me leave you to your fans," said Massey as he turned to leave. He made eye contact with Stephen and Vir, who were slowly walking toward the door. They waited and watched.

The vinyl slab in the jukebox began to skip.

"Clouds the light of the love—clouds the light of the love—clouds the light of the love..."

"Ha," laughed a student, "an actual scratched record. That's a first for me!"

Knuckles went over and tapped the jukebox with his knuckles. The song resumed.

"Aaaarrrgh!" The sound came like the roar of a grassland predator. Massey stopped in his tracks. It came from Amator's direction. Massey turned.

People rushed toward the billionaire, including his bodyguards. Amator clutched his left hand—the one he had been dabbing with the napkin.

"What's wrong, sir?" asked Big Jerry.

"He spilled something on my hand! Probably acid!" barked Amator in a more human tone.

The crowd gasped. Amator raised his hand. It was being eaten through.

Massey gave a slight nod to Stephen and Vir. They circled behind Amator's two guards; Stephen first stopped to move the front-door shade and take a quick glance into the rainy night.

Vir was directly behind Big Jerry, Stephen to the rear of the second hulk. Together, the smaller men produced identical syringes, each topped with a hypodermic needle. This was one of the many possible scenarios they had rehearsed for years. Vir, the medical professional, had taught Stephen slowly, and he had become quite proficient with injections.

With the timing of a dance team, they slammed their needles into the necks of Amator's giants, steadily injecting the animal tranquilizer. Their targets began to buck like ring bulls.

Big Jerry was out in seconds. Etorphine does that. Stephen had often asked Vir why they couldn't just put some concoction on a napkin and hold it over the nose of their mark, but Vir told him an injection was the only reasonable way to ensure lasting unconsciousness.

The crowd reacted with shouts of anger. Some moved toward Stephen and Vir.

"Please be calm," said Vir. "I am a doctor, this is called 'karma,' and I watch Blu-rays of *Dexter*, so I know what I'm doing."

One problem: Stephen got his needle into the other bodyguard, but wasn't able to inject the full amount of Etorphine before the mammoth threw him off. The guard was groggy, but managed to pull his weapon as he staggered.

"They burned me with acid!" yelled Amator again.

"It is *not* acid," answered Curtis Massey. He was holding Deputy McKenna's gun. He'd loaded it with his own clip.

"Curtis!" yelled McKenna, more astonished that Massey had taken his gun than in seeing his two other pacifist friends jamming sharp objects into flesh.

There had been four visions that one night years ago, but Deputy McKenna—the atheist who was of kind heart and pure soul—was not privy to one.

Befriend the law. Though not rife with belief, rife with purity of heart. The chosen shall not possess the instrument of salvation, but shall command it.

They knew they'd meet a lawman at the Out Door, become friends, and use his weapon when the day arrived. The ammunition was another story.

Massey had to ignore McKenna, at least for now. He turned his attention to the throng who would be all over him and his friends now if not for the gun in his hand. He hoped his explanation would calm the wobbly guard who aimed his own gun as Stephen and Vir struggled to gain control of him.

"If that were acid," Massey yelled, "it would be burning through the wood on the bar. At the very least, Grant's hands would be burning. He just cleaned it up."

"What the hell was it, then?" barked the professor.

It was the same liquid into which Curtis Massey had submerged his bullets every Thursday for four years. Three at a time via soup ladle.

"It's holy water," he said.

The Beast, proclaimed indestructible, will perish before the faithful and the blessed.

Most in the crowd grumbled. McKenna sighed. Knuckles kissed the cross that hung from his neck. Amator took a step toward Massey.

"This man is insane," he said, turning to his guard, who had thrown Stephen from his back and was breaking loose from Vir. "You may have to shoot him to subdue him. Aim for the leg. We are not murderers."

Several billows were recording everything. They glowed like stars.

The guard shook off Vir, stepped in front of his boss, and took aim at Massey. Curtis was prepared to die, but he didn't want to shoot the bodyguard, whom he figured to be an unwitting follower of Amator. He spoke to the groggy protector.

"Listen friend—Joel Amator is not a human being. He is the false prophet. Please step aside."

"No," replied the guard. His numbing finger found the trigger.

Just before he could get his shot off, it landed in his neck. Not the hypodermic needle but the barroom dart.

The shot rang off wildly and struck the piano. The wobbly guard dropped his gun and reached for his neck. Knuckles dropped the rest of his darts and picked up Grant's hefty bartending book, still damp from the holy water. He hopped around the bar and slammed it onto the bodyguard's skull. That completed his bumpy road to unconsciousness.

Joel Amator picked up the fallen gun, but rather than shoot, he ran toward the door. He opened it about two inches, but it would budge no farther. He smelled the exhaust fumes that washed through the cracked door with the rain. With no other choice, he turned to face Massey and raised the gun toward him. Pale flesh dangled from his injured hand.

"Don't be fooled by these zealots," he told the onlookers. "Money is at the root of this. Probably some ransom. Help me stop these criminals and none of you will ever have to work a day in your lives. You'll all be millionaires and heroes by the end of the night."

Some in the crowd began to head toward Stephen, Vir, and Knuckles. They figured Amator and his gun could hold off the armed Massey.

"Don't do this, Curtis," yelled McKenna. His mind was a blur, but it all sounded crazy to him, and he didn't want to have to arrest his friends for murder. "Let's all drop the guns and sort this out."

"Can't do that," said Curtis.

McKenna charged at Massey. "Then you'll have to shoot *me*!" he yelled.

Amator took this distraction as his cue to fire. Curtis did the same. Amator's bullets missed, but Massey's did not. Four hundred sessions of target practice had paid off. The genius inventor knew he'd been hit. Three times. But he didn't go down. He was contemplating his explanation when he felt it. Intense burning inside. Everything went hazy and he began to choke. His body felt like a barbeque pit. He went down just as McKenna pinned Massey's arms behind his back. The crowd had hold of the rest of them.

Some in the crowd went to Amator's aid. Another yelled out, "You'll all rot in prison! This has been recorded on billow, you bastards. It's all on NINe."

"They said they're doctors," yelled another as she pointed at the restrained Vir and Stephen. "Bring them to examine Joel. For God's sake, at least see if you can save him."

Vir and Stephen were dragged toward Amator.

"I'm not a doctor," said Stephen. "I sell cheap sunglasses and 'What happens in Vegas' shirts."

Vir knelt beside Amator, feeling for a pulse, hoping for none.

"I need you all to see this," he said.

A crowd gathered.

"Record this on your devices. It was shot several times, including in its throat. Come closer to see. There is no blood. Also, from its injured hand: mangled flesh but not one drop of blood."

The crowd gaped and murmured in disbelief.

"I suspect an autopsy will reveal the lack of other human necessities. What it will not prove is the lack of *atman*. The beast has no soul."

A student leaned in with his billow. The light was bright as he zoomed. Then it went out. The light shut off and the billow shut down. Then another billow, and another. They all crashed together.

McKenna let go of Massey, still searching for a reasonable explanation.

"I need to revive these men," said Vir, in reference to Amator's guards. "I have an antidote in my bag that reverses the effects of the drug we gave them. They are not evil, just blind followers."

Vir had just stepped away from Amator's body when an ominous sound came. Like a dampened volcano, it brewed from within the fallen entity. Then it exploded.

It was blazing like a back-alley dumpster fire when the first few billows blew up. People screamed as some suffered hand and facial injuries. Others tossed theirs to the floor just before they ignited.

"The evidence?" yelled Deputy McKenna.

"Don't worry," said Hanna, staring at Massey. "Everything we recorded is stored on the cloud. It can all be retrieved from NINe."

Maybe she was flirting, he thought.

None of them yet knew that all across the country, every single hulking computer server in the NINe network had just exploded. Nothing would be retrieved from any of them. Every billow on Earth was also ablaze. There were thousands upon thousands of injuries and, sadly, a few deaths. People the world over had sacrificed life and limb, but all—living and dead—were finally safe.

As quickly as it had begun, Amator's fire was ebbing. Knuckles was on the way with the extinguisher, but it wasn't needed. One small flame remained, and the man in the white hat took the opportunity to kindle it with his final piece of paper, a "Dear John" letter. He dropped it onto the pile of ashes that was once known as "the world's greatest genius" and walked back to the bar as it burned. Dorothy put her head on his shoulder.

"I don't know much about all that cloud stuff," said Bartender Grant as he emerged from the back room, "but if you all have trouble finding the evidence of that thing not bleeding, then turnin' into a fireball for no good reason, I got it all right here."

In his hand was a black plastic video cassette tape from his old surveillance system.

Memorex.

Outside the bar, pounded by rain and under the glow of the "Out Door" sign, an old Toyota Prius had been backed up right against the door. It had prevented Amator's escape, and it was still running. A man sat inside it as he had every Thursday night for four years since he saw that vision along with the other three and met them, all sunburned, on the desert sand. His beliefs had prevented him from ever entering a bar, but he knew he had been called upon for a reason, and tonight that reason became clear.

Hassan Darwish adjusted the white turban on his head and watched the rearview mirror for any sign that their mission was complete. He'd heard the gunfire and explosions, but knew his role was to hold that car against the door until it was over. He understood that if they had indeed killed the beast, it was in the realm of possibility that it might soon be reborn. Would it be at least a quarter century until it might emerge again as a grown man or woman bent on destruction? They'd all likely be retired then. Old men without much physical strength. But regardless, they would be ready to confront evil if called upon.

Saints 9, Lions 6.

Halftime.

~

And he causeth all, both small and great, rich and poor, free and bond, to receive a mark in their right hand, or in their foreheads: and that no man might buy or sell, save he that had the mark, or the name of the beast, or the number of his name.

—Revelation 13:17

CRY

Jeff Strand

My tears spill onto the keyboard as I write this.

It's pretty much because I just finished rubbing freshly sliced habanero peppers into my eyes, which is something I do every once in a while. It all started when I was six, and I thought "I wonder what would happen if I did that?" So I tried it, and it sucked, and I didn't do it again right away. But after three or four weeks I succumbed to the temptation, and now it's a semi-regular thing.

You're judging me, aren't you?

As you read this, you're developing an air of superiority, simply because I rub burning pepper juice into my eyes and you probably don't. That's all right. You're entitled. I mean, if I watched somebody jab themself in the face with a fork, I'd say to myself "I am more intelligent than that person."

Okay, that's a lie. I jab myself in the face with a fork almost as often as I do the habanero thing. Not hard enough that it goes in one cheek and out the other, but enough to make four red marks that leak. And then I put antiseptic on it, both to keep the wound free of infection and because of the interesting sensation that occurs.

Some might say that I have a problem. To them I say...well, I can't really argue their logic. I do have a problem. I don't stand there pouring alcohol on facial fork wounds and think that I'm being normal.

Oh, by the way, my name is Herbert Gomast, and I am twenty-six years old. I guess I should have started with that instead of rushing right to the self-torture stuff. I have blond hair, blue eyes, a bit of a gut, a unibrow that you can't really tell is a unibrow because it's blond, and I live in Seattle.

I didn't cry when I was born. In fact, the doctors weren't completely sure that I was even alive when they pulled me out because my mom had died a few minutes earlier.

My dad didn't blame me for the death of my mother. I appreciated that. Your home life is much better when your dad isn't constantly bellowing "What kind of a monster child would kill his own mother?" Technically, it was my fault, but it's not like I did it on purpose. I wasn't an unborn infant hanging out in the womb going "This bitch is toast!"

I had a relatively normal childhood for a kid with no mom. My dad did think it was kind of weird that I never cried, and he mentioned it to my aunt. She said that when somebody is given the gift of a child that doesn't wake them up at all hours of the goddamn night with crying fits, they should accept this precious, precious gift and not cause the Lord to say "You want a crying kid? Oh, I'll give you a crying kid!"

When I turned six, my dad died. It was sad enough that he died at all, but he died on my birthday, and he died because he'd inhaled too much helium from my balloons (at my urging because his silly high-pitched voice made me laugh), and when he collapsed he fell on my birthday puppy.

But I didn't cry. I was sad, yeah, but I didn't cry.

At the funeral, I overheard some relatives talking about how weird it was that my dad was dead and I wasn't crying. My own grandmother thought it was creepy. So I walked right up to the casket and I scrunched up my face and I tried to cry. It didn't work. I was more inclined to scream in terror over being so close to a dead body, though I didn't do that, either.

When they lowered the casket into the ground and everybody was blubbering, I tried to figure out what they were doing right, but I simply couldn't get my tear ducts to work that way. I faked it by rubbing my eyes and making sobbing sounds just so my grandmother wouldn't think I was creepy.

I went to live with my aunt, who treated me well and had cable. She was an amateur chef who was constantly inventing new dishes, and one day she was cutting up some habanero peppers for an exciting new dish. The phone rang, and she told me not to touch anything while she went to answer it.

I walked over to the kitchen counter. I wasn't tall enough to see the orange peppers, but I was tall enough to reach up, grab the edge of the cutting board, and pull it down. Sliced habaneros went everywhere.

Had my aunt been irresponsible? I don't think so. The knife was well out of reach. Just imagine if I'd pulled down the cutting board and a great big knife dropped onto my head. It wouldn't have mattered if I could cry or not. She'd been meticulous with knife safety, and how could she know that I couldn't be trusted around peppers?

I picked one up off the floor, looked around to make sure my aunt didn't see me eating food off the floor (an act of which she did not approve) and popped it into my mouth. Then I immediately spat it out and reacted in a manner that would have made a pretty good YouTube video if that service had been around back then.

I don't quite remember how my six-year-old mind made the leap from "That tastes terrible!" to "I wonder what would happen if I rubbed that in my eyes?" But my mind did, and my hand carried out my mind's request to satisfy its curiosity.

Tears flowed.

My first thought was that my eyeballs were melting, so I quite naturally panicked and shrieked. Moments later, as my aunt held my face under the bathtub faucet, I realized that for the first time in my life I had cried.

It really wasn't all that great.

I wasn't able to explain to my aunt why I had done that, and I think she just assumed that, like most six-year-old boys, I wasn't particularly smart. I didn't have any plans to repeat that experiment until the following month, when we were watching a really sad movie about two best friends who had two separate terminal illnesses. One of them finally died, and the other one couldn't go to her funeral because she couldn't get out of her hospital bed. In the last scene, the friend who was still alive stared at the hospital ceiling and whispered about how she wished she'd had leukemia instead of AIDS, because she would have died sooner to join her friend in Heaven.

My aunt cried and cried over this movie. I wanted to cry along with her but couldn't. I mean, I wasn't a sociopath; I recognized the sadness of this situation. I asked if I could get an orange, and my aunt said yes, so I went to the kitchen, opened the refrigerator, and quietly took a habanero out of the plastic bag. I broke it in half, rubbed each half on my eyes, and though the hellish burn made me feel like I had a blowtorch pressed against each orb, I couldn't deny the results: fresh tears!

"What's wrong with you?" my aunt asked as I returned to the living room, without an orange.

"The movie sadded me," I said. (Remember, I was six. I was not an awesome liar.)

My aunt held me under the bathtub faucet again and warned me that I could go blind if I kept doing stuff like this. It bothered me that she'd been able to see through my scheme so easily. Did real tears not burn like acid when they came out?

I kept doing it. My aunt always scolded me and rinsed my eyes out. She never took me to therapy, which in retrospect makes sense because therapy is pricey, but when I look back at my childhood it does sort of disturb me that she didn't stop buying habanero peppers.

I didn't cry when I got knocked off the swing set at school, or when I slipped on ice, or when I was forced to eat a peeled M&M that had neither the taste nor texture of a peeled M&M, or when I accidentally walked into the girl's bathroom and Jimmy Zepp saw me and told everybody and all of the kids at school laughed at me and called me a girl.

The only thing that made me cry were the peppers. And then, when I was sixteen, the fork.

I had come home, mowed the lawn, trimmed the bushes, and washed the car, so when my aunt placed that plate of spaghetti down on the table in front of me I was absolutely ravenous. I twirled some on my fork at lightning speed, and whisked the fork toward my mouth.

Before you roll your eyes, rest assured that I'm not trying to use my extreme hunger as an excuse for accidentally jabbing the fork into my cheek. I'm not trying to suggest that you would have done the same thing. Even without knowing you personally, it's reasonable to say that I'm pretty sure you wouldn't have. But I did, and as I sat there with a spaghetti-covered fork jutting out of my cheek, I cried.

My aunt, normally so kind, understanding, and politically correct, asked me if I was retarded.

I removed the fork, ate the bite of spaghetti, and then rushed to my bedroom to weep in privacy. Why had this happened? I'd felt worse pain than this, and I'd been more humiliated than this, so why did this elicit tears?

After the wound healed, I jabbed myself again. I cried.

After that wound healed, I jabbed myself again. Cried again.

The third time, I cried, but not as much, so I went back to the habanero trick. I discovered that by alternating the two methods, I got maximum tears, and I could cry on a regular basis and feel normal.

On my seventeenth birthday, when my grandmother came to visit, I overheard her say that it was kind of creepy that a boy my age was crying on a regular basis. Shit!

On my eighteenth birthday, my aunt died. She was on the way home with my cake when her brakes failed. The car she struck was being driven by a mother of six, who died instantly upon impact. Three of her children were disabled and required her full-time care, though that number would drop to two the next day when the child who'd been riding with her was finally moved from ICU to the morgue.

It was pretty sad. I did the fork thing and cried.

"He's not crying very much," I heard one of my cousins whisper to another one of my cousins. "I'm crying more than he is, and I didn't even like Aunt Betty." Shit!

I went into the bathroom, took out my pocketknife, and jabbed the blade under my fingernail. It hurt, but I didn't cry. I repeated the process with each finger on my left hand. I poked just enough to draw blood on my index finger, but by the time I got to my pinky I was sticking it in all the way to the quick. The pain was unbelievable, and I definitely made some unhappy noises, but there were no tears.

Why had the fork-through-the-face trick worked but not the knife-under-the-fingernails one?

Maybe it was the combination of pain and humiliation. Each time I jabbed myself with a fork, it reminded me that I was the kind of dumbass who had accidentally stabbed himself in the face with a dining utensil.

What could I do to raise the stakes?

Like most people, I had nightmares where I was in school wearing only my underwear. Being in my underwear in a funeral home would be less humiliating, so I'd have to go one step further and go for full nudity.

I stripped out of my clothes. This would definitely embarrass me. But though my penis wasn't gigantic, it was a pretty good size according to the articles I'd read, and that wouldn't do at all, so I turned on some cold water and splashed it over my groin until I'd shriveled to a suitably shameful length.

Hmmm. Actually, it was still too large.

There was a good way to create intense pain and deal with the size issue.

No, no, no. That was taking matters too far.

I'd just stab it instead.

After finishing, I walked out of the bathroom and over to my aunt's casket, and believe me, I'd never cried that much in my life.

For a few years after that incident, I lived a somewhat lonely existence. They didn't give me forks or habaneros in the mental hospital, so I didn't do much crying, but finally they let me out.

That's when I met Sarah.

Because Sarah needed to cut people to feel sexual excitement, she'd assumed that her love life would be less than robust. But I was all in favor of her quirky nature. Her previous boyfriend had been freakishly large, and I think Sarah would have told me that I didn't measure up even if I didn't ask her to, so I got both elements that I desired.

It's perfect. Sometimes I feel kind of lazy letting somebody else inflict all of the pain, but I make up for it by working a second job to support her twin addictions to heroin and adopting kittens.

And yes, I still rub raw sliced habaneros into my eyes on occasion, and in fact I can no longer see out of the left one, but I do that purely out of nostalgia.

Life is great. We cry together every day.

CORPSE LIGHTS

Ed Kurtz

1

Nobody knew when it began, when the light was first ignited; they only knew when it was first noticed. The MacCready Pond—perhaps inappropriately named since a small portion of the pond stretched over to Jake Needham's property—hosted the original light, the one Anne MacCready saw in the dead of night, dancing on top of the still, murky water. She was indisposed to sleep that night, and she grew curious when the usually pitch-black night was not as dark as she supposed it ought to have been. On went her housecoat, and out she went through the back door, where she espied the first blinking peculiarity beyond the hillock that shielded the pond from view.

Anne climbed the hillock in her bare feet, the cool, dewy grass tickling her heels like a thousand dead fingers. When she reached the summit, her bleary eyes struggled to focus on the anomaly before her. She was reminded of long-ago tales of Viking funeral pyres, but she knew no such thing happened in Potter's Field. Here they buried their dead by the stark light of day, as Anne had personally observed on countless occasions. Besides, the dancing flare on the water's surface was far too small to be a burning boat, much less some massive Nordic vessel. Although the several yards separating her from the weird light on the pond played tricks on her ability to aptly judge its size, she guessed it could be no greater than that of a newborn calf. Shifting and pulsing and then folding in on itself before flicking out again, the blazing light reminded her of the flame in a lamp when the whale oil was pressed and full and the wick was long. Bright and shapeless and perpetually skipping about like an anxious cricket. The nucleus of the thing was blindingly white, but it cooled to an orange tint at its amorphous edges, where tiny blue specks sparked and burst like cinders shooting out of a smoldering fire log.

At that moment, Anne MacCready deemed the light the most wonderful thing her eyes had ever seen. That was why she lifted up the hem of her nightgown and scurried down the hillock to the water's edge. That was also why she wasted no time wading out into the pond, trying desperately to swim out to the middle without splashing too much, fearful of extinguishing that stunning light.

Despite her best intentions, she did splash. A good thing, too—otherwise, her husband might never have caught her in time.

Jonah MacCready heard the wild thrashing in the pond and it awoke him with a start. He was halfway up the hillock before he even bothered to consider what was making the noise, and he was paddling back to the shore with his wife held tightly under the crook of one arm before he started to wonder what she had been doing out there. Once he placed her gently on the damp, muddy earth beside the lapping water he had left in their wake, Jonah realized that the woman was grinning like a lunatic. He knitted his brow and screwed up his mouth into a stern sneer, prepared to launch into a tirade the moment her eyes met his.

They never did.

Throughout the following day, Anne muttered and mumbled, mostly in fragments that made no sense to anyone who heard them. She was visited by the reverend and the doctor and her eldest sister Claire, and there was a great deal of hand wringing and praying and hushed conversations that consisted mostly of empty theories as to what could be the matter with her. Eventually, in the dim, dusky moments after supper, Anne smiled broadly and began talking.

Claire lit the lamp and Jonah sat down on the edge of the bed. They listened intently while Anne glared up at the ceiling with wet, glassy eyes and told of the beautiful dancing light on the water and how terribly she needed to be near it, to touch it and to allow it to consume her. She wanted it to set her ablaze, she said without anxiety, and she worried that the water would impede her hoped-for immolation. Claire broke into a fit of heaving sobs. Jonah gravely insisted that she leave the room.

The light from the lamp flickered on the wall beside Anne's bed, scuttling back and forth, beating back the shadows with each unsteady twinkle. She sat up and shot her arms forward as though she meant to seize the light in her hands. When she realized this was impossible, Anne collapsed onto the floor and wept.

Jonah was disconsolate. In the span of a single day, his good wife had become a madwoman. His heart oscillated between feelings of guilt, shame, and remorse, but mostly he was just lonesome. Soon enough he would know whether or not Anne's condition was curable; if the doctor ruled that it was not, then she was surely bound for an asylum. A lunatic wife, locked up with murderers and imbeciles, and she had never borne him a single child. Divorce was out of the question, but annulment was possible, if only faintly so. Then he could marry again and rekindle his dwindling aspirations for an heir.

He struck a match and touched the flame to the mouth of his pipe. There had not been a peep out of the bedroom for nearly an hour, a good omen. Now he felt considerably more relaxed, able to smoke and consider the future in peace. After a while he began to doze, so he extinguished the pipe, folded his hands over his belly and closed his eyes. When he next opened them—some hours later but before sunrise—Jonah found himself looking down the stubby barrel of his own single-shot Derringer.

Anne's delicate thumb pried the hammer back with some difficulty, moving the lever from half-cock to full-cock, and then she squeezed the trigger. There was a loud report and the room seemed to fill up with an acrid bluish-gray smoke, but Jonah never had an opportunity to smell it. The small, wine-dark hole above his left eye emitted a thin wisp of smoke that wafted upwards and an even thinner trickle of blood that dribbled down. He never knew that his waifish wife was adept at loading a pistol, an astonishing fact over which his rapidly cooling brain would never mull.

Anne MacCready did not smile, nor did she cry or shout or express her feelings about the murder she committed in any manner. She merely dropped her husband's Derringer onto his lap and crossed the room to the back door. From there she exited the house, traversed the moist, verdant yard and ascended the hillock overlooking the MacCready Pond.

It was well past midnight, the witching hour, and Anne's dearly loved, ghostly light shone bright atop the water's surface. Her eyes welled up with tears, which soon mingled with the pond when she dove into it. The water chilled her bones and seemed to squeeze her chest and stomach like some impossibly huge snake, but a moment later Anne came upon the light, and she was filled with its warmth. It began at her fingertips when she reached out to touch the light, and almost instantaneously the warmth spread over her arms and shoulders and folded around her head like a wool blanket on a bitter winter night. She rose into it, into the center of the light, and sighed happily, knowing nothing apart from its enveloping, protective embrace.

2

Claire ignored her teacup and thought about the marshes. In the westernmost parts of the state, the marshlands stretched on for miles. Her late husband, Mister Mason, spent many afternoons wandering the morasses, wading through the rushes and reeds with a hunting rifle in his hands and his Chesapeake Bay retriever splashing at his side. He always returned with a lovely crop of quail, duck, and pheasant and a triumphant grin spread across his bearded face. Even the dog would beam with pride after the hunt. In the evening they would dine on smoked game with walnuts and, if the summer crop had been good, Claire's own raspberry sauce. It was, she reminded herself, a heavenly life.

But now was not the time to dream about finer days. It was not the game birds and fireside meals she meant to consider but rather the weird tales Mister Mason occasionally spun over a tankard of beer when the men came around. Incredible and quite often far-fetched, her late husband's stories almost always verged on the cock-and-bull and sometimes strayed directly into absolute absurdity. He talked about the fairy people who lived in the woods and the corpse of a mermaid he'd seen with his own two eyes while working a whaler one summer in his youth. He said there was a well-known colored woman in Appalachia who was older than two hundred years, and he once swore on a Bible that he'd witnessed a man float a foot off the ground by the sheer power of his mind. Balderdash, all of it, and he would only wink and smile whenever anybody called him out on it. Each and every one of his exaggerated stories was pure nonsense, something Claire never doubted and her husband never denied.

Four years William Mason had lain in his grave before Claire considered the eerie prospect that not all of his tales were foolish. One in particular tickled the edges of her brain and made her quiver with worry over the fate of her missing sister.

The will-o'-the-wisp.

Out in the marshes, after dusk and usually well into the night, weird lights were sometimes seen floating just above the surface of the water. William claimed to have seen them only once, upon the one and only occasion that he chose to remain in the marshes after dark. At first, he reported, he mistook the two flickering lights for lanterns carried by some pair of fellow hunters. He hailed to them but received no reply. So William drew nearer, lowering the wick on his own lantern so that he might better see. What he saw defied his imagination, or so he claimed—the lights belonged to no lanterns, and there was nobody anywhere near them. Instead, these two trembling flames levitated of their own accord, never straying far from one another but floating farther away whenever William came closer. He was mesmerized by them and spent untold hours trying to determine how he might overtake them, but in the end he relented and returned home. In the ensuing weeks, as his tale of the phantom lights in the marsh made its way around the area, others came forth to confer with William Mason about their similar experiences out in the wetlands. They are the will-o'-the-wisp, one such gentleman explained in a hushed tone. Corpse lights, another man called them. Still another provided a detailed history concerning an egregious inebriate and the deal he made with the Devil.

Nothing more ever came of the uncanny event and the sinister stories the local men wove out of it. In time, its run as a favorite tale for pubs and gatherings came to an end. It was ultimately forgotten like some hazy dream.

Forgotten until poor Anne lost her mind, shot her husband dead, and then vanished into the night. And all of that after having seen a ghostly light on the pond.

Claire sipped at her tea but found it had gone cold. Returning the cup to its saucer, she wondered if she would ever see her sister again, alive or dead.

3

The midday sun did little to combat the chill on the afternoon of the funeral. The earthly remains of Jonah MacCready lay in a pine coffin that was nailed shut to keep the superstitious from touching the corpse. Mourners gathered around the pit that had been dug out of the ground the previous evening. The reverend read scripture from a leather-bound Bible and offered prayers to their communal god. Some of those present wept, but most did not. Jonah had few relatives and fewer friends, not all of whom attended the event.

Notably absent was the deceased's widow, Anne. None among the aggrieved could account for her whereabouts.

4

The small guest bed was lumpy and too narrow for even Claire Mason's tiny frame. Still, she managed to contort herself into a semblance of comfort, enough so that she gradually drifted off to sleep. Claire had spent the preponderance of the day in the MacCready house, vacant apart from herself and as quiet as a graveyard. She read and tended a small fire in the hearth. She prepared a modest meal that she ate by candlelight. Mostly she simply waited, hoping against the dark, nagging likelihood that her sister might never come home.

She dreamt that the house was full of fireflies, zipping around from room to room and filling the house with their dull, yellow light.

It was the scratching that woke her. As often happened, she mistook it for an aspect of the dream and thus paid it no mind. But somewhere in her mind the scratching was separated from the context of the dream, and some internal voice buried deep in her soul admonished her to awake and see what it was. She did awake, all fluttery eyelids and half-frozen limbs, and the noise continued unabated.

It came from outside. It was at the window, masked by the drapes, scratching at the glass.

Claire snapped up, all at once fully awake and gazing through the darkness in the direction of the room's only window. It sounded as though someone was dragging a jagged branch from the top of the window all the way down to the bottom and then starting all over again. It was high-pitched, nearly a shriek, and it terrified Claire to her core.

Slowly and silently she rose out of the bed, planting her bare feet on the cold wood floor. A shiver worked its way up from there, culminating in her twisting and shuddering shoulders. Her eyes were beginning to adjust to the darkness, and she could just barely discern the shape of the ruffled jabots above the window and the long scarlet drapes that flowed down to the floor. Together with the thin window, they were all that separated Claire from whatever was outside, making that dreadful noise.

Taking each step as if she were walking on hot coals, Claire crossed over to the window, threw back the drapes, and choked as the scream caught in her throat.

There, on the other side of the window, was the pale countenance of Anne MacCready.

Her face was a greenish-white and had a wet sort of luster to it, the same luster Claire observed in Anne's flat, sopping hair. Water spilled out of her mouth, which hung open like a door with broken hinges. There was much more water pouring out of the pallid creature's mouth than a mouth could contain. She appeared to be vomiting it up, but not even a woman's stomach could hold so much water. It just kept coming, leaking over her bottom lip and all over her moldy, sodden nightgown. Anne's eyes betrayed no unease with the ghastly malady; she merely stared without emotion at her trembling sister. And the water continued to pour out of her mouth.

Claire cried out Anne's name. When that elicited no reaction, she rushed out of the guest room, across the sitting room and out the front door. From where she ended up at the front of the house, she could see the window to her room. There was a muddy puddle on the ground just beneath it, but no one was standing in it. Claire was alone.

She stood in place for several minutes to catch her breath. It came out in short bursts of white steam. Claire frowned at this; it was a bit chilly but by no means cold enough to see one's breath. Even when her breathing slowed down to a normal pace, she could see the steamy puffs blowing out of her mouth, just as the water had come out of Anne's.

Claire shuddered and turned to go back inside. Instead, she found Anne blocking her way. Her mouth was no longer hanging open, but a little water still managed to dribble out from between her doughy lips. In the moonlight Claire was able to see the bloated, pallid face more clearly. Anne's cheeks were distended, her skin weirdly opalescent. The wetness that enveloped her appeared to seep out of every pore as though the woman was waterlogged. The whites of her eyes had turned a dull, rotten gray, and her pupils were dilated to fat, black splotches that swallowed her irises. For a moment, Claire believed that Anne was weeping, but it was only more moisture oozing out from behind her eyes.

The notion that Anne looked like a corpse occurred to Claire, as did the irreconcilable idea that she probably was one. She considered the possibility that she was still asleep, that she was merely experiencing a chimera, some dark fantasy conjured up by a troubled mind in repose. Corpses, after all, did not visit people in the night. They stayed in the ground, in pine boxes that were more often than not nailed shut. But Anne was not buried. Dead, perhaps, but never found. Until she found Claire.

The green phantom of Claire's sister gazed at her with wide amphibian eyes and pointed a gnarled finger at the sky. Claire gazed back with astonishment, and when Anne—or what had become of Anne—did not stop pointing after several long minutes, Claire followed the trajectory of the thin, wet arm with her eyes. What she saw in the sky was the brilliant waxing moon, fat and white and nearly bright enough to read by. And then the moon flared, its circumference no longer smooth but undulating like waves on the sea. Claire balked, incredulous and afraid. She refused to believe what her eyes were plainly telling her was true, even when the pulsing globe dropped out of the sky and plummeted down to the pond beyond the hillock.

Anne's head snapped back and her shoulders lurched. Startled, Claire gave a meek gasp as she watched Anne jerk and surge forward as though invisible hands were dragging her across the yard. She floated by Claire, her toes drawing through the soft, wet grass. Claire watched the eerie spectacle for a moment, long enough for Anne to reach the summit of the hillock, and then hurried to catch up with her.

From the top of the hill, Claire could see what she had mistaken for the moon dangling a few feet over the water, its scintillating twin gleaming on the surface of the pond. Anne was gone, but the lapping ripples in the water indicated where she went. Claire sighed heavily, her eyes fixed on the dancing light over the center of the MacCready Pond.

"Will of the wisp," she whispered. Corpse lights.

She tumbled down the slick decline of the hillock, not minding the grass and dirt that stained her nightdress nor the sharp rocks that rubbed her skin raw. The coolness of the pond water would soothe that, just as soon as she was submerged.

The light flickered and flared, beckoning her to swim out to it.

She did.

After that, she felt nothing apart from cold, saw nothing apart from darkness, and heard nothing apart from the deep, burbling echoes of the bottom of the pond.

5

Everyone was there. It took some time for her eyes to adjust to the water and to the blackness of the astonishingly deep bottom, but soon enough she came to know that she was not alone. The light from above, from the will-o'-the-wisp, shone down in shimming shafts that illuminated the green, bloated faces of her company. Cold, slippery weeds that grew out of the pond's floor wrapped tightly around her legs, anchoring her. The same weeds secured Anne in place as well. And Stephen Needham, old Jake Needham's boy, who had gone away in the night and who everybody said had taken that aberrant Peck girl along with him because she never came back either. The Peck girl, of course, floated right beside him.

There were others, dozens more. Some of them she failed to recognize or could not recall their names, while others were people with whom she had prayed and supped and shared her life. Folks who had been in her home and in whose homes she had been. Neighbors and friends, the heritage of Potter's Field.

All of them green, pale, distended from the water.

The people of the light on the pond.

Claire opened her mouth and let the frigid, briny water flow into her. At first it stung inside her chest, but the pressure felt good and right. Like the end of a destined path, this was where the people of Potter's Field went, at least those whose coffins were not nailed shut in defiance of their fate.

Claire Mason was exceedingly happy that she had not been put in the ground like William and Jonah, trapped forever in the dry, dark earth. They could never feel what she felt, the cool and familiar arms of a loved one reaching through the brackish depths to touch her, forever holding her in place where she belonged.

6

Having finished his prayers, the reverend stood up and walked around to the back of the MacCready house. Apart from the gentle breeze ruffling the flowers of the crape myrtles in the yard, this end of Potter's Field was quiet and still. No one remained to make any merry noises in the house behind him, having all died or vanished like the fog before the morning sun. The reverend reflected on this in his prayers, how the rate of disappearances was beginning to overtake the rate of normal, natural deaths. Later, before the sun went down, he would be expected to visit with the Sorrel clan on account of their young Abigail. Off she had gone to look for silver bells, and, by no means surprising to the clergyman, she failed to return.

He knew where she was. She was in the pond. But he had no intention of telling that to the Sorrels. They would not understand it, any of it. Nobody ever did, which was why the pond continued to send up its awful wisp.

Like the worm to the trout.

He bent his neck and shook his head, wondering if he would ever see the light and whether or not it would beckon him as it had beckoned so many before. And, in pondering that, he asked himself:

Would that be so terrible?

LIFE AND LIMB

Adriaan Ludens

He wished he was farming. Milking cows before sunup, trudging behind his draft horse and plow in the hot sun for hours, and making exhausted love to his stocky wife. But no. Charlie did not have the three-hundred-dollar sum required to exempt him from going to war. So he found himself battling for the preservation of the Union.

Two months ago he might have been pulling weeds from the earth. Now he wished for more weeds and brush to hide behind. The fire of the sharpshooters positioned on the ridge across the valley was continuous. It was also terrifyingly accurate. Weren't the infantry on the Union side supposed to have the better weapons? Charlie contemplated his British-made Enfield rifle. Had he killed anyone with it? He didn't know for sure but thought the chances were good. Farm boys from Nebraska Territory learned to shoot straight at a young age, and Charlie had killed more than his fair share of rabbits, rats, and other critters. That was before age and responsibility had lassoed and hogtied him and sent him here.

Lead minie balls whistled overhead and punctured the earth all around him. Damned things rearranged your guts if they hit you. Charlie had seen one infantryman's throat torn out by one of those balls. One of the other soldiers had screamed the dead man's name when he dropped. Slater? Tatum? Charlie wasn't sure. Everything was so hard to hear over the incessant roar of gun and artillery fire.

Memories of that awful sight still invoked in him sweat-drenched night terrors.

Charlie hunkered down and peered at the gray puffs of smoke accumulating on the opposite ridge. He saw a flash of gray that wasn't smoke and squeezed the trigger. The gray disappeared, but Charlie had no idea whether he'd helped the Union cause.

The sun throbbed with scorching ferocity, and Charlie's exhausted frame felt slick with sweat. The thought of standing so he could tear off his thick wool coat was rapidly escalating into a dangerous obsession. He compromised with himself and pulled the woolen cap from his head. True, the leather visor helped keep the sun out of his eyes as he aimed at the enemy, but right now he was intent on tending to another matter: smoking.

Charlie fumbled with his tobacco pouch. He desperately needed a cigarette to calm his nerves. His fingers shook as he tried to roll the paper without all the tobacco falling out. Charlie concentrated on his task and didn't see Captain Peters riding toward his isolated position. In fact, the captain screamed at Charlie for several seconds before the corporal became aware of his presence.

The captain dismounted but held the reins in a vise grip so his horse would not flee. He motioned frantically at Charlie. Anger and impatience seemed to fight for supremacy on the captain's face. Charlie guiltily stashed his tobacco and made a halfhearted attempt at pretending to reload his rifle. Captain Peters gritted his teeth and vehemently motioned with his free arm.

Charlie rose to his haunches and scampered awkwardly toward the captain. He straightened just long enough for a hurried salute and leaned in to hear the other man's words.

Captain Peters' face distorted, and Charlie at first thought his commanding officer was sneezing before the fragments of brain and bone splattered out the back of his head. Burgundy gouts of liquid spurted from the captain's neck in steadily diminishing pulses. The captain's body tottered with arms outstretched. He seemed to take a deliberate step forward and Charlie put up his hands to ward him away.

Then the entire battlefield flipped, and Charlie clutched at Captain Peters' broad chest as they pitched into the blood-drenched earth. Charlie's vision grayed and then faded to black.

~

Corporal Charlie Lawson clawed his way back to consciousness and immediately regretted the effort. He felt nauseous and his head throbbed.

Charlie could barely make out his surroundings. One flickering lantern hung from a peg on the far side of what he took to be a tent. Between him and the light source, Charlie noted a diminishing series of twisted wrecks of men. Some lay still while others writhed in agony. Charlie heard one man muttering angrily, another emitted long guttural groans and a third begged the Almighty in a quavering voice to strike him dead because he could no longer bear the pain. The air reeked of chloroform and gangrenous flesh. The coppery scent of blood would have been like a breath of fresh air.

Lumbering from cot to cot, occasionally checking for a pulse and more often taking a long swig from a hip flask, was a giant of a man. This Goliath swayed drunkenly, wiping the grimy back of his hand over his mouth as he drank. Charlie could see the sweat glistening on the big man's forehead and drops of liquor nesting in his beard like morning dew in a thistle patch.

Charlie had heard other soldiers tell horror stories about the amputations performed by the surgeons, colorfully referred to as "Sawbones." The grim significance of the nickname hit home for the first time when Charlie noticed the bone saw hung from a loop around the big man's belt.

Charlie swallowed hard, closed his eyes and sank back. The moans and cries of the wounded created a rhythm, dissonant and primal but a rhythm nonetheless. Charlie let the sounds usher him back into the realm of sleep and escape.

The next time Charlie awoke, he discovered another doctor—this one a thin, sallow-faced man with coal-black hair plastered to his head—wiping the circumference of his left knee with a wet rag. The rag was stained with blood, and the water in the basin where the doctor rinsed it was also red. Confused, Charlie spoke up.

"What's going on? Was I hit?"

The doctor glanced up briefly but did not speak. He reached for a cleaner-looking piece of cloth that had been folded into a cone shape. He fitted it lightly over Charlie's nose and mouth and lifted a bottle so that the mouth of the bottle touched the tip of the cone. As the doctor tipped the bottle, Charlie saw the cloth near the top of the cone darken slightly with the liquid's touch. He tried to read the label affixed to the bottle, but his eyes grew incredibly heavy. He tried to fight the stupor, but movement suddenly seemed like a meaningless endeavor. He watched dreamily as the grim, blood-spattered surgeon drew the blade of the bone saw through his pale flesh. Ignoring the blood that dribbled from the wound, the surgeon gritted his teeth and leaned into his job. As the blade shrieked and dug into Charlie's shin bone just below the knee, the young corporal fell senseless.

A large mastiff chased Charlie and pinned him to the ground. The dog clamped its powerful jaws down on his leg. The beast seemed to grow to an enormous size. Charlie's leg from the knee down disappeared into the brute's mouth. Charlie tried to scream but no sound came out. The pain was tremendous. The dog's teeth were slowly crushing his bones. The beast whipped its head from side to side, trying to separate Charlie from his leg.

The scene began to change, but the dog would not let go.

Charlie became aware once again of screams, sobs and groans. Some of them, he realized dimly, were his own. Someone nearby repeatedly screamed for "Marie." Another soldier muttered the Lord's Prayer, liberally spreading curse words throughout.

Charlie opened his eyes and found himself staring at the same portion of tent canvas as the last time he had awakened. His left knee burned as if a hundred tiny blacksmiths were practicing their craft under his skin. He pushed himself up with his elbows to look.

The dog he had half expected to find was nowhere in sight. Neither, from the knee down, was his left leg.

A pair of harried-looking soldiers moved Charlie to another part of the tent. Days and nights chased each other until Charlie lost track of how many passed while he recovered.

His fellow soldiers still raved and wept, but the timbres of their voices—and the faces that went with them—always changed. Some of those who stayed became familiar to Charlie. Most were like him, recovering from amputations. Those lead minie balls wreaked havoc on flesh and bone. About half the soldiers the Sawbones had taken a limb from lapsed into raving lunacy. Charlie had heard of "surgical fevers," and what he witnessed proved the stories were no exaggerations. Even worse off were the men whose flesh became infected and began to rot after the amputation. The stench was all but unbearable. When those men died, it was much to the relief of everyone else in the large but stifling tent. The air was so malodorous that Charlie often fought back the urge to retch. More often than not, it was a fight he lost.

Charlie watched the amputated limbs pile up each day, only to be collected by some person or persons whenever he slept. He asked the fellow next to him—Charlie couldn't guess his rank because his wool coat was missing and the fellow only wore a yellowed cotton shirt—if he knew what became of the amputated limbs.

"They get eaten," the man wheezed.

Time passed, and the fiery pain in his leg retreated just enough for Charlie to claim a tentative victory over it. He tore aside the bandages and examined his stump. The surgeon had deliberately left a flap of hairy skin from Charlie's calf. This patch had been folded over the stump and stitched to Charlie's flesh on the other three sides. He traced his fingers over the skin and decided the edges of the bone had been shaved smooth. A lance of pain that seemed to shoot up his thigh and into his gut told him his finger had found the drainage hole left by the surgeon.

Charlie spent hours lying on his back trying to remember what had happened, but the story never changed. He knew he hadn't been hit. In fact, right before the amputation, he'd seen his leg whole and healthy.

The corporal seethed silently. Day after day his anger grew. He vowed to get answers.

~

When Charlie asked for a shaving kit one afternoon, no one thought twice. The rebels might run around looking wild and woolly, but the men of the Federal Army had higher standards to uphold. Slavery was wrong, you bet, but so was poor hygiene and appearance.

Within five minutes, a heavy-lidded soldier had brought Charlie the implements he needed to rid himself of his patchy beard. He took his time shaving. No one noticed when Charlie secreted the straight razor inside his blanket.

He dozed. The sun hemorrhaged red rays from just below the horizon as the thin surgeon who had taken his leg shook him awake.

"How do you feel, Corporal?" the Sawbone asked. His double-breasted frock coat was smeared with dried blood. Charlie wondered if it had been washed even once since the war began.

"A damn sight lighter than I should be," Charlie said. His lips twisted into an angry sneer.

The surgeon's expression betrayed nothing. "Your shin bone was shattered. We had to take the limb."

"I was awake; I saw my leg!" Charlie growled. "You took a healthy limb."

"You may think that's what you saw, but I assure you—"

Charlie's fingers closed around the straight razor. He sat up quickly, grabbed the surgeon with his right arm and tugged him closer to the cot. Charlie brandished the blade under the thin man's throat. All around them came the screams, moans and ramblings of the wounded and dying. No one rose up or called for Charlie to stop. No one hurried to the surgeon's aid.

"Why'd you do it?" Charlie asked. His heart raced. "Answer true or I swear on the Virgin Mary I'll slice you worse than you did me."

The surgeon gaped fearfully into the rapidly darkening night. For a moment Charlie thought he was more afraid of what might be lurking in the dark than the razor nestled close to his throat. Finally the surgeon sagged against the cot.

"I do what I can," the man murmured. "But sometimes..."

"Sometimes, what?" Charlie spat.

"Sometimes there's not enough."

"Not enough? What does that mean?"

The surgeon's pupils had fully dilated. To Charlie they looked like twin caverns of deep darkness.

"Not enough meat. They want more."

Charlie hobbled through the camp, doing his best to navigate with the narrow crutches the surgeon had supplied. Charlie had decided the surgeon was crazy. No sane man would act the way the surgeon had. He meant to find a commanding officer and bring the atrocities to light.

Darkness had fallen, but the camp was suddenly a bustle of nervous activity.

"Strike camp on the double!" someone bellowed.

Charlie heard snatches of conversation as he struggled on his way.

"Outnumber us four to one..."

"Scouts brought the report in just a few minutes ago..."

"Gathering at the base of the opposite ridge..."

"If we don't fall back, we'll be slaughtered..."

Charlie took advantage of the confusion and reached the general's tent unimpeded. He pushed a hand through the flap and staggered inside. It took several moments for his eyes to adjust to the dim interior.

A broad-shouldered man sat alone in one dark corner. Charlie might have missed him had the buttons on his tunic not glimmered like coins in the light cast from the lantern. The rest of the tent had already been emptied.

The general gazed at Charlie and openly appraised him.

"And who are you, barging into my tent when you should be doing what you can to help strike camp?"

Charlie saluted and lost a crutch in the process. He frowned as the wooden implement toppled onto the crushed grass.

"Corporal Charlie Lawson, sir!" Charlie gave the general his company, regiment brigade, division and corps.

The general only sighed and tilted a whiskey bottle to his lips.

"Sir, one of the surgeons amputated my leg without cause."

"A healthy leg, it was, then?" The general did not sound surprised.

"Yes, sir."

"Plenty of good meat on the calf, I'd wager."

Charlie suddenly felt very lightheaded. Was the general as mad as the surgeon?

The commander seemed to rouse himself. "Corporal, your sacrifice will not go unnoticed or unappreciated."

"What the devil is going on here?" Charlie half knelt and wrapped his fingers around the crutch. He rose back up with only a little difficulty and looked up in time to see the general draining the last of the contents from the bottle.

"We've struck a bargain with certain..." The general paused and looked thoughtful. "Certain dwellers of the nearby wilderness. They spy on the rebel forces and report back to us, and we, in turn, do what we can to meet their demands."

"Demands?" Charlie's mouth went dry as a bale of cotton. His fury mounted until he felt his entire body trembling. "You want to speak of demands? Here are mine: I demand to see that surgeon strung up from a tree, I demand the tree he gets hung from be chopped down and I demand the finest limb possible be carved from the wood of that tree and presented to me to replace the leg he took!"

The general gazed at him with sad eyes. His face glistened with sweat in the lantern light.

Charlie thought of one more demand. "And I want to see these wilderness dwellers! I'll have my revenge on those cannibals, by God!"

"You don't know how right you are, son; let me collect my thoughts." The general sank back in his chair. His left hand had set aside the empty whiskey bottle and was now alternately massaging his temples. "We must all make our sacrifices. When the supply cannot meet demand, we must increase our supply."

Charlie opened his mouth to speak, but the general wouldn't give him an opening.

"Which is more important, Corporal? Life or limb? Most of us will have to answer that question sooner or later. You are one of the lucky ones. We're all part of this godforsaken war, risking life and limb. But by losing a limb, you are saving your life and the lives of countless others...on the Union side, at least.

"We have powerful allies in this fight, Corporal. But these allies could easily become enemies. And believe me: we need these wilderness dwellers on our side. From New Guinea originally, if what I've heard has any truth behind it. But outcasts, forced to flee their native land. How they ended up here, I do not know. What I do know from firsthand experience is that our unusually small allies are masters of camouflage and trackers of unparalleled skill. Mostly they dine on dead rebels, but a portion of their sustenance has to be provided by less convivial means. This practice, Corporal, is not born out of macabre cruelty. It is out of necessity.

"But let us not focus on the grisly customs of our allies. We have larger problems facing us. Trust me. Our focus—yours and mine—needs to be on the Confederate army."

The older man's words and demeanor calmed Charlie, albeit slightly. He pondered what the general had told him. The commander slowly rose from his chair. He made his way across the tent until the two men nearly stood nose to nose. The sour smell of whiskey and stale sweat curled into Charlie's nostrils. The gravity in the general's gaze could have nailed Charlie to a tree.

"Tomorrow you will get your discharge paperwork. You will go home. You will grow old. This is my gift to you, Corporal, and my apology. Take it."

The general's tone told Charlie it would be folly to argue further. He trembled, though he could not explain why. Charlie managed a slight nod of compliance and fumbled with his crutches. His breath came in quick, harsh gasps as he hobbled to the tent flap that led into the night. Charlie stopped short and spun on his one good foot to face the general for the last time.

"Thank you, sir. Good night." Charlie saluted his commanding officer again.

The general slowly raised his right arm to return the salute.

As long as he lived, Charlie never forgot how the other man's tunic sleeve hung in an oval of darkness where his right hand should have been.

WHO IS SCHOPENHAUER?

Bryan Oftedahl

John awoke, his throat rattling with a horrible scream until he clamped his mouth shut to cut it off. He found he was hugging himself for warmth before realizing that he wasn't actually cold. Whatever the dream had been about he couldn't recall, but it had been deathly cold there.

He found that, once again, he had woken up several minutes before his alarm was due to go off. Strangely, if he ever forgot to turn on the alarm, he always slept in, but if he set it, he always woke up before it went off. The thing was worthless and necessary at the same time.

At least it was necessary, he thought, *which is one characteristic I seem to lack, though I excel at the other.*

The building had been a roadside motel back when the surrounding land had yet to be overwhelmed by the expansion of the metropolis. So his apartment was little more than a single room accompanied by a bathroom. The kitchenette sat in one corner like some sick afterthought. His sofa was also his bed. Because the closet was too small to hold anything other than a broom and a bucket filled with bottles of cleansers, his clothes were hung from a variety of hooks hammered into the white walls.

Moving toward the window, he tossed the heavy curtain aside and stared out at the waking world. The twin spires were still there, of course, with their gothic décor and Roman crosses towering over the world and looking horribly out of place. He wondered if they weren't carved from some volcanic glass. Maybe that would explain the black coloring and the way they seemed to drink in the light of their surroundings.

Maybe "leach" is a better description than "drink."

For a couple of minutes, he lost himself among the wanderings of his barely conscious mind. There was really only one thing he could wonder about, and that was the circumstances surrounding his own birth. He had chewed the question over and over again, attempting to discover its hidden flavor, but the question was, it seemed, a clam which may be chewed until the end of time and still afford no further flavor.

He had been born somewhere between early morning and late night. He was born on an elevated train that was traveling over the streets of the city center at the time. It was somewhere between Alder Park and Roosevelt Straight where he arrived. For reasons he was none too sure about, he had been born at some time between his late twenties and early thirties instead of as a crying, self-fouling infant. Even at the time, he had known this was not how a man is born. He knew a lot of things he wasn't too sure he was supposed to know, except his own identity.

His fellow passengers on the train that day hadn't paid him any mind, so whatever way he had arrived must have been commonplace enough for them to ignore it. When he had politely turned to one of the passengers and asked if he happened to know who he was, the fellow traveler pulled a dollar bill from his pocket, let it flutter into his lap, and then chose a seat farther down the train. When a number of passengers had departed, he followed suit, shoving his way off the train.

The platform hovered over the streets by means of iron supports and cement stairs. The stairwell was covered in spray-painted proverbs:

"Instigated by a mind other than your own!"

"Who is Schopenhauer?"

"You must convince him it's not the truth."

At the bottom of the stairs he had fully realized just what a problem he had been birthed into. Each street seemed to extend forever and was intersected several times by still more streets. All crossroads were decorated by colored lights directing the ceaseless flood of vehicular and pedestrian traffic. Businesses lined the streets, with either offices or apartments above them. Towers of glass rose up into the clouds every few blocks, but most buildings weren't any taller than three levels.

In other words, the place was enormous and busy, and he didn't have a clue which way he should go.

After a short time of aimless wanderings, he had spotted a pair of black spires, barely visible in the darkness of night despite the collective glow of the street lamps. Feeling that perhaps something of divine nature could assist him, he had begun making his way toward the spires. Strangely enough, no matter how far or how fast he moved, the spires always remained a couple of blocks away. He could travel away from them and they wouldn't move, and he could turn about and begin chasing after them again, but they always remained stationary until he reached that borderline of two blocks.

Stopping a passerby, he had asked if they knew how to get to the church. The stranger's directions led him to a Lutheran church with a white steeple, not the twin spires. Nonetheless, the attending Lutheran pastor was kind enough to call the hospital, an act that ignited a sequence of events that eventually led him to the life he had been living ever since.

The doctor, coincidentally named Schopenhauer, was a bit mystified by his apparent amnesia since there was no evidence of head trauma and no traces of drug use to explain it. For a time the doctor simply referred to him as "John Doe," or just "John." Nobody came forward to claim him despite several newspaper articles and a few televised interviews. While filling out the paperwork that would allow him to be legally integrated into society, Dr. Schopenhauer had asked if there was any particular name he would prefer other than "John," but he couldn't think of any. He was given an apartment and a job; he was also provided a counselor to make sure he was following the unwritten rules of society.

He was given a life to live, but nobody seemed to understand what he meant when he pointed toward the twin spires and asked how one went about reaching them. He had learned to accept their presence in the background, though he still wondered from time to time why, out of the entire population, only he seemed aware of them.

When his alarm finally went off, a horrible electronic sound that violently yanked his thoughts back to the present, he hurried to switch it off before beginning his usual morning routines.

His routine generally kept its consistency from one morning to the next. Empty his bladder while waiting for the shower's temperature to change from arctic chill to temperate breeze—the warmest it ever got. If necessary, that was also when he would purge any hormonal build-up via self-stimulation. After the quick, cold shower, he would poke through his clothing in search of a dress shirt and a pair of pants a little less crusted than the others. He always locked his apartment, though he couldn't figure out why since there was nothing of real value therein.

That morning, the bus stop was the same as always. People listening to headphones while staring off into nothing or intensely texting on their cell phones so that they wouldn't have to acknowledge the presence of the people around them. For nearly two years, as far as John could vouch personally, it was always the same dozen people meeting at the same bus stop five days a week, yet none of them ever spoke to each other or even knew one another's names. He had introduced himself to one of them several months back, but she had ignored him and started waiting at the bus stop a few blocks down after that.

Just before the bus pulled in, he noticed somebody spray-painting a cement wall across the street. The vandal turned about for a second, staring over his shoulder directly at John before the bus pulled into the stop and blocked his line of vision. When he had seated himself on the bus near a window, the vandal had gone, but his work stuck in John's mind.

"Beware your perceptions of this world, as you may be telling yourself lies."

He hadn't had any coffee yet, so his mind was operating a bit sluggishly, but he could have sworn in that moment when the vandal had turned that he was looking at a reflection of himself.

The bus route carried him across the buffer zone of do-it-yourself storage units, car lots, gas stations and train tracks that separated his part of town from the commercial district of strip malls, fast-food outlets, banks, and drive-through coffee stands. In fact, the buffer zone separated his neighborhood from the rest of the city as if it were some disagreeable stepchild. The bus had nearly emptied just a couple of blocks into the commercial district. Everybody hurried off to their jobs as though they were enthusiastic about their work, which John doubted.

Walking across the parking lot, intentionally ignoring the movement of the twin spires that towered over the place from just a few blocks away, John began preparing himself for the circus that was about to commence.

On with the three-ring sideshow! he thought.

He didn't even make it five feet past the automatic doors without a problem arising. An old, boney hand fell onto his shoulder and squeezed, hard. From behind him came a voice that conjured images in his mind of a two-thousand-year-old mummy with a lisp.

"You'll hafta leave that with cuthtomer thervith."

In a perfect world, Norton would be drinking rum-spiked lemonade somewhere in Florida while screaming at neighborhood kids, but instead he had fallen victim to a decade-long confidence scam that had drained his retirement and left him with only Social Security. Because he needed to eat, he had to go back to work, and the only job he could land at his age was as a greeter at the Circus gates. No matter how much management berated him for it, he never wore his dentures to work.

"Actually," John growled while shrugging off Norton's attempt to remove his backpack, "I'll be leaving it in my locker, the same as I always do."

The old man's eyes narrowed, and for a moment John thought he saw a speck of evil burning behind them. "You cauthing me trouble, boy?"

"Relax, Norton," said a feminine voice from behind John. "He works here."

The old man's scowl melted away like ice cream in Arizona as his face stretched into a big, toothless grin. "Good mornin', Julian."

Norton never seemed to forget her, just all the rest of his coworkers. Julian looked like what would result if a forest sprite got drunk and ransacked a Hot Topic, so one really couldn't blame the old man. Julian had a tendency to be unforgettable.

"Come on, Johnny," she said, throwing an arm around John's shoulder and leading him deeper into the store. "You'll be late for the séance."

According to company policy, all incoming shifts had to gather around to discuss any upcoming changes, any customer complaints, or any number of other things none of them really cared about. At the end of each meeting, everybody was expected to begin clapping while calling out the company cheer. The closing cheer reminded John of an H.P. Lovecraft story he had read the year before, in which a number of police officers raided a heathen gathering in the depths of a swamp.

In the middle of the clapping and chanting, Julian leaned in and asked, "When do we get to sacrifice the virgin?"

Without missing a beat, John countered, "Not until pay day."

Once the séance had ended, the incoming shift workers dispersed to replace their doppelgangers out on the sales floor. John, however, was grabbed by the manager of the electronics department.

"You didn't shave again, John," she said. Behind her back, everybody referred to the manager as the bearded toad because her chin looked like a toad halfway through a "ribbit" and was spotted with curlicue hairs, like pubes. "You keep showing up with that scrag on your face and I'll write you up."

A write-up. Could I ever survive a write-up? Oh the humanity!

"I'm sorry," he said. "I'll shave tonight."

He hurried off to the sales floor, but he wasn't even able to make it to his own department before another problem presented itself in the form of a little old lady dressed head to foot in pink. She was standing in the housewares section inspecting a display of pillows with lacey edging and floral designs. She kept turning one pillow over and over again as if looking for something that wasn't there but should have been. Her hand, nails polished pink, fired out and grabbed hold of John as he attempted to slide past.

"Excuse me, but do you know the price for these?"

If all else fails, look in front of your face.

"I think those are nine ninety-nine, ma'am."

"Well, don't *think*, honey." Suddenly, the granny facade melted into something one would expect to find in a gingerbread house with children's bones in the fireplace. "Is that the price or not?"

He simply pointed above the display, where a sign read "$9.99" with a smiley face beside it, and then hurried off to his department.

In electronics, he was greeted by a gentleman dressed as if he were preparing for political domination. The man complained that his son's birthday was coming up soon and he needed some games for the kid's Wii. Before John could unlock the case with the Wii games in them, the man wandered past.

"What about this game?" He pointed into the case at the end of the aisle. "This one looks cool."

"Actually, those are for the Xbox," John explained. "The Wii games are down here."

"Zelda." The man couldn't even make it back without becoming sidetracked again. "I know he mentioned something about Zelda. Can you open this one?"

Through gritting teeth, John said: "That's for the handheld, not the Wii. I have Wii games down here, though."

Where the big "Wii" sign is.

"Are you sure?" The man's eyes scrutinized him, seeking any evidence of lies or betrayal. Again he became distracted by another display. "Hey, I think I saw previews for this one, how about this one?"

"Playstation."

This is why there's a big "Playstation" sign above the display and why all the products are marked with the Playstation icon!

From behind his back, John started signaling Julian for help. Ten minutes into his shift and already his patience was drained. She grabbed the intercom, and her voice rang throughout the circus. "Johnny from electronics to the back, please. John to the back."

Turning to the business man, John smiled. "I'm so sorry, but I have to get that. Julian here can help you though."

"What's the deal?"

She grinned like a monster beneath a toddler's bed while John hurried off the sales floor and back to the warehouse to count to thirty and recompose himself. Upon returning, John found Julian and the man at the register with a half a dozen games, none of which were for the Wii. The transaction finished, the man walked away. Once he had rounded a corner and was out of sight, she began laughing.

"What would the world be like without idiots?"

Paradise.

"You do realize those were for his son's birthday, right?"

"Yeah, he told me." She folded her arms and shrugged. "So?"

"So?" For a moment John was speechless until he remembered who he was talking to. "So the kid is going to open his presents and realize his dad is a moron, and then the guy is going to come back here demanding blood."

"I fail to see the problem."

Really? You fail to see...

"Uh, you'll get fired."

"I have a few chances." She counted them off on her fingers: "Either he'll be too embarrassed to return them, or he'll come back on my day off, or he'll forget I was the one who sold them to him."

"Sure, he'll probably say it was me."

"Relax." She craned her neck and gave him a quick, raspberry–Chap Stick flavored peck on the cheek. "Prescribe a chill pill."

Ha ha.

Giving her a scrutinizing glare, he asked, "You have beaded curtains in all your doorways back home, don't you?"

"Wood and hemp," she said, shrugging him off again. "Not plastic and nylon."

By the time another customer arrived, Julian had managed to vanish into thin air. It was a trick she refused to teach him, explaining that a true magician never reveals the science of their illusions.

"I need some help," the customer growled from deep inside his grease-stained coveralls, leading John out of electronics and into automotive.

God help me.

John didn't understand whatever the customer was complaining about, so the man's temper rose higher and higher toward the boiling point until he was nearly screaming. John felt like one of those petite characters in cartoons with cheeks flapping in the wind while a larger character, almost entirely mouth, stands over them yelling.

"Don't you know anything?" The man roared.

I know that members of Heaven's Gate used the barbiturate phenobarbital in order to reach "the level above human." The socialist Jonestown movement used the all-too-famous poison cyanide to escape this "inhumane world." Do the world a favor and take your pick.

"It's very simple," the man said. He explained everything again as if repeating it word for word would suddenly trigger understanding. "Do you understand?"

Nope.

"Sir, as I've been trying to explain, I don't work this department," John said, trying to keep himself composed. "I don't know anything about cars. I work in electronics, not automotive. If you'll allow me, I can return to my department and call for somebody from this department to help you."

Without waiting for an answer, he left the man. Just a few aisles down, he was nearly run over by a man with a basket full of spray-paint canisters. The two stared at each other in horror. No amount of rubber or latex could create such similarity. No works of light and shadow, mirrors and smoke, could cause such an unnerving mutual resemblance as the two witnessed in each other at that moment.

John's double dropped his basket of spray paint, spun around on his heels and threw himself down the aisle, leaving John feeling dazed. The moment the double was out of sight, a strange sound, like the striking of an enormous gong, reverberated throughout the building. He glanced about to see if anybody else had heard the sound only to find that nobody else was in sight. Back in electronics, he found that Julian was still gone, along with the usual kids playing the video game samples or staring at the banks of televisions.

What...the...hell...

Moving from one aisle toward the next proved the building was completely empty. Even Norton had abandoned his station at the front doors. Once outside, he was again met by the hollow metallic sound, echoing across the lifeless acres of parking lot. For some time he glanced around, seeking its source.

My God, it's the cathedral!

He broke into a run across the parking lot and down empty avenues, chasing after the black cathedral, somehow certain that this time he would succeed where he had failed so many times before. It was along Johnson Street between Seventh and Eighth avenues that John found himself standing at the bottom of the cement stairs of the elevated platform, the same stairs he had stumbled down the night he had been born.

"Who is Schopenhauer?"

Across the street on the Seventh Avenue corner of the block stood a couple of townhouses. The first floors were combined into a bookstore titled "Parnassus," and the second floors of each were cut up into efficiency apartments. On the Eighth Avenue corner was a retro diner, The Pioneer, complete with a marquee and office space above. The two businesses were separated by an alley, a strange fact that caught his attention.

He had eaten at that diner before. There was a little doorway that had been knocked into the wall between the diner and the book store so that people could buy a dime novel to read while waiting for their meals. He had passed through that doorway each time he ate at the diner to see what books occupied the sales rack. Somehow the two businesses were separated by an alley that had never been there before.

Why does this feel so damn familiar?

Hurrying across the street, still somewhat dazed, he entered the alley. There were no garbage cans or dumpsters. None of the surrounding buildings had doors, windows, or fire escapes into the alley. The walls were spray-painted with the same phrase over and over: "open your eyes open your eyes open your eyes." The alley extended to the center of the block before turning at a right angle. Around the corner, the alley stretched for two more blocks and ended at a pair of wrought-iron gates, on the other side of which a dirt footpath wound up a small rise to the front doors of the black cathedral. None of it matched the dimensions of the city outside the alley.

John reached his hands out to the gate. The moment his fingers touched iron, the last peal rang out. His heart could barely contain its own excitement as he shoved the gates open, rushed up the hill and threw himself through the double doors of the cathedral. Once inside, his heart missed one or two beats.

Whatever he had been expecting, it certainly was not what he found. The main cavity of the cathedral was filled with pews occupied by faces both familiar and strange, faces that turned and stared without expression toward him. The people from his bus stop and the bus driver himself were there. Norton, Julian, and the businessman who couldn't choose the right video games were among the crowd as well. They all watched in silence, their faces devoid of life.

He kept his eyes fixed forward as he hurried down the aisle toward the altar, which also was not how he expected it to be. If there was anything Christian about the structure, it was not evident. He was quite sure no Eucharist had ever been performed there, no order of service sung, no prayers offered nor sermons preached. There was no imposing cruciform suspended over the altar, no heavy, leather-bound copy of the Scriptures. The altar was occupied by a single piece of furniture, a large mirror sitting in an ornately carved wooden frame.

In its reflection, each pew was empty despite the sounds of rustling and sniffling he heard from the crowd around him. Inside the mirror his double stood at the altar, watching as he approached. The double was smiling, but tears streaked his cheeks. His arms were spread wide as if he wished somehow to embrace John through the glass.

It's so good to see you. The double's voice, which emerged between joyful sobs, somehow bypassed his ears, arriving directly inside his head. *I've been waiting for so, so long.*

"What do you mean?" John asked. He began hugging himself, shivering. "What is going on?"

You're inflicting on yourself what you believe you deserve. You're lying to yourself. He dropped his hands as he approached his side of the glass. *I'm so glad it's over...for me.*

"What...does that...mean?" John could barely speak through the almost convulsive shivering of his body. His breath was visible as he spoke. "Please...tell me...what's...happening?"

Behind his double, on the other side of the glass, a rippling motion spread through the hall, leaving the empty pews full. He didn't have to look over his shoulder to know the people were no longer with him on his side.

Open your eyes. The double had taken to shivering as well. *Open your eyes.*

"Open your eyes." A moment passed before John noticed that he was copying what the double was saying while the double mimicked his movements, as a mere reflection now instead of as a separate entity. For a while he simply stood and watched his reflection while whispering to it again and again: "Open your eyes, open your eyes..."

When he opened his eyes, it was all gone.

The panic was overwhelming. He couldn't move or breathe or see much of anything because of what he was encased in. It was freezing. It was solid.

Oh God! Let me out!

The claustrophobic panic began burning into his mind.

I need out! Please, let me out!

The mind, that's where it had all been? Suddenly he knew things he wasn't sure how he could have ever forgotten. He remembered his name was John Schopenhauer and that he had been a doctor. He remembered that it was a sense of responsibility, the need for retribution for his sins that had driven him to his current circumstance. He knew he had been there, in the ice, for so, so long but that his damnation was far from finished. He had objectified his fellow human beings to a degree surpassing that which a surgeon needs to operate, tumbling into a sadistic lust for the god-like power of life or death, and his sins would warrant nothing less than eternity.

Hell, it turns out, is all about self-infliction, not fire and brimstone. He had been frozen into the glacial bowels of the abyss and left with his own devices to pass eternity by himself. The first several millennia passed rather painfully as his mental stability deteriorated into dementia. After witnessing his own self fall apart piece by piece, he attained a Zen-like insight into his very being, into how and why he was the way he was. He eventually caught an intuitive glimpse of just how long eternity really was, and he realized that he would need something to keep him occupied. This realization inspired creativity.

Within the depths of his mind, he began constructing a somatic machine that would pit his being against itself in a looping motion not unlike a figure eight. The playing field would be a compilation of settings from his past: the neighborhood he grew up in; the restaurant just across from the elevated transit platform where his parents took him after Sunday church service; the apartment where he lived through the first two years of college; the location of his high-school job. The playing field would be populated by his hopes and fears: his high-school crush, a bohemian forest sprite he had never had the gall to approach; the doctor he hoped to aspire to; the grumpy old man he feared he would one day become; and that sickening state of uncertainty in which he felt most of his life had been wasted. All these would be present.

Once finished, he had thrown the switch and leapt into the machine. The thought had never occurred that a time would come when he might wish to shut it off. Then again, ell adores consequences.

You're inflicting on yourself what you believe you deserve, the double had said. *You're lying to yourself.*

John sealed his eyes shut against the ice and fell back into his somatic machine, where he found himself screaming at his reflection in a mirror, his voice echoing through the empty cathedral. Through the glass, he watched as the occupants of the pews rose from their seats and shuffled out the doors and into that world on the other side, leaving the reflection of the main hall just as empty as the space behind him, leaving him alone to scream at his own reflection.

"How do I turn it off? I want it to stop!" A thought occurred to him, something that had been painted on the stairwell the night he was born: "You must convince him it's not the truth."

Oh god, it's going to start again! Another cycle.

John jumped from the altar and down the aisle. Once outside, he ran down the small hill and back into the alley. The moment his feet hit the sidewalk, he felt a rush of air and a loud *whump* as the alley closed itself off, disconnecting the cathedral from the rest of the playing field until the end of the new cycle. A can of red spray paint was waiting at the bottom of the stairwell.

"I can make this work." His double had been too subtle with him, a mistake he hoped not to repeat. "I will make this work."

Where he stood, furiously spraying the walls, the streets were lifeless and the rails above were silent, but soon, he assured himself, the worlds on either side of the mirror would cross each other's paths once again. It was a figure eight with two loops meeting at the center, one loop being the lifeless state of realization he stood in, the other being the populated world of uncertainty he had left behind and where his double would soon be born.

It was somewhere between early morning and late night. He was on a train traveling over the streets of the city. He was certainly new to the world but, strangely enough, was aware that his birth was unnatural, although his fellow passengers showed no signs of anything out of the ordinary having taken place.

When he politely turned to one of the passengers and asked if they happened to know who he was, the person pulled a dollar bill from his pocket, let it flutter into his lap, and then chose a seat farther down the train. When a number of people left the train against a crosscurrent of boarding passengers, he followed suit and shoved his way off the train.

The platform hovered over the streets by iron supports and cement stairs. The stairwell was covered in spray-painted proverbs:

"They all know because they're all you."

"Look between Parnassus and the Pioneer."

"You are Schopenhauer."

PHANTOMIME

Gregory L. Norris

The change, at first, wasn't obvious. Eamon was Eamon when he entered the little room at the back of the house, what had once been a detached summer kitchen, he was told, eventually encompassed by the big house during one of the renovations in its storied past. But he was less Eamon when he left.

In the shape of an L, with one wall covered in ancient bricks and a closet that used to be a pantry, Eamon O'Rourke thought the room would make the perfect home office. At least that's how he had sold it to her. Start one of those small businesses he was always trotting out verbally on bad days and after long shifts or when he complained about the nonspecific pains he suffered more frequently now, his body still youngish at thirty-five but starting to creak and settle like a house. When they met, she had been supremely supportive of his ambitions. Now on those rotten days when he blathered about his plans to invest, or help others, and turn a tidy profit, or open new restaurants, he caught that sour look, heard that condescending snort from deep in her chest, especially when the latter idea was mentioned.

A home office was an easier sell than a man cave, which he knew it would degenerate into easier than an actual functioning work space. He already spent enough of his day chained to a desk, locked out of the Internet's more salacious destinations. Eamon was cursed by that office at his day job.

In time, the not-man cave/home office at the back of the house cursed him worse.

~

They moved into the apartment, which occupied half the ground floor of a rambling Federal-style house renovated several times throughout its past, one of those major fixes engulfing the summer kitchen and an outdoor bathroom, scooping them up, hemming them in, adding square footage and one or more unexpected, undesirable features, such as the situation brewing in the L-shaped room at the very end of the hall.

The previous tenants stored unopened boxes and furniture in that room and had left behind an antique dresser that boasted an oval mirror suspended between carved wooden posts. The people before them simply kept the door closed.

Eamon asked for the room. She granted it to him, though he sensed it wasn't a victory for him so much as for her. Relegating him to the room at the back of the house meant she wouldn't have to spend so much time with him.

Eamon entered the room. Hours later, Eamon and something else walked out.

White walls and one made of brick. An ancient plank floor streaked in fading ribbons of cobalt-blue paint, a dash of sunny yellow beneath a window, a blood-red hatch mark where a desk could sit, the space presently occupied by a dresser with an oval mirror.

A summer kitchen once. Maybe he would guide talented chefs in opening new restaurant concepts. Wasn't that a fitting goal? After moving in, the office still wasn't much of one. There was no desk. Nor was there a chair, nor artwork, nor anything to personalize the space beyond the few cardboard boxes he'd lugged in, usually one per visit, acquainting his junk with that which already sat abandoned in the room.

Once inside, Eamon fell into the pull of the mirror, and his features altered. He forgot he was a man with a few fractured dreams of his own, and he began dreaming someone else's.

Most of the borrowed dreams involved leaving the room at the back of the house. When Eamon eventually walked out after several long hours spent staring into the mirror, he wasn't entirely himself.

The mirrored dresser had sat in the room above that spatter of red color for some dozen years, if the facts according to the building's manager held true. Put there by a previous tenant. Abandoned along with everything else stored in there when he moved out.

"I left it," the manager said, avoiding Eamon's gaze. "You know, in case you could use it."

A box filled with old high-school and college bowling trophies—useless junk, really—and another heavy with business texts bookended the dresser. Eamon dragged in a chair.

He often went into the room while she read or knitted, her latest obsession, and the TV droned on in their living room. He sat and listened and sometimes heard soft, little echoes that almost sounded like voices. And when he stared into the mirror, what he saw reflected was, with increasing frequency, not the room as it was in the present.

An early-November twilight fell. What started as frigid rain on the long commute home was ice by the time he pulled into the driveway, and another chunk of Eamon's soul had been sliced away by yet one more brutal day at work. He felt its absence on the march from the car to the front door. He was too young to feel this cold, this old. His insides were riddled with great, gaping holes, a patchwork of vacant nothingness no longer able to stay warm or survive the approaching winter.

Create a database of known and trademarked restaurant names to help establish a concept. Then archive, region by region, the best and most reasonable restaurant-equipment suppliers and locavore-based produce sources, including farmer's markets, meat providers, and fromage artists. The ultimate achievement in this particular pipe dream, which didn't seem so unattainable while inserting key into door and turning knob, would be the creation of a new social network devoted completely to experts in the culinary field. Top chefs from around the country would create profiles, online resumes, culinary point-of-view statements. Somehow, he'd turn a profit on the database. It was brilliant.

She snorted under her breath, didn't meet his gaze, slurped at her soup. He forgot her name, forgot that he loved her, and only remembered that feeling of emptiness, those gaps in the fabric of his soul.

Rising from the table, his dinner mostly untouched, he plodded into the room at the back of the house and slammed its door behind him.

He paced and then sat backwards in the chair, assuming that stance of tough guys and cowboys. Eamon's eyes drifted into the glass, his reflection crimped and flawed around the silver edges. He met his own eyes, a muddy hazel. At one point, their color turned blue, the same rich shade as the paint streaks on the floor, as that of delphiniums and jay feathers.

There were holes eroded into his soul. While Eamon stared, something in the room filled them in with its residue.

It was summer in the dream, not fall. A warm breeze redolent with the surrounding trees and gardens drifted in through the window screens. While food cooked in the wood-fired stove set among the bricks, Eamon painted. A canvas bearing the image of a beautiful woman in an effortless pose stood on the easel. Eamon, who wasn't only Eamon, fell into the hypnotic pull of her gaze. Eyes like summer thunderheads bewitched him. He drew in a deep breath. Among the pine was the scent of exotic flowers, of her. A section of a half-remembered melody materialized in his mind, jaunty like her pose. He hummed it, but the voice didn't sound fully his.

Eamon blinked, stood. He ambled out of the room at the back of the house, crossed the hallway, and entered the bedroom. She sat in the bed with pillows behind her back, a book opened, its spine balanced on her bent knees. She glanced up. Her scream brought him fully back.

"What?" Eamon snapped.

She clutched at her chest and drank in big sips of air. "For a second I thought you were somebody else."

~

The face in the mirror, he realized, had altered.

On a brisk Saturday afternoon, as the honey-gold sky outside the room's windows colored his reflection in shades of sepia and platinum, he put it through the motions, looking for the slightest misstep: a smile that showed plenty of teeth, an exaggerated frown, a sudden lurch toward the mirror, a slow drag away from the glass. That old stage and TV trick mimed by people pretending there was a mirror in front of them, not another actor made up to look like an identical twin.

There was a mirror and two actors here; one looked like Eamon, only his hair was shaggier and sometimes he wore glasses. His nose had broken and healed at a slightly askew angle, his lower lip slightly plumper than its topside twin. When Eamon blinked, the blue eyes behind the glasses blinked in unison. Still, he searched for some clue, a slip-up where the other actor flubbed his choreography.

Eamon blinked again, and for an instant the chair was empty. After the next blink, his face stared back. He felt less riddled with holes, less empty, because, he understood after leaving the room, the thing that the mirror had somehow captured, absorbed, was now inside him.

He was the mirror.

At work, he talked openly of his ideas.

"Restaurant concepts. An idea that's going to revolutionize the industry," he said over tea, to which he'd only recently switched, forsaking his usual coffee. "And if that doesn't take off, I'll, I don't know, paint."

"You look different," said the woman in the bullpen beside him, her name lost in the ether and excitement. Simone? Cynthia? "Something about you's changed."

He laughed it off, labored to get through the work day, took an extra twenty minutes for lunch, and walked out ten shy of his shift.

~

Eamon entered the house and saw that most of her clothes were gone from the closet, its door intentionally left open as a parting shot. The note said she would be back for the rest of her things. They'd worry about the bigger details later, such as claims to the furniture and finances. It wasn't working out, for which, she claimed, she was sorry. He was disconnected. Different.

He grunted a swear beneath his breath and punched her side of the bed. The fragrance of flowers wafted up. He breathed it in and, saying nothing more, walked into the room at the back of the house and sat in the chair, cool-guy fashion, and gazed into the mirror.

There he waited.

After four days in the room, he heard her enter the house though, in his confusion at staring into that other room beyond the glass, the one in the mirror where food cooked in the summer kitchen and the walls stood open to sultry breezes and a makeshift art studio had sprung up in one corner, it could have been hours or even decades. He'd spilled a bit of cobalt-blue paint on the floor in that version of the L-shaped space, a bit of sunny yellow at another time too. Steaks rubbed with a crust of salt, cracked pepper, and some garlic sizzled on the grill. And there were leafy salads with vibrant-red garden tomatoes and a homemade dressing and potato salad with sliced eggs and onions, and cold beer to accompany the meal.

She was back. Plates for two. They would work it out. Only he could tell by the look on her face when she poked her head in from the threshold that everything had changed. The deed was done. She was not back to mend wounds but to finish severing those which she'd partially cut.

The image in the mirror was fully Eamon's, he noted. The face and form of the body in the chair, he sensed in a disconnected way, were not.

"Eamon," she snapped.

The body stood up from its Joe-cool crouch, giving the chair a spin on one leg. Eamon's reflection, however, remained frozen in the glass. From the corner of his eye, understanding that the mimes had at long last messed up the routine, had shown the audience that there was no mirror but just two actors following a script, he saw himself lunge for her; heard her screams. He smelled the flowers and then the blood.

A patch of red stained that one corner of the L-shaped room at the back of the house. Like the other marks, it had been there for years, soaked into the ancient plank floor, absorbed by the room, a reminder of events long past but not quite fully ended.

The mirror had shattered. Eamon wasn't exactly sure how, but fresh red liquid dripped down the splinters of glass, some of the disparate shards reflecting the room as it was in the present, others as it had been. His own face smiled back from various pieces still held within the mirror's frame, a living Cubist study.

Restaurant conceptualization, from that first spark of inspiration through the plating of food placed in front of hungry diners. Or investments. He had great ideas. They only needed to be acted out.

Instead, dipping his fingers in the red, Eamon began to paint.

NEVER SAY NO

Angela Bodine

The entire world disappeared until all that was left was this perfectly manicured hand holding a red envelope. The color of her sixty-dollar nails matched perfectly, bled onto the paper, fusing Alaina Heathermann with the inevitable.

"It's here," she thought aloud, her voice echoing oddly in the high-ceilinged foyer.

Outside, downy snow fell silently onto the big house, mixing with the fifteen-hundred-dollar Christmas lights and nativity scene in what would have made a perfect holiday postcard. Inside, the decorations had not yet been staged and the absence lent a hollow feel to the house.

Alaina had been waiting a long time for her invitation. Years.

She turned the envelope over and over in her hands. No return address. There were just her name and address, written in silver that glittered like attractive lies. She had almost begun to hope that she had been left out, but no such luck. Alaina Heathermann was always on the VIP list of every important party, and it seemed that this would be no exception.

She finally slid her flawlessly manicured index finger under the sealed flap of the red envelope and gasped with the sudden, flaring pain of a simple paper cut. She put the finger to lips painted with Revlon lipstick, seventeen dollars, and laughed a little. *How fitting.* Even opening the long-awaited invitation brought pain. Yet it was nothing compared to the pain that would come.

The card was simple but elegant. It wasn't a Christmas card, of course. Dead people can't send Christmas cards.

Only invitations.

The words on the front of the white cardstock read simply "You're Invited" in elegant, embossed script. She opened it and allowed a sheaf of delicate gold tissue paper to flutter to the ground. Inside the card there was nothing. No picture, no printed words, no handwritten words. Just a blank card. Empty.

A sharp rap on the door caused her to pull the card to her six-thousand-dollar implants in surprise. She felt her heart thudding beneath the curled fist and crumpled invitation.

She turned to the door, dismayed to see that the large, fifty-dollar wreath obscured the frosted-glass panes on the door, hiding whoever was outside. She would have to open it to find out who had knocked. She wished that someone else was in the house with her, anyone else, but she had given orders for all the help to be gone today. She had wanted to be alone.

But now she wasn't. Three more sharp raps on the door, insistent, refusing to be ignored. *Rap. Rap. Rap.*

She looked around herself, trying to prolong the inevitable. Hundreds of dollars' worth of bouquets, plants, and cards of condolence littered the antique table in the foyer, spilling onto the marble floor. She thought vaguely of all the thank-you cards she would need to fill out later, but then she chuckled morbidly as she realized this would probably be the one time she wouldn't have to worry about fulfilling her social obligations. Her mother had taught her from a very young age that one always sends a thank-you card after receiving a gift. She had taught Alaina many things about social etiquette, such as which silverware one uses when and what kind of gift one brings to the host of a party. And she had taught her that one must never, ever, turn down an invitation.

Alaina looked at the crumpled invitation in her hand. The red envelope had fallen to the floor to mingle with the overflowing funeral flowers; she only held the white card now, as unnaturally white as the fist that clenched it. She tried to smooth out the card, smiling wryly, thinking to herself that her mother would be proud. She never said no to an invitation.

As if in response, the rapping on the door came again, stronger and more insistent this time. Alaina sighed. She looked at herself in the eight-hundred-dollar mirror that hung above the antique foyer table. She normally used that mirror to check her reflection before answering the door (if the butler wasn't there to answer it for her), and the habit calmed her somewhat now. She smoothed the blonde locks that cost her two hundred dollars every six weeks, and pinched her pale cheeks to bring color to them because her twelve-dollar rouge seemed to be falling short at the moment. No pink blush came to her cheeks; her face was as pale and blank as the empty invitation she still clutched.

She turned to the door. Took a breath. Invitation in the left hand. Knob in the right. She pulled the door open and—

—rummaged through the contents of her locker, looking for her trig book. It was no easy task; her locker was an absolute mess. Her mother would have been disappointed if she knew.

"Hey, gorgeous."

Alaina smiled and turned to embrace another thing her mother would have been disappointed about if she knew. Oh, she didn't disapprove of Chance himself. He was from a substantial family and was already on the fast track to a career in politics, even though he was just a senior. He was also handsome and popular.

Chance squeezed her butt through her acid-washed jeans, and Alaina slapped his hand away, looking around the crowded hallway to make sure no one had seen.

That was what her mother would have been disappointed about. Chance was the perfect future son-in-law on the surface. He was, however, a seventeen-year-old male with raging hormones, as well as a secret inclination towards alcohol and the occasional "soft" drug. Alaina had learned since they had started dating as sophomores that it was best to avoid him when he was drinking. As for the hormones, she had given him her virginity last year after the homecoming dance in the hope that it would help extinguish his public groping, but instead it had seemed to fuel it. She figured that once he was a little older he would outgrow all that childishness and dismissed it as much as she could. Boys would be boys.

She gave Chance a quick peck on the cheek after slapping his hand away.

"Oh, come on. Is that all I get?"

"You hush. I am not risking detention so you can fondle me in the hallway," she whispered in a hiss but then smiled. "We'll have some private time Saturday night anyway."

He grunted.

"I don't want to wait till Saturday. How about Friday?"

She turned back to her locker to retrieve her trig book.

"No can do. Friday's Bradley's party."

"You've got to be kidding me. You're not really going to that loser's party, are you? He actually handed out invitations like some old woman. He's the joke of the school, babe. Lame."

Alaina eyed the invitation tucked into the door of her locker before shutting it. She secretly thought it sweet that a teenage boy had passed out written invitations to his party, putting them in every locker in their small school, leaving no one out. She didn't know Bradley very well; he was quiet and didn't hang out with her popular clique, but he seemed nice enough.

"I'm going, Chance. Maybe it'll be fun to do something other than hit the drag like we do every single weekend there's not a football game. Besides, I never turn down an invitation. It's rude."

She was surprised by how much the last two words sounded like they had come out of her mother's mouth and not her own.

"You never turn down an invitation, huh?" Chance got that familiar, mischievous grin on his face and tried to grab her. "I got an invitation for ya."

She laughed and ducked out of his arms before she could be ensnared.

"Saturday." She slapped his hand away as he tried to grab her butt again. "I'm going to the party on Friday. That's that. I'll talk to you after third period. I've got to get to class before the bell rings."

As if on cue, the bell rang—

—and rang, playing a discordant, electronic version of "Jingle Bells" to an empty porch.

Alaina shivered against the cold and shock of the empty porch, wishing she had never agreed to have the holiday music installed on a motion sensor. What was once charming was now creepy. A sudden gust of snow-laced wind made her shut her eyes. She reopened them, trying to blink a sixty-dollar colored contact back into place, and looked for any sign of who had been on the porch, rapping on the door. There was no sign. No footprints in the snow, on the porch, or in the yard. No car parked in the cul-de-sac directly before the house. Even the front gate remained closed.

Alaina shut the door, returning to the foyer with its bright and expensive reminders of death, and looked at the invitation again. The snow had wetted it, making it look as though tears had fallen on its wrinkled surface.

She glanced at all the flowers in the foyer. She wondered if Bradley had received so many condolences when he had died. She lifted one of the cards out of a random arrangement. It was a nice one; it must have cost at least a hundred dollars. The card on the outside read: "Our prayers are with you during this difficult time."

Inside, the card was blank.

She felt her breath growing short. Breathing seemed to be a huge task.

Her body felt limp beneath her, and she glanced down at the marble floor briefly before her legs gave out and—

—she landed on the dirty linoleum in a heap. The red plastic cup full of strawberry daiquiri spilled over the floor like wasted blood.

"Holy crap, Alaina, are you okay?"

Bradley rushed over to help her to her feet.

She giggled and straightened her red party dress.

"Yeah, sorry. I'm not much of a drinker. I never do it. Wow, I made a mess."

They looked at the slushy pile of daiquiri on the linoleum floor, and both laughed this time.

"It's okay. I don't think it's gonna hurt that floor much anyway. I'll clean it up later."

Alaina noticed that Bradley had a cute dimple on one cheek when he smiled, and how attractive he looked when his longish bangs fell into his eyes.

"It sucks no one came to your party."

She had been too sober to mention it before. At first, they had been awkward and Bradley had seemed embarrassed, but a few daiquiris had taken care of that problem. For the past three hours, they had listened to music and browsed his bookshelf, and Alaina had even talked him into showing her a little of his artwork. She had made him promise that he would paint her picture one day.

"It's okay," he said, shrugging it off. "I'm just sorry for you. You're probably not used to such sucky parties."

"Hey, I'm really having a great time." She giggled and picked up her spilled cup. "Besides, this is the only party I've ever been to where I could just be myself. I haven't had to worry about how to act or what to do or what to say. It's kind of a relief."

He smiled, dimple flashing.

"Honestly, I'm kinda glad no one came too, or I wouldn't have had time to get to know you."

Alaina's flush had nothing to do with the daiquiris. Embarrassment flooded Bradley's face.

"I'm sorry. I know you have a boyfriend. You don't have to worry about me trying to hit on you or nothing. It'd be good enough just to have you for a friend." His blush deepened. "I mean, if you want to be friends."

Maybe it was the liquor. Maybe it was the homey little trailer that Bradley lived in or the music that seemed to pulse in time with her heartbeat, but in that second, Alaina decided that she'd much rather have a boyfriend like Bradley than Chance. They'd actually had a conversation that was about *her*; Chance was more interested in, well, Chance. And, most importantly, she hadn't realized a teenage boy could be capable of reigning in his hormones. It made her feel as though he actually saw her as an equal, not just a tool to use for his own pleasure.

When she leaned across the sticky puddle of daiquiri on the floor to kiss Bradley, her mother's voice came into her mind. *He has no future. I haven't been training you all these years to have you wind up in a trailer park with a nobody.*

She pushed the voice out of her mind and kissed Bradley demurely.

Even for such a discreet kiss, the heat that suddenly flooded Alaina was phenomenal. She felt simultaneously lightheaded and grounded.

By the look on Bradley's face (mixed with a hint of surprise), she could tell he felt the same.

They stood and looked at each other, and Alaina tried to reconcile her conflicting emotions with what she had just done. Ultimately, she decided to just remain in the moment and enjoy it.

She was just leaning forward to meet Bradley's lips again when the front door burst open. She whirled around and stared in disbelief as Chance stormed towards them across the trailer's living room, face full of rage and aggression. He must have seen them through the uncovered front window.

"Chance, wait!"

Chance grabbed Bradley by the cuff of his shirt and lifted him off the ground, spitting in his face.

"I'm gonna kill you, you little fucking loser. Teach you not to touch what doesn't belong to you."

Everything after that happened too fast for Alaina's shocked and alcohol-addled brain to fully register.

Chance's arm thrust back to strike like a tightly coiled spring. Alaina trying to grab it. Missing. The expression of surprise on Bradley's face replaced by the fist. The sound like a gunshot. Awful. Alaina trying to grab Bradley as he fell. Slipping in the spilled daiquiri. Chance trying to grab her. Falling. Then the most awful sound ever. *Crack*. On the ground, covered in daiquiri. Covered in red. Covered in, *where did this come from*, blood. Chance moving, trying to stand. Alaina frozen. *No, no, no*. Bradley still, *why isn't he moving*, deadly still with his eyes closed and his nose bleeding and his neck at an odd angle.

Chance was back up, standing above them, hands on his hips, the fury in his face replaced with irritation.

"Well, shit. Look what you've done, you slut."

Alaina remained on the floor, unmoving. Bradley on the floor, unmoving. *It should end here*, Alaina prayed.

It didn't.

Chance leaned forward, his anger clearly rising again, grabbed her face, and—

—the same hands that had killed Bradley stroked her cheek gently.

"Alaina, hon. Alaina, wake up."

She opened her eyes and they focused on a concerned face that had, seconds ago, been filled with rage. *No, not seconds. Twelve years.*

Chance Heathermann. Handsome and distinguished. Accomplished and well respected. If only the voters had known who he really was, what he was really capable of.

"There you are. Can you sit up?"

She did.

"You had me scared for a second there, hon. What happened?"

She shook her head and looked around. She was still on the marble floor in the foyer, surrounded by funeral flowers.

It suddenly struck her that the flowers had no fragrance. She should have been overwhelmed by the different aromas, but she smelled nothing. Nothing except a very faint hint of strawberry daiquiri.

Chance was still looking at her. She noted that his mask of concern was growing thin; beneath it, his usual look of irritation and annoyance was peeking through. Once he found out that there was no one in the house but them, he would drop the façade entirely.

"I got invited."

She held her hand out to him, still clutching the ruined invitation.

He took it. Read it. Handed it back.

"What are you talking about, Alaina? What is this? Who sent it?"

She smiled.

"Bradley."

He rose suddenly and scoffed at her. "You're crazy."

And with that single admonishment, Chance was gone. He left the foyer, with its expensive flowers that didn't smell and the well-put-together trophy wife whose legs didn't work.

And Alaina remained on the marble floor and wondered why she was here. She wondered why she had married a murderer, why she had never told anyone what actually happened. Why she spent so much money on clothes and furnishings and things that didn't matter. They were all questions she'd asked herself before, and, as always, no answers presented themselves.

But now she had an invitation to her last party.

Alaina would finally pay for her complicity in Bradley's death.

She found the strength to rise off the marble floor, and—

—Chance and Bradley were gone. She felt her neck gingerly and imagined the bruises that would inevitably rise there. She knew she was lucky Chance hadn't strangled her to death. *At least it's winter and I can wear turtlenecks*. She looked at the mess on the linoleum floor. Red everywhere. *Festive, like Christmas*. There was also a little blood on the edge of the counter where Bradley's head had struck.

Automatically, unaccountably, Alaina did the only thing she could think of.

She cleaned up the mess.

Once done, she walked to the door of the trailer, still open from when Chance had barged in, and left.

She probably would have gone home and huddled in her bed and tried to convince her brain that nothing had happened if not for one thing. Chance's car was still there. He must have been in the backyard with, *with Bradley*, with the body.

Alaina walked toward the back of the trailer numbly, not feeling the cold or the snow falling on her.

Behind the trailer there was a small backyard decorated with a cheap barbecue and four plastic chairs, all covered in snow. There was also a large cliff about fifteen feet from the yard. *How convenient*. Chance stood at the edge of that cliff, a still form—*Bradley, his name is Bradley*— beside him on the ground.

Alaina found herself standing beside Chance with the heap—*Bradley*— between them. Forty feet of rock between them and the bottom, with only a slight slope.

"What are you doing?"

Her words were small and laced with vapor from the cold. Chance didn't look up from the view.

"He's still alive."

Alaina suddenly felt as if she had awoken from a nightmare. *Still alive!* Thoughts raced through her brain so fast she was certain the friction would cause her head to burst into flames. They needed to act quick. *He was alive*. They could call an ambulance. *He was alive*. They could somehow make this all right. *He was alive, alive, alive! Bradley wasn't a body or a still form or a heap. He was alive!*

When Chance bent down to pick up Bradley, Alaina assumed he was picking him up to carry him inside, where they would call 911. She didn't suspect anything sinister until she saw Chance's arms suddenly empty. *Stupid girl*. She tried to scream, but her bruised throat only allowed a squeak.

She looked down and saw—

—her six-hundred-dollar high-heeled shoes standing on the marble floor.

Stupid girl, she thought. *How absurd you look in your expensive costume*.

She slipped the heels off her feet. Better, but now she stared at a forty-dollar pedicure. *You won't be able to see your toes in the snow.*

It seemed like a good idea. She numbly left the foyer, which smelled nothing of flowers because there were never actually any flowers there. She walked into the unbroken landscape of snow in the yard, feeling no cold, remembering how she had felt no cold on the day Bradley died. *How fitting.* She looked down at her three-hundred-dollar dress. *That will have to go too.* It did. The bra and panties too, top of the line and just as expensive as the rest of her clothes, even if no one ever saw them. She stood naked in the snow, feeling nothing, and looked at the invitation now in shreds in her hand. She noticed her sixty-dollar, blood-red manicure. *Silly girl. Foolish girl*. She fell to her knees and thrust her hands into the snow to bury the nails. *Better, but not enough.* She still had her two-hundred-dollar haircut, her expensive makeup, and even her colored contacts. *The snow should be deep enough if you lay flat.* Alaina burrowed into the snow, face first, like an animal trying to dig through the ground. She knew she wasn't completely buried, but the heavily falling snow would cover her back soon enough. She tasted the snow and the earth in her mouth and thought of Bradley—

—lying in the snow at the bottom of the cliff.

He looked so small, just a dark smear in that sea of white. He looked so lonely there. So little and alone. Just a boy who threw a party that no one came to. She wished she could join him—

—there in the snow, naked and buried. Inside, Chance was probably opening a two-hundred-dollar bottle of wine to enjoy while he watched the news on their fifteen-hundred-dollar flat-screen television with 3D features. She heard her mother's voice in her head: *This isn't what I raised you for, Alaina. To end up with a boy in a trailer park with no future.*

Yes, momma, but sometimes things don't turn out the way you planned. Sometimes—

—you throw a party and no one comes."

"What in the world are you talking about?"

Chance was looking at her incredulously, but she didn't see. Her eyes were fixed on Bradley, at the bottom of the drop. Waiting for her.

Alaina smiled—

—but no one saw it as she lay buried naked beneath the snow in front of her million-dollar home. She was still now, deathly still, except for her legs, which moved as if she were trying to take a step—

—to the edge of the cliff.

Chance grabbed her arm.

No," he said, firmly, fiercely, resolutely.

In another life, she would have listened. In another life—

—she would have maybe even married a murderer, become his accomplice, lived a full life of vanity and vice, trying to bury that awful day they buried Bradley. So she would spend and spend, and smile and preen, and attend all the best parties. At least until the day she would crack and wander naked into the snow. . . But in this life—

—Alaina simply shook Chance's hand off her arm and said, "I have an invitation to answer." She stepped off the edge of the cliff and plummeted to the inevitable, her last get-together forty feet below.

SATURNALIA

Maria Alexander

Something chittered and cackled as it danced in the shadows of the naked trees. Maria skirted her dead Jeep, putting it between her and the noise, afraid the creature would burst through the foliage. She tried to make out what it was, but the trees flanking the road confounded her eyes with their twisted limbs. Thick, smoky rivulets streamed from beneath the battered metal hood, further obscuring her vision. Yet something rustled beyond the sharp, frosty branches of the forest walls. Something feral and utterly frightening.

Maria took off at a run, crunching the oyster shells strewn over the swamp-soaked dirt road with each step. Duffel bag in one hand and water bottle in the other, she abandoned the doorless old Jeep Wrangler, her breath escaping in frosty puffs. The faint odors of sulfur and rotting vegetation wafting from the forest put her stomach on edge.

Just a few days ago, an anonymous, handwritten letter had asked her to come to Ville D'Or—a village some ways from Thibodaux—to pick up her brother's belongings. The letter had also said she was to talk to someone named "The Preacher." She'd called the sheriff's station in the Lafourche Parish, but they had not heard of any deaths in that community.

"Doesn't mean anything," an officer said. "Folk in these more rural communities keep to themselves, if you know what I mean."

Winter break had just started at the California community college where she taught American history, so she packed up and came here. Alone.

The last town she'd seen was thirty miles back on the outskirts of Thibodaux. The guy who'd rented her the old Jeep wore a shirt that said "Proud to be a Coonass," with a cartoon coon proudly displaying its rear end. His rundown car-rental office had been littered with cheap Christmas decorations, tinny carols playing in over the office sound system. The big holiday was only a few days away...

The rustling kept to her left for some time but faded as the road widened and the trees thinned to make way for the village. Dilapidated bungalows and trailers squatted on stilts above the wet ground, resting quietly around the perimeter with vegetable gardens, chicken coops, dogs, and tree swings that twitched in the moist breeze. Everything stood well away from the forest of gnarled cottonwood trees, towering cypresses and weeping willows, a levee glistening wetly between them. As Maria crossed a damp stone bridge, churning gray clouds clustered above, threatening to drench the village further. The rotting smell gave way somewhat to pungent farm odors.

A hand-painted sign hung from a splintered post in the rapidly approaching town square:

"Welcome to Ville D'Or"

The Village of Gold.

Since her older brother Joshua had disappeared all those years ago after college without so much as a goodbye, he'd carved an aching emptiness into her soul. Both parents had been killed in a car accident during elementary school. They were fostered by Mr. and Mrs. McGregor—a decent but stern couple who never formally adopted them.

As young orphans, Maria and Joshua clung to one another as if drowning.

Brooding, brilliant, rebellious and reckless, Joshua went to Yale on a scholarship for a degree in philosophy. Maria, however, only managed to enter CSU Fullerton for her history degree and eventually earned a teaching credential. Still, they kept in close contact, ever a lifeline to one another, until Joshua began to pull away with his ever-increasing use of drugs and alcohol.

Mrs. McGregor's disapproving frown had burned a deep degree of discipline into Maria's life. While Joshua rebelled, Maria continued her catechism, much to the pleasure of her foster parents. She lived a highly sheltered life, even living with the McGregors until she graduated. Joshua was the only man she'd cared about until she met her now dearly departed Alejo. Although they had shared ten years of marital bliss, Maria never entirely overcame her shyness.

Shy or not, when she received that chilling letter a few days before, she knew she had to come.

The town square appeared deserted. A chorus of voices seeped from a stone chapel at the far end of the village. Located on a peninsula of dense foliage, the forest swelled against the church, reminding Maria of the ancient chapels she'd seen when the McGregors took her to Ireland, with dark glass windows and granite archways carved by long-dead masons. The church appeared very much out of time and place, with stone walls that sank into the hallowed ground.

The bell tolled, the doors opened, and the parishioners meandered down the stone steps.

Maria stopped beside a row of food and supply shops, closed and shuttered this Sunday. Was this because of "blue laws"? She thought that only pertained to alcohol. She noted the lack of Christmas debris that passed for decorations in the previous towns. Didn't they celebrate Christmas? Maybe they were Jehovah's Witnesses? Potbellied men and women in winter caps and thick scarves wrapped around their necks strolled gaily past her without a look, chatting to one another; the children scampered and shouted happily.

She wiped her neck with a handkerchief, exertion beading on her skin, feet aching as she watched an old black man in a coal-black suit wander from the church doors and make his way into the town center. He seemed to be one of the few African Americans here. He placed a threadbare fedora on his head as he strode toward her, eyes gleaming wet like the levee under the sunlight of the breaking cloud cover. As he came into better focus, his priest's collar shone bone white under his gray-stubbled chin.

"Excuse me, sir, but are you the *padre*? My name is Maria Burbano."

"Why, yes I am," he said with a guttural voice, extending his hand. His words were thick, and a strange laugh punctuated the sentence. Maria nodded, and he exhaled a breath of surprise. "Glory! You Maria? Joshua's sister? I never expected—heard a *lot* about you. And the family resemblance is mighty strong."

Maria nodded, taking his hand. Cold and dry.

"I'm Samson Reynolds, preacher in these parts." He laid a hand on her shoulder. "I'm awful sorry 'bout your brother, Mrs. Burbano. I assume that's why you've come to D'or."

She showed him the letter, which said they'd buried Joshua behind the church, as he'd wished. "Do you know who wrote this?"

The preacher scanned it and handed it back to her. "I've no idea," he replied. "But I buried him myself. Come this way."

He led her toward the graveyard, where the ropey cypress trees thickened, boney wooden "knees" jutting up from the wet ground. Up close, the church appeared even older. The arching stained-glass windows told stories one could only read from inside when sunlight leaned against the panes. Maria wanted to ask the preacher when it was built, but something hardened in his eyes as they rounded the mammoth walls.

The marble mausoleums shouldered against one another in the swamp grass, surfaces worn smooth with age. The remains of withered bouquets littered some, while others lay bare, lost in memory and time. Maria stepped carefully between them, her hiking boots sinking in the dirt as she approached the grave. She laid a hand on Joshua's glossy, white marble mausoleum and crossed herself.

"Was he religious?" Maria asked. "How did he die?" Tears blurred her vision as they slid down her cheeks. She wanted to ask many more questions, but the grief prevented it. She hoped he'd not lost his faith, even if it hadn't been strong enough to keep him out of trouble in school.

Dead leaves rolled over the crabgrass as a wind snaked across the graves. The preacher took his time answering, hands in his pockets as he watched her. "He took his life."

"What?" she gasped. "How do you know?"

"I have the death certificate, signed by the county coroner. Would you like to see it?"

Before she could answer, something crackled faintly from deep in the forest. The preacher's attention snapped toward the woods.

"What is it?" she whispered, terror-struck. "I think it tracked me on the road."

He frowned. "That's the forest spirit," he said. "That's what the folks call it here, anyway. Sometimes it gets children if they wander too close. Adults, too." He leaned against her, drawing his leathery, whiskered face close to hers. His eyes creased. Tobacco tinged his breath. "Best you stay away from the forest. You hear?"

Maria nodded again. The rustling faded into the depths of the woods.

The preacher led her from the graveyard to an old pickup. As they drove, they passed children wearing grotesque papier-mâché masks chasing each other down roads and adults drinking beer on the sidewalks as they joked and embraced freely. No Christmas lights, holly, mistletoe, red bows, or any other decorations, yet conviviality lit every street corner of the otherwise decaying town. She noted acres of blighted fields stretching beyond the village and what looked like an abandoned plantation.

"Is there a farm here? What does it grow?"

The preacher silently watched the road. Then, after a moment: "What are your plans tonight?"

"I don't know. The Jeep I rented in Thibodaux died a couple miles back."

"It's getting late. I'll take you to Thibodaux tomorrow morning."

The pickup soon rumbled into the gravel drive of his home—a clean, olive-green house with a large vegetable garden—where a plump woman named Delilah in pressed white skirts introduced herself as the preacher's wife. She chatted amiably as the preacher served them cheese sandwiches and lemonade in a spotless, old-fashioned kitchen. Maria thought it curious that he never looked his wife in the eye and addressed her as "Mistress" with that guttural voice. Whenever he did so, Delilah grinned with wild delight and rolled her eyes. As Maria finished eating, Delilah excused herself to get ready for the night's celebrations.

As Maria looked around the kitchen, the spectral memory arose of her grandmother making tamales on Christmas Eve, the *thwack-thwack* of her palm on the *masa*—dough. Maria was only six when she died. "What's happening tonight?" she asked the preacher through a mouthful of white bread, mayonnaise and Velveeta.

"Saturnalia," the preacher said as he gazed out the window, quickly finishing a glass of lemonade. "Now, if you'll excuse me a moment." He winked at her, hiccupped with that strange laugh, and left through the kitchen doors after his wife.

Saturnalia? That was some kind of ancient celebration on the longest night of the year. Why did these people celebrate it? What about Christmas? Perhaps the preacher was joking.

As the sky outside dimmed and russet leaves blew past the kitchen window, Maria heard a rustling, then amorous groans through the doors in a distant room. She checked her cell phone: no reception. She sat uncomfortably at the small kitchen table for the next hour.

Leaning in the rain like a stack of forgotten magazines, her brother's tin shanty sat slick and oily on stilts, with an earthy smell rising around it. The preacher stood in the mud below with an umbrella as Maria pushed open the unlocked metallic door. She flipped the greasy switch, drawing light from a bare bulb that swayed from a thin chain in the middle of the cramped room. Dingy gray sheets spattered with a dark fluid lay crumpled on a narrow mattress, which sat on a rusted frame beside an oversized metal cabinet. Six hunting knives of various sizes were mounted to the cabinet door. A faint organic odor unlike anything she'd smelled before stained the air.

Maria leaned out the door to the preacher. "Have the police been here, padre?" she said, her voice quavering.

A wind blew across the empty yard.

She closed the door and edged her way around the chilly room, unsure if she should even be there, but her curiosity raced ahead of caution. Was this truly his home? The preacher said it was okay if she wanted any of his belongings, so she felt that she ought to see his home, even though it felt like an invasion. Bookshelves covered every spare patch of wall space: tattoo magazines, violent pornographic Japanese comics, true-crime paperbacks, all interspersed with intellectual and philosophical treatises on retribution, religion and anthropology. She flipped open one of the true-crime books, revealing grizzly black-and-white photographs of murder victims strewn carelessly across blood-spattered sheets. Flesh torn, gaping inky on celluloid, eyes staring at vanished killers. Remnants of cruelty, sadism and evil.

Maria replaced the book, shivering and sickened. Sitting on the bookshelf was a snapshot of Joshua holding a dead snake and wielding one of the hunting knives. His nose was like hers, too long and bulbous for his face, and his head was bald.

As she moved away, her toe stubbed a crude wooden box with a bulldog harness lock. Swallowing lakes of dread, she pried one of the hunting knives from the cold metal cabinet and knelt beside the box. Splinters barbed the unvarnished surface like the sharp, bristling forest-tree limbs beside the road they drove along that morning. With all her strength, she pounded the thin hinges with the knife point until they came loose from the heavy box. The lid opened, releasing a faint musty odor.

Her calves throbbed as she crouched for several minutes in front of the open box, heart pounding, knife in hand. Textbooks, photo albums, and dated notebooks layered one another inside. Resting on the heap lay an abridged edition of Frazer's *The Golden Bough*, a book documenting magical and religious practices all over the world. Multiple pieces of cloth and scraps of paper heavily marked dozens of passages. The book shook in her trembling hands as she lifted it. Yellowing with age, the thin pages fell open to a place marked with an X-rated playing card:

...we must conclude that the human victims at the Thargelia certainly appear in later classical times to have figured chiefly as public scapegoats—sacrificial victims who carried away with them the sins, misfortunes, and sorrows of the whole people. At an earlier time they were looked on as embodiments of vegetation...

This passage, which fell under "The Periodic Expulsion of Evils," was underlined with a blue ballpoint. Several pages later, marked with a frayed green ribbon, Maria found the following passage underscored with thick pencil lead:

...The Roman celebration of Saturnalia, on the other hand, was celebrated in December. In darker times, altars to the ancient Lord of Misrule are said to have been stained with the blood of human victims to take away the sins of the community...a criminal was tied to a stake, gagged and strangled, his neck being placed between two poles, which are then violently compressed, all the people eagerly helping to squeeze the criminal to death...

Below the book lay a jewelry-box-sized tin and several spiral-bound notebooks. The black notebook on top, titled "Meteorological Data" and dated the current month, glared under the light of the swaying bulb. Flipping back the front page, Maria glimpsed several lines of writing, then closed the cover quickly. She decided against reading it; she wasn't ready for that yet. Instead, she set aside *The Golden Bough* and cautiously opened the tin.

Faded Polaroids burst from beneath the canister lid. Tender young boys bound, gagged, screaming, weeping, kneeling, straps of leather, knives, brutal clips, sawhorses, anally inserted rods, children spreading their tender legs to camera lenses, cum dribbling from their tiny, bruised lips, blindfolded, burned, bleeding, beheaded...

With a man. Always one particular man...

Joshua.

Staggering to her feet, Maria fell to the floor once again and vomited the bread, the distance, a million wishes for his life, games of hide-and-seek, Saturday mornings, the tree fort behind their house. Everything she had kept, everything he'd neglected.

Icy pain seized her gut and washed up through her lungs. Her shaking hand numbly dug in her pants pocket and extracted the anonymous letter. Brushing aside the Polaroids with wide sweeps of her arms, she crawled back to the box and threw that black notebook to the floor.

Maria held the letter alongside the scrawls on the first page: the handwriting was identical. And while the letter was dated two weeks ago, the last entry of the notebook was dated only yesterday.

Twilight descending, the denizens of the town gathered in larger crowds around the pubs, drinking and laughing loudly to joyful Cajun folk tunes. Children played in the other roads, blissfully unsupervised. Some squinted at Maria through their masks as she tore through the crowds.

"Reynolds!" she screamed into the damp air. "Reynolds! Where is he?" Her patience, which she'd exercised far too liberally with these bizarre people, had lost its grip on her actions. "*Where is he*?"

A tall, freshly painted white fence wound around one yard under a dense copse of trees. Children were playing within, but they were rather subdued compared to the others roaming the streets. Maria's instinct about the mischief of quiet children drew her to stop and press her face close to the slot between painted boards to peer within.

An eight-year-old girl with dirty-blonde hair stood blindfolded before the massive trunk of a willow tree shading the yard. The blindfold tied over her pigtails crushed down the fine locks. Three boys, two girls—the oldest boy, with strong Creole features in his nose and brows, took a long stick and, standing behind the girl, feigned cutting her throat...

Stone spires rose against the horizon as Maria ran for the church. Sunlight no longer leaned against the stained glass; prostrate shadows clutched the threshold. Her legs wobbled as her feet plunged one after another, pain and confusion guiding her steps to this place where God was mortared in stone.

Maria grasped the black iron handles of the heavy oak doors and pulled them open. Oily incense smoke draped the stony entrance. Touching her forehead, she started to cross herself until she noticed the life-sized stone carvings that flanked the dark vestibule entrance. Casting an uneven glow over the walls, bowls of flame sat beneath images not of the Virgin and Son, but of a Roman man with flowing robes, holding a scythe and scales.

Beyond the vestibule, candles perforated the darkness of the sanctuary, beckoning those who entered down a wide, carpeted pathway to the dimly lit altar of black and white marble. As she stepped cautiously down the path, the stained-glass windows reached high above against either wall, jewel tones stained with the stories of not Jesus and the saints but of ancient dramas involving gods and mortals, carnage and bliss. Eyes jeweled, wings blackened.

Maria collapsed into one of the pews, crying and shuddering with long, heaving sobs. She wanted to leave but was afraid of the night closing in. Pulling the cell phone from her pocket, she opened it—she had to call the sheriff she'd spoken to—but her cell still had no reception.

The pew pockets bulged with more dull gray copies of *The Golden Bough.* She reached for one of the books and opened it directly to where the shiny blue ribbon marked every book:

...Lastly, the scapegoat may be a man. The Gonds of India worship Ghansyam Deo, and at the winter solstice festival the god himself is said to descend on the head of one of the worshippers, who is suddenly seized with a kind of fit and, after staggering about, rushes off into the jungle, where it is believed that he would be killed one year later.

From behind the candles, the preacher emerged from inky seclusion. "Elijah Owen," he intoned. He stopped only a few feet away, resting his hands on the wooden pews. "He was eight years old when your brother kidnapped, raped and strangled him. Joshua spent ten years in prison for that crime alone, where he learned the undeniable truth." The preacher paused as the last sheet of sunlight fled from the windows. "That he was a monster."

Outside, an ominous rumbling shook the earth as if something titanic were being dragged across the ground.

"This *place* is monstrous," Maria growled, throwing the book down on the pew seat. "You could have warned me about Joshua's past. And where is he, Padre? What have you done with him? Is he to be your sacrifice?"

"Mrs. Burbano, you don't ask the right questions," he drawled, leaning towards her as he did in the graveyard. "In 1792," he continued, "a man by the name of William Beaucage came here with a handful of escaped convicts from the colonies. A former Jesuit priest, Monsieur Beaucage himself was a confessed child sodomite, sadist and opium addict—"

"Beaucage la Bête," Maria whispered, fear slipping like ice floes in her stomach as she remembered the infamous colonial criminal. Beaucage the Beast.

"Monsieur Beaucage knew that the story of Jesus, his Mother and the Holy Ghost worked for those simple souls with ordinary sins who needed to be cleansed in the name of a gentle, loving God. But for those of us with more savage souls, he knew we needed rituals and beliefs less refined, something more primitive, if you will, to take away our more barbaric sins. An annual ritual like our ancient forefathers enacted, for example.

"So he built this church with money he raised from the cultivation and sale of opiates and founded this community for all time to—"

"Wait. *Our* more barbaric sins?"

The preacher smiled congenially as that chill stung her gut once again. "We are all criminals here in D'or, Mrs. Burbano. We are all either monsters of society or the children of those monsters, convicted by the gods or the state of the most heinous crimes known to civilization. And all we want is salvation."

"But the blood of Christ was shed to forgive *all* sins, Padre. How can you determine where Christ's blood ends and another's begins? It is not right with God."

"There are some crimes worse than Jehovah's premeditated murder of his Son, Mrs. Burbano. There are some sins so dark they bleed over the sun and eclipse the moon. Sins you have no idea of. Sins you are not even capable of conceiving. But those of us who have conceived of them—even partaken of them—we know better than you ever will in your bleakest, soulless nightmares."

"I don't care what obscene logic you use to pervert the Word of God. You can do as you like. But the children, they're innocent. They don't know these crimes. They cannot imagine such things unless they experience them. And I pray they never will."

"You are wrong again, Mrs. Burbano. The Lord visits the iniquity of the fathers on the children, and on the third and the fourth generations of those who hate Him," The preacher said. "So the sacrifice we make is as much for them as it is for us. And for you."

"Me? I have committed no mortal sins."

"You broke into a man's home and destroyed his property. That's a crime. You're a criminal."

"That's outrageous! I—it was my brother! You said he was dead!"

A hollow bass drum thundered steadily somewhere outside in the dark. *Whooom. Whooom. Whooom...*

Saturnalia.

The preacher's face darkened. "You best stay inside here, Mrs. Burbano. Given your more traditional religious views, you won't like what you'll see. Not at all."

He closed the church doors behind him when he left. Outside, deep voices chanted what sounded like a passage from Latin mass, but none Maria recognized. Wooden flutes sang wildly above the chant as the tempo of the drums increased.

Compelled by curiosity, a distrust of the preacher, and the misplaced belief that the voyeur in no way truly participates in an event, Maria crept to the doors and opened one a sliver to watch the ritual.

To witness Saturnalia.

Gathered at the edge of the forest, where it swelled against the town nearby, the population of D'or chanted among torches, held high in the damp air by women and children bundled against the cold. The men grasped clubs, rifles, and hunting knives, shifting anxiously from foot to foot like caged animals as they stared into the trees.

Whooom. Whooom. Whooom. Whooom...

WHOOM!

The drumming ceased, followed by a moment of silence. Then the women spoke in unison:

"Bring us the forest spirit. Bring back the source of our evils. Bring us the forest spirit—*kyaaayayah!*"

The sharp ululations signaled a raw burst of savagery as the men charged into the crackling forest—tree limbs snapping, brush rustling, swamp water splashing, rifle shots exploding through the tangled web of vegetation.

Then she heard the shrill chittering from the road where her jeep died. Maria gasped at the inhuman sounds. One man after another cried out in terror and agony within the cover of trees. Within moments, the men emerged with the whitened, struggling body of an emaciated creature that bit, shrieked and clawed at its captors. Its long, blackened hair almost covered a scrawny, hairy chest, naked flesh scarred from cheek to heel. One eye squinted from under an old wound at the brow. Its pale skin was spattered with dark fluid. Tears flooded Maria's face as she realized it was not an animal but an insane young man.

The forest spirit. Their scapegoat.

"It got Blake and Jeb, and Nate lost an arm," they yelled. Some of the men were bloodied, and others never emerged. "Hopefully this won't be a problem next year," another quipped. The others laughed. They carried the terrified young man up onto a wheeled wooden platform and, standing him upright, tied each hand and foot to one of two poles, arms stretched Christ-wide as his teeth snapped at his captors. Blood matted his hair above one ear but ran freely down his cheek like rusty tears from a place he'd likely been struck by the butt of a rifle.

Children buried their faces in their mother's waists, and even some men looked away from the hideous creature that now howled pitifully at its bonds.

They've pieced this together from The Golden Bough. *What will they do to him? Crush his neck between two poles? Que cristo nos ayude. What of Joshua?*

Maria considered running. Maybe she could get her jeep to start. Maybe she could just keep running. But her heart ached to see Joshua.

An unusual figure appeared in the crowd.

Deep-brown buck skins swayed around the man's naked body as he cavorted through the crowd to flute and drum music. The massive horns twisted and stretched from the buck's scalp like brambles; its eyes were black holes where the hunter carved the beast's skin from its skull. As the beast man danced with a small scythe, everyone shouted for joy. "The Lord of Misrule approaches! Dance for us, Lord!" Children dared to touch his horns, immediately dashing back to their mothers. The Lord of

Misrule lunged playfully at the older children with the scythe, then squeezed their mothers' tits. He feigned mock battles with the men, alternately climbing on their backs as if to fuck them from behind.

The creature bound to the platform watched, a glimmer of what seemed like sanity burning in his eyes. The Lord of Misrule turned toward him and, a thousand breaths between, he lunged up the platform steps, scythe raised over his head—

Maria cried out, but it was too late.

The creature threw back his head as the scythe swiftly shaved the scalp of long black hair from his skull, blood spattering his pale shoulders. Then the blade landed on his chest, dipping into his sternum and ripping downwards to his belly. The gore trapped behind the delicate walls of his flesh rushed forward. The creature's screams rippled from forest canopy to the deepest grave before he slumped over.

"Aaayaaaaaaaahh!"

The Lord of Misrule swiftly hacked from one side to another, too deftly for Maria to see what he had cut, then turned back to his people, holding the creature's severed hands high. "The forest spirit who causes our ills is dead!" the Lord of Misrule called out. His erection throbbed at his loins, glistening in the firelight. "The forest spirit is dead! Long live the forest spirit!"

Horror overwhelmed her and, like morning dreams, Maria's mind slipped away in blinding whiteness. She left the church and shuffled toward the spectacle, drawn into the shining night. The congregation parted for her as she approached.

Shadows swayed at the edges of the congregation. Their terrible voices chanted *basso profundo* from the murky woodlands in languages long dead to Earth as the Lord of Misrule grasped the buck's snout of his skins and pulled back the skull.

"Joshua?"

The sight of her brother's face destroyed her humanity, and the hand of a god she'd never heard of in catechism set the burning crown of collective sin on her head. Maria then plunged madly into the woods as commanded by the god's voice. Into the holy realm that was now hers for the year.

And as the branches cut her flesh, gentle Maria felt the searing horror of those heavier sins the preacher had mentioned. Those sins that bled over the sun. That's when she knew: at next Saturnalia, she would not fight the hunters.

She could not wait to die.

THE BUTTERFLY

K. Trap Jones

There is a beautiful butterfly gliding in the cool breeze of the valley. It has no care in the world and lands wherever it so desires. A small gust of wind is all that is needed to lift the butterfly from its perch and force it into flight. There is no concern as to where or how far it will be carried. When the wind dies down, the butterfly takes back control of its destiny and lands to rest until it is bullied once again.

The butterfly is close enough to me now that I can see the wonderful patterns detailed on its wings. There is a striking red hue that blends perfectly with the orange and yellow. It is a wonder of life, and a true testament to nature's creative genius. With all of the beauty and passion that the butterfly represents, there is a heavy contrast with how it sits upon the skull of the dead. It serves as a stunning symbol of the living in the tormented atmosphere of this cruel world.

The dead litter the valley where I reside, yet the butterfly is left unharmed and free to spread its wings. As my collapsed lungs struggle to gain enough air to suffice my slowing heart, I cannot help but be gifted with the creation of jealously within my mind. How could such a delicate insect survive the torturous realm that our land has become? How could such a tiny species fly through the thick, death-consumed winds of the valley without a hint of hesitation or fear?

I can only lay one eye upon the spectacle of the butterfly; to raise my face from its encased tomb of mud and earth would be far too much effort and a waste of whatever energy I have remaining. Where my body lies is where my final resting place will be. My youth was spent within these fields as well as my older years. I have made a living from the soil where I now find myself, and it is fitting that I should die within it.

Much like the others, I tried to escape the winds of death. Much like the others, I was unable to outrun it. There was no warning, no inclination of what was approaching from the horizon. The day was like any other day. The sun rose above the tree-lined mountains and cast warm rays upon the village. We all began the day with our usual chores, but something beyond our vision was brewing. It was hidden well from our eyes; it was hidden far from our curious minds. Beyond the mountains, something was approaching.

As the day proceeded, the mountains spilled a creeping fog that hid the trees. The sun vanquished against the thickness of the sky and left us alone with a sudden change in weather. Everyone noticed the quick alteration in temperature, so much so that it halted our daily tasks.

We saw it approaching, but were unaware as to what we were looking at. We had plenty of time to escape its path, but ignorance guided our thoughts and actions. It rolled down from the mountains as if someone was unraveling a blanket. It had a slow, crawling speed, but it was the sheer size of the entity that struck us with amazement. Never before had anyone witnessed such an awe-inspiring vision as the sky opened up and produced a heavenly plow with the clouds.

Like the others in the village, I could only stare at its beauty from afar. The thickness of the clouds consumed both the trees and mountains. There was no concern at that time as it was still far away and moved at an innocuously slow pace. Most of the others went back to their work, but I did not. I walked to the fence that served as the boundary of our village and watched. The colors of the clouds were beautiful and had an unnatural swirling motion like a pit of tangled snakes. There was a calmness and a surreal creativity about it that makes it difficult to put into words. It was heavenly in its design but powerful in its structure. We had seen our fair share of rolling thunderstorms before, but the sheer density of the framework was almost dreamlike to behold.

The mass of clouds consumed all vision of the mountains as if they had disappeared. Like a river finding a new path, it flowed downward with ease and entered into the beginning of the valley where our neighboring farmlands lay. From a distance I noticed something odd, which prompted me to jump the fence and walk further into the pastures to get a better look. A group of deer exited from the gray haze and were sprinting towards the village. Some were stumbling and unable to run, but from that distance I could not understand what I was seeing. It was not until a few of them came closer that I began to understand why they were running. Their coats were stained with blood, and portions of their flesh were missing as if they had recently survived a bear attack. They were terrified and wanted desperately to outrun whatever was chasing them. The wounds on their legs prompted some to fall to the ground and be engulfed in the haze. One ran past me, and I could see its ribcage through a hole that was dripping flesh. Another dropped just before me. Although it was still breathing, the fur of the animal was rapidly disappearing. More deer leaped over our village fence and collapsed sporadically throughout the courtyard. I remember turning back towards the pastures and seeing the cattle also trying desperately to run. I witnessed each of them get swallowed by the thickness of the clouds. Birds were falling from the sky with their wings completely barren of feathers.

As I stood on the outskirts of our village watching the destruction of nature, fear set in with a grip beyond control. It overshadowed my rationale and ignored all of my reasoning. There was no justification to be considered; there were no questions to be answered. Time would not allow any of us to doubt what we were witnessing. Pure terror was all our minds would permit.

I quickly jumped the fence and sprinted back into the village shouting for everyone to run. There would be no reasoning behind my warnings, no additional words to ease the panic that would soon set in. At that particular moment, everyone just needed to run. There were those who heeded my words and those who ignored them. Even I could not completely understand what exactly I was saying, but I knew that something was just not right.

The village went from calm to unbridled chaos as people grabbed their young and screamed uncontrollably. Some wanted to take their possessions and some simply dropped everything, even leaving loved ones behind. A few decided to go inside their homes and test their fate by sealing their doors and windows, but I saw no value in that decision. I ran; mostly all of us just ran.

We ran through the roads, over the fences and into the plains of the adjacent farmlands. We could see all of the animals ahead of us. Every single species that had once made the mountains its sanctuary left them behind without much thought. With no plan or time to think, everyone blindly entered the pastures. Normally, we would have prayed for rain to feed the roots, but at that moment we prayed only for solid ground to tread upon. Our feet sank heavily into the waterlogged terrain. Mud caked onto those trying to escape. The slowness of our steps enabled us with brief moments to look back. The haze had entered the village as people still tried desperately to collect their belongings. They thought they had time; they thought they could grab one more relic. I did not look upon them as greedy; I looked upon them as dying sooner than I.

Fear has a remarkable way of making even the simplest of actions seem difficult to achieve. I bypassed many who fell, having stumbled over their own strides. I dodged those who had found themselves imprisoned within the mud. They clawed at me as I passed, but I could not help them. No one could help another. It was not personal; it was mere self-preservation. Horses neighed as they struggled to raise their legs, hoping to achieve one more stride away from the approaching storm. Screams filled the wind and transported the sounds of the dead as if to push the echoes against my back. The horrific bellows of the nearly deceased watered my eyes and choked my throat. I saw myself coming to grips with my own demise. I feared something which I could not control. I feared a fate that had already been chosen for me as the clouds swallowed the entire village and erased it from existence, but still I ran.

If I merely stopped, it would all end, but the torturous resonances of those clinging to life kept my legs strong and moving forward. There were others ahead of me and some behind. Occasionally, I would catch the eyes of my fellow runners as we all wanted to achieve the same goal. Our hearts bled with sorrow when one of us collapsed or could not physically continue. It was only a matter of time before we all felt that disappointment.

The mud clinging to my feet, legs, and clothes became terribly heavy and slowed my speed. I soon passed a man who had stopped running and was just sitting, watching the clouds approach. I saw peace in his eyes, but it was not enough to make me stop. I passed cows that were stuck in the sludge and birds that could not take flight. There were many runners ahead of me, which granted me some hope of salvation. I would have loved nothing more than to be atop one of the mountains and watch the grayness envelop the ground below, but the valley was where I found myself, struggling for more time to enjoy life.

My burning legs carried me slowly forward as I felt the beast upon my back. I dared not turn around, keeping my eyes focused towards the fence line just up ahead. I soon caught up to a group of runners, but there was no time for kind words. It was not my speed that enabled me to join them; it was the thickness of the terrain that had slowed them. With one step, I felt my entire right leg sink down and watched as it disappeared into the mud. Our forward progress stopped, and we all scraped at the ground in order to continue. Our movements were reduced from running to crawling. The cries from even the strongest of men reverberated through the field as the cool air encased us. There was no noise once we found ourselves within the skin of the devilish clouds. Fear enthralled our tongues and compressed our throats, squelching any sound.

The valley filled with gray and disoriented us so much that some started to crawl back toward the village. The cool, damp air engrossed our exposed skin and began to feast. With my mind focused on my approaching death, I chose not to concentrate on the fact that I could see my bones through the devoured flesh of my legs, nor that my left hand had become skeletonized. I could barely hold my head above the ground and felt the wind funneling through my open wounds like a blistering winter storm. I could hear the crackling of my ribcage with every breath I took. My neck muscles struggled to hold my head upright, and it soon slumped down and buried half my face in the mud, restricting my vision to one eye.

Through the distorted, horrific fog of the land, I saw her. She had a white gown that flowed freely through the air. With one hand, she pulled a wooden wagon; with the other, she toted a large staff that she used to collect the bones of the dead. Tossing the corpses of my comrades, she was cleansing the land. I held her in my vision for as long as I could until her gown blended effortlessly against the gray. Her vision consumed all the remaining fear that I had left. Her essence swallowed my tears and dried my eyes.

The butterfly floated again, assisted by the murderous wind, and landed upon the protruding arm bone of a fellow runner. My one eye wanted to close, but I desired the company of the butterfly to carry me into the afterlife. How could something so beautiful exist within this field of death? The colors of the wings were so vivid and bright it seemed as though heaven itself resided within them. So let it be written that I tried desperately to keep the butterfly within my vision until I could no longer see it. My torment from the unforgiving winds of death, so let it be done.

THE LEAVING

Matt Moore

Drawn by the tinkle of the bell above the door, Georgina blew out a relieved breath—Paul. At his feet, just before he closed the door, a scattering of leaves—black and curled like burnt scraps of paper—blew across the old, faded linoleum.

Aside from Mrs. D'Angelo wiping down some tables, they had Georgina's small diner to themselves.

Good. Just what she wanted.

Late afternoon sun through the big front window illuminated his grin, stubble on his chin, and undone buttons at the neck of his flannel shirt revealed dark curls.

Smoothing down her apron and hoping she looked better than hideous after a day's work, Georgina moved to the counter and said, "Hi, Paul."

"Good afternoon," he replied, grin growing.

Then the barnyard stink struck Georgina, overpowering the diner's salty, deep-fried smells. The decade-old memory of Colin pounding on the back door flashed across her mind's eye.

But Paul was here. Now. Safe. Four days ago, when the Leaving had started, she'd looked up every time the bell rang, wanting it to be him. So far, there had only been word of that one boy being killed. But no matter how many times she assured herself that someone must have told Paul by now, she worried over whether anyone would know if something had happened to him.

He sat in the stool opposite her.

"We're closing in about fifteen," Georgina said. "Kitchen's shut down, but I could get you a beer."

"Yes, please. I'm just here to say hi."

Halfway down the narrow aisle, Mrs. D'Angelo looked up and cocked an eyebrow.

Georgina grabbed a mug and poured his favorite draft. "Haven't seen you around. Began to worry something'd happened." He *had* to know, she told herself, setting the mug on the counter. Word would've gotten around—new man in town, all alone, cleaning out his newly inherited grandmom's farmhouse.

"I've been working on the barn," he replied. "There are so many things to sort through." He took a quick sip. "So what is with the notice from the police on the door? A coyote attack and curfew? Is it related to the smell and the leaves turning black?"

Georgina's stomach dropped. He didn't know. But if he was in the barn last night...

Down the aisle, Mrs. D'Angelo made her way toward Georgina.

Georgina realized she'd be the one to tell him. That was okay. She had prepared for it, rehearsed what she would say. Been prepared since Jefferson Hollow had awoken to find the leaves on all the trees fading from brilliant green to matte black, a month earlier than their usual transformation to fiery brilliance. She would explain the smell, the leaves, and the rules everyone in Jefferson Hollow knew—stay indoors at night.

Georgina waited for Mrs. D'Angelo to come round behind the counter. The older woman had lived all her seventy-two years in the Hollow and explained the Leaving to others, including her late husband. Between the two of them, Paul would have to believe.

Georgina opened with: "A boy was killed last night. Out in Sunrise Village. That new housing development?"

Paul leaned forward. "Oh my God. What happened?"

She expected he'd want details. Paul worked as a medical examiner in the city. Taking a deep breath, she began: "We don't know—"

Mrs. D'Angelo laid a hand on Georgina's shoulder.

In the parking lot, two pickups turned into spaces. Brawny men wearing reflective orange vests over sweat-stained T-shirts climbed out of the beds and cabs.

Mrs. D'Angelo gave a squeeze. *Hurry*, she seemed to say.

Paul looked at Georgina, waiting.

She'd wanted to take her time, explain it, answer his questions. She sputtered: "At night—"

Loud, deep voices on the steps.

"Should I tell them we're closed?" Mrs. D'Angelo asked.

Paul turned toward the door.

"No," Georgina said, letting out a breath. "But one round."

The bell clanged as the men came in, heavy boots thumping, black leaves blowing in on a breeze carrying the animal smell.

Mrs. D'Angelo let out a frustrated snort, readjusted the clasp holding a bun of silver hair in place, then set her shoulders in her "I work for tips" posture before approaching the booths where the men settled in.

Paul touched her hand and said, "You were saying about that boy?"

Georgina hadn't rehearsed it like this. As Mrs. D'Angelo explained that the diner was closing, Georgina scanned the men's faces, not recognizing a one. Not locals. They'd call her story of leaves and smells and death crazy. And might convince Paul.

"Coyotes caught him as he was walking home," she said, echoing the police chief's official statement, a statement that newcomers in Sunrise Village would accept. "Best to keep indoors—"

"You closin' early 'cause a'*coyotes*?" chuckled one of the men, turning to face Georgina.

"To a pack a' them, you'd be a tasty morsel," Mrs. D'Angelo spat over her shoulder, passing the order pad to Georgina. "Grab the beers, sweetie?"

Smiling at Paul, Georgina moved to the cooler.

"They're from the construction crew working Highway 27," Mrs. D'Angelo muttered to Georgina as they assembled the order. "Far enough south of Fellow's Point now it's almost the same distance to get here. We'll be seeing more like them soon."

Georgina couldn't blame Mrs. D'Angelo for her resentment. Despite its dangers, despite her children leaving decades ago, the older woman loved Jefferson Hollow. Said she'd die here. Felt the Leaving forced a hardy, self-reliant character on its residents that most small towns had lost. But Highway 27 would change all that, and this crew symbolized that inevitable change.

"It looks like you have your hands full," Paul said as Georgina placed bottles on a tray. He stood, reaching for his wallet. "I'll come back tomorrow."

"Stay inside after dark," Mrs. D'Angelo said, carrying the tray to the men.

Paul grinned. "I'll be okay. It's just twenty feet to the barn."

Panic leapt up, icy and sharp. "Paul," Georgina began, not sure what to say. "Really, you should..."

His eyebrows knit.

"What are you doing for dinner?"

"The same as usual," he said, grinning. "Something in the oven or on the barbecue. Did you have other ideas?"

Heart thudding. "You could come to my place."

His grin widened. "I would love to. What can I bring?"

"Just yourself," she replied.

"When and where?"

"Six o'clock?" Georgina gave directions to her house.

He handed over some bills, covering his beer and a generous tip. "I'll see you soon."

Georgina watched him go.

"You're glowing, sweetie," Mrs. D'Angelo said, coming behind the counter with the empty tray. "Are you planning on having supper in an hour and sending him on his way before sunset? Or...?"

Georgina grinned, heart still a heavy beat in her chest. It had been a while since she'd had a man in her life. But all of them had pursued her, asked her, made the moves. And they'd all been happy here in the Hollow. Farm kids. Sons taking over their dads' stores. Tradesmen servicing cottages up and down County Road 626. High-school educated or dropouts. None wanted something better. To get out.

Not since Colin, anyway.

"I don't know," Georgina said. "But I've got to get something for supper and take a shower—"

"Then go. I can handle these guys."

"Are you sure?"

"I've done this plenty of times when your mother got sick. Go."

Georgina kissed Mrs. D'Angelo on the cheek and hurried to her car.

From the parking lot, Georgina turned right onto County Road 626 and drove south toward town. This far outside the town center, only a few trees were bare. Someone passing through would hardly know anything was wrong.

Ahead of her, it was different.

But behind her, 626 followed a twisting path north into the city, over an hour away. Highway 27—straight, smooth, four lanes wide—would cut that time in half. Already it had transformed the small towns along its route into bedroom communities. Sunrise Village was the first step toward monotonous, vinyl-sided neighborhoods, restaurant chains' neon signs, and massive box-store parking lots.

Though she understood Mrs. D'Angelo's feelings, Georgina welcomed the change. Since she'd been a girl—hell, since Mrs. D'Angelo had been a girl—the town had remained the same. Even her girlfriends were the same ones from high school. She'd almost gotten out. Hard work in school, despite after-school shifts, netted scholarship offers. But her mom's condition got worse. So she'd stayed, working the diner and taking classes at the community college up in Fellow's Point.

Then Colin—

Then her mom—

In town, oaks, maples, and elms stretched bare, gray branches to the sky. Cars hurried up and down Main Street as people finished errands before sunset. Black leaves blew through the parking lot behind the grocery store as Georgina got out and rushed inside.

The same store, Georgina reflected, run by the same family. Only the high school kids at the cash register changed.

But Paul was new. When he'd first arrived, intent on cleaning up the farmhouse and selling it before going back to his life, she'd allowed herself impossible little fantasies of city life—managing a small restaurant, visiting little boutique shops, going dancing. And dating Paul.

But after a week, he'd taken a liking to the town. "Never been here," he had said. His grandmom always visited them. "Might keep the house for weekends and vacations. Maybe ask a friend in the county office up in Fellow's Point about openings."

That's when she started shaving her legs again and wearing makeup to work.

An announcement that the store would be closing in five minutes, on account of the curfew, pulled Georgina from her thoughts. She got in line at the checkout, rehearsing what she'd tell Paul about the Leaving. Reaching the register, she didn't recognize the girl tallying up her things. Probably another kid from the Hollow starting an after-school job, but what if she was a newcomer living in Sunrise Village? Had someone warned her? A teacher? A friend?

Paying, Georgina thought about how many others wondered the same thing across Jefferson Hollow.

Heading for her car, black leaves crunching under her feet, she considered what would happen when Highway 27 finally passed through Jefferson Hollow and hundreds—or thousands—moved here. When the next Leaving started, it wouldn't just be one boy the first night.

But she'd tell people just as she'd tell Paul. And after tonight, Paul would help spread the word.

Tonight. Even with what she had to tell him, the thought of what else might happen tickled her all over.

Georgina stowed the vacuum in the closet just as the doorbell rang. Opening the door revealed Paul, slacks and a polo replacing jeans and work shirt, a bottle of wine in hand. Beyond, daylight was a marmalade stain on the western sky, painting everything in a fiery glow through the bare trees.

"You look fabulous," he said, smiling.

She wore a simple white blouse, jeans, and flats. No time for anything else. And not like she had anything nicer. "So do you."

Georgina shut the door against the shifting leaves and animal smell.

Wine was opened, brie and crackers set out. They sat in the glass-walled sun room off the den, watching the black leaves stir and chase themselves across the lawn. They talked, debated, bantered. He asked about the boy in Sunrise Village, a topic well suited to his curiosity about rare, bewildering deaths. He loved solving puzzles, fitting seemingly unimportant pieces together. Like unraveling the full life his grandmom had lived by her books and photos and mementos.

He asked about Georgina's life in Jefferson Hollow. She explained how her mom had died before Georgina finished college, leaving her the diner and the house. Plus a mortgage, student loans—Paul could sympathize—and staff. Because her mom had used her savings on drugs and experimental therapies, Georgina had nothing. Except the diner. Thankfully, Mrs. D'Angelo knew the business inside and out, but for seven years Georgina barely made ends meet and had been unable to find a buyer.

With the sun down, the sun room's glass walls became black mirrors. Georgina admired how the two of them looked together—cozy, comfortable. Sunset also meant he was spending the night.

She had to tell him.

Then Paul's stomach rumbled. They laughed and he apologized. Georgina put the finishing touches on dinner—a simple chicken recipe. While she did so, Paul browsed her bookshelves, commenting on titles they had in common.

Dinner served, he raved about it, wondering aloud why it wasn't on the diner's menu. "Because," Georgina replied, "the Hollow's a deep-fried-chicken kind of town." The conversation shifted and flowed. Wine poured. Georgina repeatedly took a deep breath, preparing to explain the Leaving, but every time she came close, Paul described some outrageous memento he'd found tucked into a closet or crawlspace and have her laughing.

More wine opened; Georgina's head—and other things—buzzed pleasurably. He was smart, confident, funny. She loved the way his eyes lingered on her.

Dishes in the sink, they moved to the couch. Logic born of wine and lust concluded that since Paul was spending the night, there was no need to ruin it with talk of the town's curse. She straddled him, kissing him, feeling him swell beneath her. His warm hands cupped her neck, stroked her skin. She slid off, reached for his pants, undid them, teased him. She kissed his neck, nipped his earlobe, and said, "You'll need to come down *every* weekend."

"Georgina…" He pulled her hand away. "I should… I need to tell you something."

She pulled back. "What?" A wife? Kids?

Straightening up, he said, "I'm selling the house. The Sunrise Village developers approached me. They're buying up everything past Fuller Avenue. They offered me…quite a lot. I couldn't say no. These past few days I've been working out the details. Last night, I was in the city signing papers. I wanted to tell you earlier, at the diner..."

Georgina stared. "So what does that mean?" *For us*, she wanted to add.

"With the money," Paul continued, "I can repay my student loans and pay off a good chunk of the condo. I still want to buy another place in the country. It would probably be smaller and closer to the city—"

"Closer—"

"That doesn't mean…" He shut his eyes. Shook his head. "I'm not explaining myself well."

Alcohol and shock and the longing to be touched coiled and spun, wanting to scream at him to get out.

Just like Colin. Right in this room.

He was standing, buttoning his pants. "I should go."

"No," she said, fighting back an irrational rage that wanted him to go out into the darkness. "You've been drinking—"

He was down the hall. Georgina followed. He opened the front door. The animal stink flooded in.

—slamming his hands against the backdoor, flaps of skin hanging from his face—

Georgina grabbed Paul's arm. Turned him around.

"Don't..."

Outside, a ripple moved through the black leaves that blanketed the lawn.

—His motorcycle just steps away. He could make it. He'd promised—

"My car is right—"

"It's not coyotes," she blurted.

Paul shifted his weight. "I don't—"

"The kid. In Sunrise Village. It wasn't coyotes."

"What are you saying? You know what killed him?"

She'd prepared for this. Rehearsed it. But not after two bottles of wine and every bit of her aching for him. "We don't know what it is. We call it 'the Leaving.' Every couple of years, in September, the leaves turn black over a couple of days, and then, overnight, they fall off the trees and this smell comes. When it happens, you don't go out at night until the smell fades. Usually a few days."

Paul rolled his eyes.

"I'm serious!" She took a breath, straining to keep it together. "Eleven years ago. Someone found a teenager under a porch out round your grandmom's place. Every inch of him'd been sliced up. Turns out he'd run away from home and was trying to reach his uncle, who lives here."

Paul drew a breath, his expression skeptical. Before he could speak, she said: "A few years before that…" She paused for an instant, letting her nerves settle. He wouldn't take her seriously if she lost it. And if she lost it and he left, Paul was dead. "A drifter…" she continued. "Out where the train tracks used to be…throat sliced so deep he'd almost been decapitated."

"What were the causes of death determined to be?"

She had him. At least enough to keep him inside. Shutting the front door, she shook her head. "During a Leaving, no one asks too many questions."

"There must have been coroner's inquests or police investigations."

Georgina crossed her arms, hugging herself, wishing Mrs. D'Angelo were here. She'd have explained it better, had the answers. Damn it, Georgina scolded herself, she should've told Paul at the diner. Brought him in the back or something. "I don't know. This is just how it is. The stories go back over a hundred years."

He took her by the shoulders. "Georgina, my grandmother left me a letter in the will. Told me if the leaves went black and a smell came up, to ask someone I trusted in town about it. That I wouldn't believe her. You're telling me it's a spook story?"

"It's not a story!" she shouted with a venom she didn't expect, pulling away.

"The leaves are likely some cyclical disease," he continued. "As for the deaths, some psychopath or cult could be using the legend—"

"But I've seen it!" she screamed. "Nine years ago. It killed my boyfriend in front of me!" She wanted to stop. No one knew this. But a momentum had her, yanking out the words, hurling them so they hurt. "My mom was in the hospital again. So Colin was spending nights with me. It was like revenge 'cause Mom hated him. Long hair and drove a motorcycle. Worked at a garage. Always talking about getting out. Mom told me I could do better. 'Men like him, like your father, are unreliable,' she said. She said if I kept seeing him, she'd kick me out. Cut me off. All my money for school gone. I'd have nothing. But I loved him. So we kept it secret. And when he had enough money, he'd get me out of here." Tears welled up. "But the Leaving started. It was afternoon and Colin was over. Said he'd made a pile fixing up this old Mustang. Wanted us to take off the next day. But I couldn't leave my mom in the hospital. So he asked 'When?' and I didn't know, and he said I'd never stand up to my mom. I yelled at him, and he said he was going to leave without me and tell my mom about us anyway. I told him to get out."

She took a breath, holding back the tears. Paul's arm was around her shoulders, and somehow they'd wound up on the floor. "He—" Her breath caught and a sob escaped.

Words tumbled from her mouth about Colin opening the back door. And the smell. Georgina had been too proud to tell him not to go, and Colin didn't say a word. It was just dusk—probably safe. Colin ran across the small porch and down the steps, disappearing from sight. There had been a moment of nothing—just the small, wooden porch and deepening darkness.

Then screaming.

"I called the cops in the morning. Not sure what I did for the rest of the night. Said he tried to break in at sunrise."

"Did they believe that?"

"I guess. My mom never asked me about it." She wrapped her arms around his neck. "Do you believe me?"

"Yes," Paul replied.

Silently, they held each other.

Eventually she led him upstairs. Without a word, he disappeared into the spare bedroom.

Georgina sat on her bed, holding her pounding head.

Something pulled her up and out of sleep. A siren, far away. Pale, gray light illuminated her small bedroom.

The front door opened. Clicked closed.

Paul, Georgina realized. Leaving.

She flew to the window. Trees—dark-gray angles against light-gray dawn. Below, Paul got into his car, started it, backed out of the driveway.

After a moment to be thankful it was bright enough, she wondered if she'd see him again.

At least, she told herself, he knew. He'd be safe.

Unlike whomever that siren was for.

By the time Mrs. D'Angelo arrived for the breakfast shift, the usual crowd was assembled at the counter. Rumors drifted over coffee and eggs and toast. Two boys in Sunrise Village. Camping in their backyard. Parents discovered them come morning. Tent shredded, boys cut to ribbons. House had a fenced-in yard. Probably thought they were safe.

Mrs. D'Angelo tied on her apron. "How was your night?"

Georgina over-poured a mug, spilling coffee over the edges. "I told him about the Leaving."

"And?"

She had known Mrs. D'Angelo would ask, tried to prepare for it. "He sold the house, Mrs. D. Getting some place closer to the city." She grabbed a rag to wipe up the spill.

"Oh. Well." Mrs. D'Angelo's hands went to her bun of hair. "I've been meaning to tell you this, sweetie, so maybe with this news, now's the time. I'm moving to Austin."

Georgina almost dropped the cup.

"One of my boys got a job with Dell. He can pay for the move. And I've enough stashed away to afford my own place."

"But..." Georgina sputtered.

"I know what you're going to say. But the town I love is gone, sweetie. People like Paul, selling it bit by bit. And this place won't last when they open an Applebee's or Fuddruckers right off the highway.

"And I don't want to be here for the next Leaving. With all the new people, either we'll warn them and word'll get out, or we won't and there'll be too many deaths. Then what? The army? Guys in lab coats?" Mrs. D'Angelo shook her head. "Time for me to go, sweetie. Maybe for you, too." She went to a table to take an order.

Georgina placed the coffee before a local plumber. "Terrible tragedy," he said to the man next to him. "Should've listened to the police," the other replied. "Might be someone else tonight," someone offered. Going to be worse next time, they all agreed.

But someone would tell them. Sure, someone.

Headlights arced across the walls of Georgina's living room. She moved to the window, feet aching from a long shift. Paul's car sat in her driveway. Finally. She'd been trying his cell all day.

She hurried to the front door and pulled it open. Almost sunset. The western horizon was bruise colored. Paul moved up the walkway, black leaves crunching.

Georgina held the door open. "Come inside."

"I'm not planning on staying."

"Then...? It's almost dark..."

Paul rolled his eyes. "It's a *legend*, Georgina."

"You said...you believed me."

"I believe something happened, but not that some mysterious force killed your boyfriend. And I'm going to stand here and prove it."

Georgina took a step backward.

"I spent the morning at the library," Paul continued, "scanning the town paper going back twenty years. There's no mention of 'the Leaving' or the smell or black leaves. No articles on drifters or teenagers being killed. But I did find an obit for a Colin Keenan. Was that him, Georgina?"

"Yes. Paul—"

"So I went up to the county coroner's office in Fellow's Point. There are no records of mysterious deaths in Jefferson Hollow. In the case of Colin's death, the police and a local doctor signed off on natural causes, which means no autopsy or coroner's investigation. You said Colin was killed at dusk, but you told the police he tried to break in at dawn."

"I didn't want my mom—"

A ripple passed through the leaves out near the road.

"Even a rookie can tell a freshly deceased corpse from one that's been out all night by skin temperature. So I looked into that boy from Sunrise Village. Those wounds were clearly not from an animal attack. I have to ask myself: how can these errors be made repeatedly by the police?"

Georgina held up her hands. She didn't know how it worked, just that—according to Mrs. D'Angelo—for over a hundred years they'd been able to avoid attention. Keep outsiders from turning their town upside down. Staying inside a few nights every couple of years was a small price to pay to keep their town from becoming another anonymous suburb. "What do you want me to say?"

"I then recalled that you said no one asks questions about deaths during the Leaving. And that no one would go out after dark. So I have to ask, Georgina: rather than Colin leaving, did you kill him?"

She went cold. "No."

"You two had had a fight. He said he was going to reveal your relationship to your mother. So in a heated moment, knowing you could get away with it, you somehow got the better of him, killed him, and said it was the Leaving."

The leaves in the yard shifted despite the lack of wind.

"That's insane!" she cried. But she'd left him out there. After Colin had screamed, he'd charged back up the stairs, bloody gashes in his face. Seeing him, she'd locked the door.

"Help!" he had screamed, yanking on the door. "Please, Georgina!"

She had frozen.

He had slammed his palms against the heavy glass door. "Georgina!"

She had backed away. A flicker of darkness and his cheek flapped open—gums and teeth visible. Had she screamed? She must've shut her eyes because a sound made her open them to see the porch, empty. Maybe a flicker of motion going over the railing? Then nothing.

She hadn't wanted him to die. But if she had opened the door they both would have been killed.

Was that true? Could he have leapt inside, then slammed the door? They might've talked it out, forced to stay inside all night.

"Then explain it," Paul said.

The leaves rippled, shifting towards them.

Georgina charged down the steps, taking Paul's hand. "Paul, please. I'll explain the best I can. But we have to get inside."

She pulled.

He set his feet. "The sun is down, Georgina. It's a *story*." He shook his head. "I have no choice. I have to refer this to the chief medical examiner. At the very least, they'll reopen an investigation into Colin's death. They'll want to talk to you."

She yanked his hand hard enough to pull him off balance and up a step. "Listen to me!"

With a roar, the leaves exploded into an obsidian cyclone, engulfing them. The animal stink assaulted her. Paul's hand yanked out of hers. She threw up her arms to protect her face as leaves whipped past.

Paul's scream reached her through the noise. Eyes shut, face buried in the crook of an arm, she reached out. Pain, razor fine, crisscrossed her arms, her legs, her body. The sound was deafening. "Paul!"

The top of her ear separated and fell. Pain blossomed. The panicked, animal need to flee turned her round, propelled her up the porch steps and into her house. She slammed the front door, stood stunned for a moment, and then wandered into the living room. Thick, warm wetness dripped from her fingers.

The light in the living room was wrong. Like it came sideways. From outside. She had an instant to realize what it was, car headlights through the sun-room windows, before the panes exploded. She dove behind the couch as chunks of glass flew around her. After a few moments, she pulled herself to her knees, shards sliding off her back and hair, and looked over the couch. The crumpled hood of Paul's car poked into her living room through the remains of the sun room.

Georgina found herself next to the car. Within, Paul slumped back with a grimace frozen on his face, eyes flat, dark leaves choking a wide, blood-smeared gash in his neck.

Something black shot by her. Warmth trickled across her scalp. Another.

The stink filled the living room. Just as she realized that the barrier between her and the outside had been breached, thundering blackness enveloped her.

With arms wrapped around her face, she ran for the bathroom, pulled open the door, and tumbled in. She kicked the door shut but not before leaves flowed through the closing gap—spinning, diving, slicing. She dropped to her knees, grabbing for a towel. It fell from her grip. Reaching for the other, she saw her right hand was missing all fingers but the pinky. She snatched the towel with her left hand and snapped it upward. Fragments of leaves rained down like ash, releasing the barnyard musk.

She leaned against the vanity, panting. Cold. Clammy. Nauseous. The world—cock-eyed grey.

Something made her open her eyes. Scratching. In the space between the door and the floor, tips of black leaves wriggled against each other, fighting to get through. Strength leaving her, vision going dark, Georgina pressed the towel, swollen with blood, into the gap. She tried to brace it with her heels, but her legs felt heavy, far away. And something pushed back.

Beyond the door, she heard a sound like a thousand tiny claws trying to dig through.

And ringing. A high, sweet sound swelled in her ears.

Like the bell at her diner. Its cheerful tinkle made her look up to see Colin, safe and handsome, coming in. His bike was out back, he'd tell her. Just a short walk and he'd take her away from this small town. Untying her apron, she'd tell her mom she was starting her own life. With Colin.

They'd be together.
They'd be leaving.

THE TRAPDOOR

Douglas J. Lane

They'd been in the house six months when Jude decided she wanted to pull the carpets and restore the hardwood.

"When it freezes, you're going to feel it," Darryl told her. The place was a pier-and-beam bungalow, a kit house. It was sixty years old, and its underside was open to airflow year-round.

"Then you can buy me slippers for Christmas," she said. Darryl watched her rise from the couch and walk into the kitchen. He loved to watch her walk, the way she moved. She topped off their coffee cups and brought them back. "Besides, hardwood is hot right now. It'll add triple the value to this place when it comes time to sell."

He knew she had no interest in flipping the house. She'd wanted something more suburban than the condo, someplace to put roots and build a family. It had been almost a year since the miscarriage, and Darryl saw evidence of Jude's desire to nest, despite her insistence that the second bedroom be intended for guests.

His mind lingered on the miscarriage, and Darryl pushed the memory deeper inside, guilt tearing at him like a swallowed fishhook. "I don't know the first thing about stripping floors."

"You don't need to," she said. "You'll be at work for most of it anyway. It'll keep you from getting underfoot." She poked the sole of his bare foot and he squirmed. "But you can help me move furniture and pull up this ugly carpeting."

It *was* ugly. Worn on the edges, with an odd mix of colors and geometric patterns, it reminded Darryl of something salvaged from an old hotel two steps ahead of the wrecking ball and given new life in their suburban hideaway. Staring at it gave him a mild headache.

"That'll be a pleasure," he said.

They found the trapdoor in the center of the living-room floor.

It was flush with the floorboards, two feet square, built from a series of angular, interlocking pieces of a lighter wood. The design reminded Darryl of a pinwheel. A ring handle of black iron was set in a notch on one side. In the center of the ring was a keyhole. Darryl didn't see any hinges.

"Why would anyone put a door here?" Jude asked. She knelt beside it.

"Maintenance access, probably. Easier than shimmying all the way under the house." Darryl hooked a finger through the handle and pulled. The trapdoor was locked. "Not very useful if you can't open it."

"Maybe that's why they covered it." Jude traced the inlays with her slender fingers. "The design is nice. Someone put a lot of work into it, considering what it is. It's almost a shame to stain over it."

"We don't have to decide anything right now."

"Ow!" Jude jerked her hand away. A drop of blood stained one of the inlays.

"What happened?"

"I must have caught an edge." She sucked on her fingertip and then studied it. "Damn, that's deep."

She held it out to Darryl. He didn't see a splinter. There was a gouge where the skin had been torn. He watched the blood pool in the wound. Another drop ran down the side of her finger and fell to the floor.

"That's not how we want to stain the wood," Darryl said. He grabbed a tissue from the box on the side table. He wrapped it around the fingertip. "Let's get it cleaned out."

Jude studied the seam where her finger had caught. Darryl saw her frown. She blotted the blood spots on the inlay with the tissue around her finger.

"Weird," she said. "It looked so smooth."

~

He lay awake in the dark, cataloging the sounds of the night. Jude snored beside him. It varied from a light, wheezy breath to the occasional thirty-second burst of buzz-saw intensity. The refrigerator compressor clicked on and hummed twice an hour in the kitchen. Beyond the walls, the whistles of freight locomotives in the distance split the night.

He lay awake and thought about how he'd poisoned Jude.

No, not Jude. The baby. Clifford's baby.

Clifford was the muscle head who lived upstairs in the condo building, with the bright blue eyes and the best smile money could buy. He was always there with compliments for Jude and what felt like digs at Darryl, asides about how he could tone this or tighten that. Darryl wasn't in bad shape. There were a few pounds he could stand to lose. But Clifford made ten sound like fifty.

Darryl didn't realize Jude and Clifford were getting together. He was wrapped up in work, missing whatever signals she was sending that they were adrift from each other. He did notice that she was more quiet and giving him space. He presumed it was because work had made him prickly.

He discovered Jude was pregnant from the discarded test. He might not have found it if the garbage bag hadn't snagged on the bent corner of the chute and torn open. The plastic stick jutted from the pile of debris that landed on the floor, a plus sign in mute testament to her condition.

He knew the baby wasn't his. He had cut his share of health classes in school, but the requisite activity hadn't occurred with his wife in at least four months.

After finding the test, he spent the next few days watching, paying attention, waiting for Jude to tell him something. Instead, she drew closer once more, engaged with him, seemed recommitted to him. He could tell that whatever had been going on had ended. It wasn't until he realized that Clifford couldn't meet his eyes any longer and that his digs had turned to silence that Darryl put it together.

Then Jude began musing aloud about children. Were they ready? Did a child fit in their lives? Could they manage?

"Is there something you want to tell me?" he asked after one such round of contemplation over dinner.

Jude shook her head and shrugged it off. "Just thinking out loud."

It was then that Darryl decided he didn't want Clifford's legacy to determine the course his life with Jude was going to take. He still wanted her. But he didn't want the baby.

A propeller plane droned past overhead. The dog up the street barked at the wind. Lying beside Darryl, Jude rolled in her sleep and draped an arm over him. He caressed it and closed his eyes. He wondered if the buzz in his head was actually the sound of self-loathing.

That Saturday morning, Jude woke him with a shake and an excited smile. "I found the key!"

Half-awake, Darryl had no idea what she was talking about at first. He hadn't given the trapdoor much thought. He looked up at the object she dangled above him, a shaped piece of metal the same color as the door's lock and handle. It was on a piece of dirty twine.

"Huh. Where was it?"

"On top of one of the kitchen cabinets," she said. "The one by the sink has a recessed top. I was putting up your old Warner Brothers cartoon glasses. It was in the dust."

Darryl propped himself on one elbow. "Have you tried it yet?"

"Yeah. It's unlocked, but it won't budge. I'm thinking it might have been nailed closed outside, or it's rusted shut." She gave him a coy grin. "I was wondering if you wanted to take a trip under the house after breakfast."

He could hear the *tap tap tap* of the broom handle on the floor boards. He had told Jude to tap the trapdoor in three-rap intervals so that he could find the right spot as he worked his way under the house on his back. He picked the path that had the fewest obstacles—low-hanging pipes and discarded bricks or stones—but there still wasn't a direct line to the underside of the living room.

Darryl was able to follow the sound until he was positioned beneath it.

"Can you hear me?" he asked. Above him, Jude tapped once on the floor for "yes." Darryl shined the beam of his small flashlight on the bottom of the house. He didn't see any sign of the trapdoor.

Even if the underside was plain wood instead of the ornately inlaid wood displayed on the top side of the panel, the same seams should have been visible. There should have been hinges, at least. "Honey, am I in the right spot?"

There was another single rap of the broom handle on the floor above Darryl. Then there was a metallic thud and a creaking noise, and something struck Darryl in the face.

A peal of thunder woke him.

He opened his eyes to darkness. The night air was damp, and he could hear rain rattling the gutters. Darryl's back ached from lying on the uneven ground. He could hear Jude somewhere above him inside the house, sobbing.

"Baby?" he called. Jude didn't answer.

Darryl worked his way back to the edge of the house, his head throbbing. Had the trapdoor come unstuck and hit him? If so, why had Jude left him under the house all day?

He slid from beneath the dwelling and lay on his back in the wet grass and falling rain. He felt his forehead. There was a lump, painful to the touch and tacky with blood from a gash he couldn't see. He stood and fought off a wave of nausea.

Darryl entered through the back door and made his way across the kitchen and dining room. He turned the corner into the living room. All the lights were on. Jude was huddled in the far corner. Her knees were pulled up to her chin. Her eyes were red and swollen from crying. She didn't seem to see Darryl.

"Jude? What happened?"

Jude was somewhere else. She sobbed, eyes fixed on the trapdoor. Darryl crossed the room, knelt beside her.

"Jude, look at me."

He touched her arm. She recoiled and screamed. She turned her gaze on him. The scream stopped. She gasped. Then she hugged him as if her life depended on not letting go.

"It opened," she said later, when she had calmed down. They sat on the bed. He'd brought her a beer, but she hadn't taken more than a sip.

"I know." Darryl pushed the hair on his forehead out of the way to show her the gash. Cleaned up, it felt worse than it appeared. He was still debating whether he should have it x-rayed for a fracture. "Why didn't you check on me after it hit me?"

She shook her head. "You weren't there."

"I sure as hell didn't go anywhere, being unconscious and all."

Jude had stopped crying, but her body seemed compelled to the fetal position. "No, I mean you weren't wherever the trapdoor opened into."

Darryl stared at her. "It's a door in the floor. It goes to the outside."

"No it doesn't," Jude said. "It opens to somewhere else. To steps that go down."

"There are no steps under there," Darryl said. "There's no room for them. It's eighteen inches high. Stairs couldn't go anywhere even if—"

"You're not hearing me," she interrupted. "The trapdoor doesn't go under the house. It goes somewhere else. There are stairs that lead down in a spiral."

"That's physically impossible."

"Oh, it's possible. It's very fucking possible."

"Did you go down these steps?"

"No," she said before pausing. "He came up."

Darryl studied her. She'd been in shock when he came inside. Now she was collected and alert, but what she was saying was bat-shit crazy. "*Who* came up?"

Her gaze was hard. "The baby." She swallowed. "The baby that you killed. That *we* killed."

Darryl's heart skipped. He opened his mouth, but nothing came out.

"He knew all about it," Jude continued. "How you poisoned me. He knew about the celandine and feverfew you mixed into my food to encourage a miscarriage." Darryl saw a sheen of tears build in her eyes. "And he told me that he knew I let you."

"You *what*?" It came out despite his dry tongue and lips. He'd done his homework when he'd decided he didn't want her to have the baby. There were a number of herbs that would encourage a body to miscarry. Very simple, very natural, readily available at the health-food store up the street from the condo. He'd wanted it to seem an accident.

She nodded. "You think I didn't know about your hiding places. I was looking for money to visit a doctor. You think I was stupid? I knew the timing. I knew if I was knocked up, it was Cliff's. I was terrified. Cliff wanted no part of it. And I thought if you found out, you'd leave." She sniffled, and he thought she might cry again. "I found the bottles. In a way, I was relieved you figured out on your own." She frowned. "I presume you found the pregnancy test."

Darryl nodded. He felt as if he was falling.

"I did some reading when I found the herbs. I realized what you were doing. At first, I thought your method of dealing with it was fucked up. But the more I thought about it, the more it felt like the perfect solution. It let us both live with the lie. It let us stay together. And it let me off the hook. For a while."

Darryl took a deep breath and exhaled. "I'm sorry."

"So am I," she said. "Because now we need to care for him."

"What are you talking about?"

"He lives in the twilight between worlds. We destroyed him, and now we have to atone. That's why he made the door here in the floor. Why he came through it. To tell me that we needed to go to him. He was our blessing. We were selfish and we murdered him, and now he's our curse. Forever."

"Jude, this isn't possible. You've had a shock. You've imagined something."

"He's coming in three days," she said. She stood from the bed and walked into the bathroom. "For both of us."

She closed the bathroom door behind her.

He picked up the phone and dialed 911.

~

"Is she going to be okay?"

Darryl looked across the desk at Mikey, his boss. He'd had to tell Mikey about Jude being hospitalized. He'd concocted a story to cover the gash in his forehead—*Oh, that. Got dizzy getting out of the tub, fell and whacked it on the sink*—and had omitted the rest.

"They're going to keep her a few days for observation," Darryl said. "They think it's some kind of response to the anniversary of the miscarriage." As they wheeled her through the hospital corridors to her room, Jude had repeated continuously that her baby was returning in three days. The doctor had her on a mild sedative and had requested to keep her for some tests.

"Take the time you need," Mikey said.

Darryl traveled from work to the hospital to the house the first two nights. He held her hand and talked to her, but Jude didn't notice he was in the room. She muttered unintelligible words and stared at the ceiling. At night, back in their bed, Darryl was one with the darkness and tried to ignore sounds he didn't recognize.

When Darryl arrived to see her on the third evening, the nurses were frantic. Jude was missing. She'd gotten dressed and simply walked out of the ward, then the hospital. The only person with whom she'd spoken on her way out was Mrs. Glennon, an elderly woman in the room two doors down who was hooked to an IV and clutching a walker when Darryl spoke with her.

"Oh, yes," Mrs. Glennon volunteered. "I saw her. Such a nice girl. She was talking about going to see her baby."

The front door was open wide in the sweep of Darryl's headlights. He parked out front and ran from the car to the house. He flipped the switch inside the door. Light filled the room.

The trapdoor was open, leaving a square space yawning in the floor. A figure in a hooded gray robe stood beside the opening, leaning over it, peering down.

"Jude?" Darryl asked.

The figure in the robe turned towards him. Where Jude's face should have been visible under the hood, there was a deep, dark emptiness. On a woven cord around the figure's neck hung a life-sized face that might have been sculpted from alabaster. It was Jude's face, eyes wide with terror, mouth open in a silent scream.

Darryl heard a scratching sound from the opening. Small hands gripped the edge of the floorboards. A second figure climbed into view. This one was thin, naked. Its skin was sallow, its hair fine. Its genitalia declared it a boy. It appeared to be a year old, and yet its blue eyes had an intelligence that transcended age.

It took Jude's hand and guided her to the opening. Darryl watched his wife disappear, slowly turning as she spiraled down the staircase. As she descended from view, Darryl stepped closer to the opening. There was light coming from below. He saw the top of the impossible staircase. He heard the murmur of distant voices, a garble of sounds that made him uneasy. Jude was gone.

The child moved between him and the opening. A sound arose, not in Darryl's ears but within his head, a wail that coalesced into a voice.

You must come too.

"Come where?" Darryl said. He felt an itch and rubbed his nose. His fingertips came away stained with blood.

The boy ignored him. *But first, your mask.*

The wail rose again. Darryl felt as if someone was squeezing his head in a vise. His face stretched, shredded. He opened his eyelids long enough against the pain to realize he could no longer see. His eyes were gone. He began to scream. Then his mouth was filled with blood, and the scream became a terrible gagging.

The boy cooed. *Testify.*

Darryl realized he was seeing himself through the child's eyes. Darryl's face was a churning pulp, skin fraying and muscles splitting against bone. His skull pushed forward, out from the bloody mass, but instead of eye sockets and teeth, it had his features. Darryl recognized the cold gaze, the haunted expression. It was the face he'd seen in the mirror the night he'd given Jude the dose that finally pushed her body into the miscarriage.

He watched his clothes change, transform into the same style of robe Jude was wearing. As the hood formed around the destroyed flesh of his face, the pulpy-mass face began to retreat, swallowed by the pitch black within the hood. It was like watching the ruin of who he was sink into a dark sea.

The face of bone with its sorrowful expression hovered in the air. Then a cord wove itself from the fabric of the robe and threaded itself through the back of the face. The cord slipped behind his neck and connected in a loop. Darryl watched the face fall against his chest and felt the sensation at the same time. When the face struck him, as if he were watching a movie, his vantage point switched from that of the boy's eyes to that of the face hanging against his chest.

Now your shame has no mask, the boy said.

The pain in Darryl's head had vanished. His heart thudded in his chest. He felt the boy take his hand. The flesh was cold. He wanted to run, but his feet ignored him and took him instead to the trapdoor. The murmurs filtered up from the silvery light at the bottom of the staircase. There was a scream somewhere in the distance, terrified, forlorn. He wondered if it was Jude.

Where are we going? Darryl thought as he took the first step down. *Where does this lead?*

Behind him, the boy answered in a voice of grim joy. *Home. Daddy.*

ABOUT THE AUTHORS

Maria Alexander has committed a number of literary crimes as an author of horror, suspense and humor. Her deeds have appeared in award-winning anthologies and magazines beside greats such as Chuck Palahniuk and Clive Barker.
Like your horror hot? Then check out her newest e-collection, *By the Pricking: 5 Dark Tales of Passion and Perversion.*
For the full literary rap sheet, visit her website: www.mariaalexander.net.

Angela Bodine currently lives in the mountains of West Virginia with three monsters she calls her children, a spoon gremlin, a temperamental muse and plenty of ghosts. When she's not working, chasing heathens or pursing a degree in psychology, she keeps sane by writing or reading. You can find her at angelabodine.wordpress.com

Monique Bos is the author of the novel *The Dark Jests of Lost Ghosts* and numerous short stories, several of which have appeared in previous Blood Bound Books anthologies. She loves the TV show *Bones*, reptiles, thrift stores, bad creature movies, morbid music, and gargoyles. Her favorite local hangout is the zoo, where she enjoys honing her photography skills. A freelance writer and editor, she lives in Colorado with a big black dog, two cats, and several lizards, amid precarious wall-to-wall, floor-to-ceiling towers of books. She (sometimes) blogs at moniquebos.wordpress.com.

Nathan Crowder is a horror writer, dime-store diplomat, and karaoke superstar living in Seattle. He enjoys a good Sidecar, loves his friends, and has never been comfortable swimming in lakes. His short fiction has appeared in the anthologies *Rock 'n' Roll is Dead*, *Cthulhrotica*, and *Rigor Amortis*, among others. Online, he can be found at nathancrowder.com or on Twitter at 140 characters or less as @NateCrowder.

Christopher Hawkins lives in the Chicago area where he, along with his wife, edits the critically-acclaimed *One Buck Horror* anthology series. When he’s not writing, he’s an avid book collector, role-playing gamer, comic book reader, and serial complainer. His previous work appears in the anthologies *Night Terrors II*, *The Big Book of New Short Horror*, *Read by Dawn II*, and numerous others. For more information, visit his website at www.christopher-hawkins.com.

Brad C. Hodson is a writer living in Los Angeles. His first novel, *Darling*, is now available through Bad Moon Books. He also co-wrote the award winning cult comedy *George: A Zombie Intervention*. When not writing, he’s usually dragging heavy sleds and throwing sandbags in the park while pretending he’s a Viking. The mead helps. For random musings on the horror genre, life in Los

Angeles, or to find out other books to find his short fiction in, please visit: www.brad-hodson.com. You can also check out his new horror novel at www.darlingbook.com

K. Trap Jones is an award winning author of literary horror novels and short stories. With a strong inspiration from Edgar Allan Poe and Dante Alighieri, his passion for folklore, classic literary fiction and obscure segments within society lead to his creative writing style of "filling in the gaps" and walking the line between reality and fiction. More information can be found at www.ktrapjones.com

Ed Kurtz is the author of the novels *Bleed* and *Control*, in addition to numerous short stories. His work has appeared in *Needle, ThugLit, Dark Moon Digest*, and the anthologies *Psychos, Deep Cuts*, and others. Kurtz is also a contributing writer to Paracinema Magazine. He lives in Austin, Texas.

Douglas J. Lane's work has appeared in *Tales of the Unanticipated, Bards & Sages Quarterly*, online at *PureFrancis.org*, and in the anthologies *Machine of Death, Seasons In The Abyss and Kindle All-Stars Present: Resistance Front*. He lives with his wife in Houston, TX. You can visit him online at: www.douglasjlane.com.

Adrian Ludens is the author of *Bedtime Stories for Carrion Beetles*, available as a quality paperback or for Kindle from Amazon. His work has appeared in *Alfred Hitchcock's Mystery Magazine, Morpheus Tales* and *Big Pulp*, among others. Recent anthology contributions include *Blood Lite III: Aftertaste, Zombie Kong, Slices of Flesh,* and several titles from Blood Bound Books. Adrian is one of only two South Dakotans who are members of the Horror Writers Association. Visit Adrian at: curioditiesadrianludens.blogspot.com

Brian Lumley is the author of the bestselling Necroscope series of vampire novels. An acknowledged master of Lovecraft-style horror, Brian Lumley has won the British Fantasy Award and been named a Grand Master of Horror. His works have been published in more than a dozen countries and have inspired comic books, role-playing games, and sculpture, and been adapted for television. When not writing, Lumley can often be found spear-fishing in the Greek islands, gambling in Las Vegas, or attending a convention somewhere in the US. Lumley and his wife live in England.

Chad McKee is an American Southerner who splits time between medical research and writing genre fiction. His contributions can be found in the anthologies *The Best of House of Horror, Day Terrors, Seasons in the Abyss*, and *D.O.A.: Extreme Horror Collection*, among others. He currently resides in Oxford, England.

Joe McKinney has been a patrol officer for the San Antonio Police Department, a disaster mitigation specialist, homicide detective, administrator, patrol commander, and successful novelist. Winner of the Bram Stoker Award, he is the author of the four part *Dead World* series, *Quarantined, Inheritance, Lost Girl of the Lake, Crooked House* and *Dodging Bullets*. His short fiction has been collected in *The Red Empire and Other Stories* and *Dating in Dead World: The Complete Zombie Short Fiction.* For more information visit his website at http://joemckinney.wordpress.com.

John McNee is the author of numerous strange and disturbing stories, published in various anthologies, including *Ruthless, Tales From The Bell Club, A Hacked-Up Holiday Massacre* and the Blood Bound Books collections *D.O.A.* and *Steamy Screams*. He is also the author of *Grudge Punk*, possibly the only dieselpunk-bizarro-horror-noir anthology on the market. He lives in the west of Scotland, where he is employed as a reporter covering strange and disturbing news.

An Aurora Award nominee, **Matt Moore** is a horror and science fiction writer living in Ottawa, Ontario. His columns and short fiction have appeared in print, electronic and audio markets including *On Spec, AE: The Canadian Science Fiction Review, Leading Edge, Cast Macabre, Torn Realities, Night Terrors* and the *Tesseracts* anthologies. His novelette *Silverman's Game* was published by Damnation Books in 2010. He is also the Communications Director for ChiZine Publications. Find more at mattmoorewrites.com.

Lisa Morton is a screenwriter, author of non-fiction books, award-winning prose writer, and Halloween expert. After appearing in dozens of anthologies and magazines, including *The Mammoth Book of Dracula, Dark Delicacies,* and *Cemetery Dance*, her first novel, *The Castle of Los Angeles*, was published to critical acclaim in 2010. She is a four-time winner of the Bram Stoker Award®, a recipient of the Black Quill Award, and winner of the 2012 Grand Prize from the Halloween Book Festival, and she recently received her seventh Bram Stoker Award® nomination for the collection *Monsters of L.A.* A lifelong Californian, she lives in North Hollywood, and can be found online at www.lisamorton.com.

Gregory L. Norris lives and writes at the outer limits of New Hampshire. A former columnist and feature writer at Sci Fi, the official magazine of the Sci Fi Channel (before all those ridiculous Ys invaded), he once worked as a screenwriter on two episodes of Paramount's *Star Trek: Voyager* series. He is the author of, among others, *The Q Guide to Buffy the Vampire Slayer* (Alyson Books) and *The Fierce and Unforgiving Muse: A Baker's Dozen from the Terrifying Mind of Gregory L. Norris* (Evil Jester Press, 2011)

Daniel O'Connor lost his mother when he was four years of age, and his father two years later. He lived with his grandmother until she passed when he was ten.

Rather than purchase a clown mask and a chainsaw, he kept the demons at bay through books, movies, music and writing. His first novel, *Sons of the Pope*, was released by Blood Bound Books to great acclaim in 2012. His short story, Between Catskill and Cooperstown will appear in the 2013 anthology: *Serial Killers 2*. He is currently working on his second novel. CONTACT DAN: AuthorDanO@aol.com

Bryan Oftedahl was raised in the depths of the Tongass rainforest on the edge of human civilization and the wildernesses beyond. Occasionally he exercises his skills as an amateur author to compose a tale, more often than not its crap but every so often he manages something more than. "Who is Schopenhauer" was inspired by the hellishly pessimistic works of the philosopher by the same name.

Mark C. Scioneaux is employed as an industrial hygienist by day and a horror writer by night. He is the author of numerous short stories appearing in anthologies by Blood Bound Books, Severed Press, Evil Jester Press, and others. And coauthor of the thrilling zombie novel, *Insurgent Z*. He is the founder of *Horror for Good: A Charitable Anthology*. Teaming up with Cutting Block Press, they will send all proceeds from book sales to amfAR, an international AIDS charity. He is a co-owner of Nightscape Press, and a member of the Horror Writers Association. He is a graduate of Louisiana State University and currently resides in Baton Rouge, Louisiana with his wife, Jessica.

Jeff Strand's novels include *Pressure, Dweller, Wolf Hunt, A Bad Day For Voodoo, Graverobbers Wanted (No Experience Necessary)*, and a bunch of others. He has never rubbed habanero peppers into his eyes, though he did burn the crap out of his tongue trying just a teeny tiny little drop of the hottest sauce at Tijuana Flats. Visit his Gleefully Macabre website at www.jeffstrand.com.

Aric Sundquist is a graduate of Northern Michigan University and holds an MA in Creative Writing. His stories have appeared in various publications, including Evil Jester Digest, Twit Publishing Presents: PULP! Anthology, and Dark Moon Digest. He loves 80's horror movies and playing the guitar. He currently lives in Marquette, Michigan.

Desmond Warzel is the author of a few dozen short stories; these are mostly science fiction and fantasy, but he is occasionally called upon by unseen forces to enter the realm of the horrific, as evidenced by his previous appearances for Blood Bound Books (in *Night Terrors* and *Night Terrors II*). Recent work has appeared in the dark fantasy anthology *Love and Darker Passions* (Double Dragon Publishing) and the venerable *Magazine of Fantasy & Science Fiction*. He lives in northwestern Pennsylvania.

CPSIA information can be obtained at www.ICGtesting.com
Printed in the USA
BVOW001113130513

320580BV00003B/19/P

9 780984 978274